D1431605

3 23
STRAND PRICE
5 00

EUREKA

EUREKA

$$\cos A = \frac{b^2 + c^2 - a^2}{2bc}$$

$$y = \sqrt{x^2}$$
$$y = \sqrt{x+1}$$
$$y = \left(-\sqrt{x}\right)^2$$

DINA NEUMAN

MENUCHA PUBLISHERS

Menucha Publishers, Inc.

© 2022 by Dina Neuman

Typeset and designed by Rivkah Wolfson

All rights reserved

ISBN 978-1-61465-571-8

Library of Congress Control Number: 2021949487

No part of this publication may be translated, reproduced, stored in a retrieval system, or transmitted in any form or by any means, electronic, mechanical, photocopying, recording, or otherwise, without prior permission in writing from both the copyright holder and the publisher.

Published and distributed by:

Menucha Publishers, Inc.

1235 38th Street

Brooklyn, NY 11218

Tel/Fax: 718-232-0856

www.menuchapublishers.com

sales@menuchapublishers.com

Printed in Israel

This book is dedicated to my sisters,

Yaffa, Leah, Rivky, Malky, and Menucha,

Because no matter how far from each other we roam,

When we get together, it always feels like home.

(And you know it's true because it rhymes.)

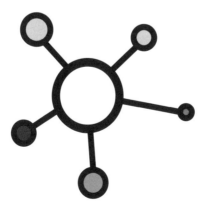

CHAPTER 1

The whole way there, from the heart of the city to the heart of nothing at all, Rachelli found herself thinking that whatever her father's top-secret experiment was, if it didn't work after all this, she might go up onto the nearest rooftop and scream.

And that was even before the PNAAD (Personalized Navigator and Automatic Driver), who went by the name of Pinny, had a glitch and nearly plowed them straight into an oncoming cow.

"It's not so much that we nearly died, Daddy," Rachelli was explaining, her hands on her hips, her overly large red bow hanging limply from her long, straight ponytail. She was addressing a pair of legs that were sticking out from under the minivan. "It's that we were nearly killed by a cow. It's humiliating."

The legs slid out, revealing a torso, arms, and a head. Professor Shore squinted in the sunlight. "Death by cow," he said, looking up at his family. "That would be a terrible way to go."

"Mom would kill us if we got killed." Effie, fixing the brim of his brand-new hat, knelt down to help his father to his feet.

The Shores were standing on the edge of the road, the black asphalt nearly glowing in the heat. Three cars had passed by in the last hour.

All around them, as far as the eye could see, were cornfields.

"Cornfields," Rachelli said.

"What about them?" Effie kicked at a pebble.

"I was thinking about them, and I think I hate them," Rachelli said.

Effie laughed.

"You can't hate cornfields." Alex, who was leaning against the fence separating the field from the road, was shocked enough to take his nose out of his book.

"Well, why not?" Rachelli made a face at her younger brother. "What are they good for, anyway?"

"You mean besides for corn?"

"When you kids are finished discussing the relative merit of cornfields, I think it'll work this time." Professor Shore opened the car door and pressed a button on the dashboard.

The dashboard of the minivan was covered in buttons, each one activating an invention of Professor Shore's. They did various things, such as pop pillows out of headrests for weary travelers or turn the car into a flotation device in case of an emergency. One button activated the solar-powered microwave, and another the coffeemaker magnetized to the car's console.

And yet another button, the one that Professor Shore had just pressed, activated Pinny, the Personalized Navigator and Automatic Driver.

Hopefully, anyway.

Everyone, even Lolly, held their breath.

"Good afternoon, Shore family," a mechanical voice echoed from the speakers. "My, that's a lot of cornfields."

Effie pumped his fist in the air. "Eureka!"

"I dunno." Rachelli held Lolly's hand and peered suspiciously at the car. "Pinny sounds weird. Doesn't he sound weird?"

Professor Shore rubbed at his head. His yarmulke fell over one ear. "I had to play around quite a bit to get the PNAAD operational again. But it should be fine, at least for now."

"Hey," came the voice of Pinny, sounding oddly miffed for a machine. "I can hear you. I have ears, you know."

"No," Rachelli said. "You actually don't." She shot a meaningful glance at her father.

"Thanks for rubbing it in." Pinny sounded like he was going to cry.

"Everything is fine, Pinny," Professor Shore said. He patted the dashboard. "Just drive us straight to our new home. There's a good PNAAD."

There was a sound from the speakers that was very much like a sigh. Then the doors to the car opened, and Professor Shore, Effie, Lolly, and Rachelli climbed into the cool interior.

"Twenty seconds," Rachelli said.

Effie nodded. "Start the countdown."

Just as Rachelli reached one, Alex looked up from his book. He blinked at the cornfields, at the empty road in front of him. Finally, he focused on the car that was filled with everyone in his family — other than his mother (away on business as usual)…and him.

He opened his door to a chorus of laughter. "Ha ha," he muttered back.

"Start, please, Pinny," Professor Shore said from the driver's seat, and as the minivan pulled onto the road and began driving, he opened up a *sefer* and was soon lost to the world. Alex got swallowed up in his book again, Effie pulled out a Game Boy, Lolly ate the apple slices that Rachelli handed her, and Rachelli herself stared out the window and kept a sharp eye out for cows. Her thoughts soon wandered, once again, to the mysterious experiment that was the cause of all this trouble.

Professor Shore was not, as the neighbors in their old neighborhood were led to believe, a candy-machine repairman. He was a scientist, and some of his experiments were extremely important. So important, in fact, that the Shores were driving halfway across the state and through an unbelievable number of cornfields for him to complete the most important experiment of all. Mrs. Shore was away on business — she ran the practical side of the Shores' science team, seeking patents and clients for her husband's inventions — and would join them later.

Rachelli was used to her absence, but right now, as everything familiar receded behind rows upon rows of corn, she missed her.

"We are now entering the town," a mechanical voice interrupted her thoughts. "Welcome to our new home!"

"Eureka!" Professor Shore said in delight. He put down his *sefer* and pointed a finger up at a sign planted in the cornfield to the right of the car.

As one, everyone in the car leaned forward to look.

"Welcome to Sundale, Population 4,000," the sign read in large blue letters, and then continued: "Home of the Second-to-Largest Ball of Twine."

"Home of the underachievers, it should say," Rachelli said. "Seriously, second-to-largest ball of twine?"

"Would you like to know some interesting facts about Sundale?" Pinny asked.

"No," Rachelli and Effie answered together.

"Fine," said the PNAAD snippily. "Then I won't tell you."

Lolly swallowed her last bite of apple slice. "Are we there yet?"

"Almost, sweetie," Rachelli answered.

"I'm still hungry," Lolly said plaintively.

"Want some corn?" Rachelli pointed out the window, but the rows upon rows of corn, without warning, had given way to a small one-way street with several stores on either side. They passed a gas station and then made a left onto a tree-lined street.

The car sputtered to a stop in front of the third house on the block. "We are here," the Personalized Navigator And Automatic Driver said, triumph in its mechanical voice.

"We are?" Rachelli frowned in disbelief. "We just drove through the whole town? It's a good thing I didn't sneeze. I would have missed it."

"Gesundheit," Alex said absently, his eyes never leaving his book.

Professor Shore turned around to look at his children, and ran a hand through what remained of his hair. "I know that this move came out of nowhere," he said. "And I know that we left behind friends and family. You have all been amazing about this, especially you, Rachelli."

Rachelli shrugged modestly.

Professor Shore scratched his nose. "I don't know how long this is going to be, but we can think of it, for now, as a summer vacation. My point is, with the right attitude, this is going to be great."

He smiled, and Rachelli, despite everything, couldn't help but smile back.

"Let's get this summer vacation started then, yeah?" she said, and pulled open her car door and stepped out, squinting, into the near-blinding sunlight. Her father followed suit, as did Effie and Alex and Lolly, once Rachelli had released the straps on her car seat.

They found themselves standing in front of a lawn the size of what would have been a small park in the city, if the city would have let their parks get this overgrown. There was a tire swing attached to a tree beside the house, and it seemed to swing sadly in the faint breeze.

As for the house itself, it was impossible to see due to it being completely blocked from view.

"Eureka!" Professor Shore said, his back to the house as he closed his car door. "The privacy that I need to finish my experiment in peace! This is going to be wonderful!"

"It depends how you define privacy, I guess," Effie said.

"What?" Professor Shore straightened up. "What do you mean?"

"Daddy, did you tell people that we were moving in today?" Rachelli asked casually.

"Well, the landlord of this place knows. Why?"

"No reason," Rachelli said. She gestured toward the crowd surrounding the house. Some of the kids were waving at her. "It's just that if this town has a population of four thousand people, I think we're about to meet all of them."

CHAPTER 2

Dear Ones,

I miss you so much! I think about you every day and every night. How are you settling in? Isn't the house so much fun? I just know that you will love discovering all of its secret little nooks and crannies!

Things are going well over here. I'm having many meetings with many important people who are very interested in Daddy's newest experiment. I'm sure I'll have some good news about grants and patents really, really soon!

In the meantime, I hope you're all enjoying the peace and quiet in Sundale! The privacy is a refreshing change from life in the city, I bet.

All my love,
Mommy

The people surrounding the house turned as the Shores approached them.

For a moment, besides for the slight rustling sound of the grass underfoot, there was silence.

And then the silence exploded into high-pitched shrieking of many voices extending greetings.

"Well, hello there!"

"Welcome to the neighborhood, new neighbors!"

"We are real pleased to see you!"

The Jewish community of Sundale was small and tight-knit, the real estate agent had told Professor and Mrs. Shore. Everyone knew each other's names; everyone went to the same three shuls and two schools. They were warm and friendly and loved visitors.

"Oh," Rachelli had said when her father had repeated those words to her. "That sounds nice."

But she had the sudden realization — as the crowd closed around her, as foil-covered casseroles were thrust into her hands and stacked so high she couldn't see ahead of her — of what those nice-sounding words actually meant in real life.

"It's *like* privacy," Alex said as someone, in an effort to shake his hand, nearly knocked his glasses off his face. "It's very *similar* to privacy."

"How do you figure?" Rachelli asked him.

"As in, the antonym of."

"Speak English!" Rachelli yelled as she was hugged by a woman in a huge red sun hat and a huger smile and handed yet another warm aluminum tray. Off to her left, Professor Shore clutched Lolly tightly in his arms and smiled his absentminded smile at everyone who came over to welcome him.

"He *is* speaking English," Effie said, holding onto his hat with two hands. He had to call out to Rachelli at the top of his lungs to be heard.

"He's saying that it seems that Sundale will be the perfect exact opposite of privacy. And I have a kind of a feeling that he might be right."

"It's a castle," Lolly said in awe.

"Well," Rachelli wrinkled her nose. "It's definitely old enough to be one."

The house, when the last of the neighbors had taken their leave — well, their relative leave, being that a few of them were still standing at the edges of the lawn, and a kid was swinging on the tire swing — was revealed to be a large Victorian that had probably, once upon a time, been painted white. The wraparound porch was held up by large pillars, and the heavy double doors that led into the house scraped at the floor alarmingly when they were opened.

"Hello?" Rachelli called into the empty hallway, and her voice echoed back at her.

"Hello!" Lolly called in delight, testing out the echo. She ran forward into the dim recesses of the house. "Hello! Hello! Hello! Hello! Hello! Hel—"

Her voice abruptly stopped, and the rest of the Shores ran after her.

"Lolly!" Rachelli cried. She crouched down and deposited the leaning tower of 9x13 pans onto the dusty floor. "Lolly! Where are you?"

A muffled cry was her only answer.

"Does anyone see a light switch on the wall?" Effie called.

Professor Shore reached into his pocket and retrieved what looked like a small white pill. He tossed it against the floor, and there was a loud popping sound before the room was suddenly flooded with streaks of light.

"Nice, Dad," Alex said appreciatively. "Chemiluminescence?"

"Essentially, hydrogen peroxide in a tablet!" Professor Shore beamed. "Simple, but effective. I just need a name for it."

Alex pondered. "Hey, how about 'InstaLight'?"

"Hey!" Rachelli looked from her father to her younger brother with her hands on her hips. "How about Lolly?"

"Oh!" Professor Shore grimaced and tapped himself ruefully on the forehead. "Sorry—"

"Found her!" Effie's voice echoed loudly from somewhere deeper in the house. "Hey, I need some help!"

They all rushed further into the cavernous abode, past several rooms shrouded in darkness and down another long hallway. They screeched to a halt when they finally saw Effie kneeling on the floor of what was probably the living room. There were three extremely dusty couches beneath an enormous chandelier coated in spider webs.

Effie looked up as Alex, Rachelli, and Professor Shore knelt down beside him. There was a wooden panel jutting out of the floor. Below the panel was a hole, and in the hole was Lolly. "Trapdoor," Effie said. "I guess it was open."

Professor Shore popped another one of the InstaLights from his pocket, revealing a short set of stairs in the hole below them. Lolly scrambled up them. She was covered from head to toe in a layer of dust.

"Are you okay?" Rachelli knelt down and gently wiped at the little girl's face.

"I fell down," Lolly explained. "The floor has a hole."

"Usually, if a floor has a hole, Lolly's the one who finds it," Effie remarked.

Lolly stuck out her tongue at her big brother.

"Dad, where are you going?"

In the glowing light cast by the InstaLight, Professor Shore raced down the staircase, the kids hot on his heels. They found themselves standing in a huge, empty room; the only light was from the dim remnants of the InstaLight upstairs. That, and the gleam in Professor Shore's eyes as he swooped down and swung Lolly over his head.

The little girl shrieked with delight. "Why, Daddy?" she asked when he put her down. "Why are we so excited that I fell down the stairs?"

"Don't you see it?" Professor Shore demanded.

"The dust?" Rachelli asked.

"The spiders?" Effie asked.

"I'm hungry," said Lolly.

"I see it, Dad," Alex said. He smiled in the gloom. "This secret room is perfect for your laboratory."

"This secret room," Rachelli mimicked in a high-pitched voice as she dipped her mop into the soapy bucket and attacked the floor with a little more aggression than was strictly necessary, "is perfect for your laboratory."

It was bright and early the next day, and the cleaning had begun.

"Alex doesn't sound like that," Effie said. He leaned against the wall, then yelped when he was hit with a wet, soapy *shmatte*. He caught it before it hit the ground.

"You are not standing there with your arms folded," Rachelli said as she retied her oversized hair ribbon so that it sat perkily, if rather dustily, atop her long pony. "You are not on arm-folding duty. You are on spiderweb-cleaning duty."

Effie got to work. "Who," he asked, "are you going to boss around when I go to yeshivah tomorrow?"

Rachelli kept her face carefully hidden. Effie would still be coming home for Shabbosos for the rest of the summer, but she would miss him during the week. Not that she would ever admit that or anything. Instead, she tossed the mop to the floor, where it fell with a rather satisfying clatter. "This house is enormous," she said. "It'll take me a week just to clean out this room!" Rachelli glared at the fallen mop. Then she sneezed on the fallen mop.

The house they were renting came furnished, but before the Shores could even begin to settle in and allow Professor Shore to begin working on his mysterious project, they would have to find the furniture buried under blankets of dust and cobwebs. So while Alex kept Lolly entertained, Professor Shore, Effie, and Rachelli were working on getting the enormous house, or at least sections of it, into a livable state.

After a few minutes, Rachelli and Effie fell into a comfortable silence as they both sprayed, wiped, and sneezed in turn. The house was so quiet, in fact, that when Rachelli went upstairs to get some fresh paper towels and bumped into a stranger, she was startled into a scream.

CHAPTER 3

"And then" — Rachelli paused for emphasis and shifted the phone into a more comfortable position between her shoulder and ear — "and then it turns out that the person who ran straight into me was our new next-door neighbor! Ma, she just walked into the house! She said the door was open, but, Ma, I don't think it was!"

Rachelli inserted half a dozen eggs, whole in their shells, into the bulky metal contraption on the stove. The contraption beeped. "Analysis complete. No bloodspots," read the screen on the top, so Rachelli pressed a button and watched as the machine cracked open the eggs with a mechanical claw. Soon the room was filled with the smell of scrambled eggs.

"My point is, Ma, that it's a good thing Daddy is setting up his lab in the secret room below the living room, or his secret experiment will be as much of a secret as the fact that Alex did not brush his teeth."

"Hey!" said Alex. "I did so brush my teeth!"

"Oh, he *is* listening this morning. Anyway, we're fine, Ma, just coated in a fine layer of neighborly goodness like breadcrumbs on a piece of schnitzel. Sorry you missed Effie; his bus came early this morning. I'll tell him you called when he comes back for Shabbos…

I love you too." Rachelli hung up and watched as Alex passed a metal wand-like object over pieces of bread laid out on the counter. The Toast Stick hummed as it instantly turned the bread into toast.

"I'm hungry," Lolly's voice echoed as she padded into the over-sized kitchen in her nightgown. "I'm starving."

Rachelli brought a plate filled with scrambled eggs and toast over to the table for the little girl. She opened her mouth to ask Lolly if she needed help washing, when there was a sudden sharp rapping sound.

"Is that someone knocking on the door?" Alex asked absently, pushing his glasses up the bridge of his nose.

"Not possible," Rachelli said. "No one in this town seems to know what it means to knock on a door."

The rapping sound was following by a muffled thump and then a muffled shout and then the distinct sound of an explosion. The whole house seemed to rock slightly.

There was the thump-thump of the trapdoor opening and closing, and Professor Shore walked into the kitchen, wearing a white lab coat and a dazed expression. He was splattered from head to toe in a greenish gooey substance.

"Is that eggs and toast I smell?" he asked.

"Is that stuff acidic, Daddy?" Rachelli asked with her hands on her hips.

"It shouldn't be, why?"

"Because," Rachelli said, "it's eating your lab coat."

Professor Shore looked down at himself. In the places where the greenish gooey substance had been were several large holes that were smoking slightly.

"Ah," said Professor Shore. "Interesting. I wonder if..." But he never finished his sentence; he bolted from the room.

"Is that your secret experiment?" Rachelli called after him. "Making lab coat–eating goo?"

"Nice try," Professor Shore called back, and a minute later, Rachelli, Alex, and Lolly heard the thump-thump of the trapdoor open and close.

"What do you think the secret experiment is, Alex?" Rachelli poked her eggs with her fork before making a berachah and taking a bite. "And why," she asked around the bite, "is it secret even from us? Ew, did the Egginator undercook these eggs?"

"Something government-related." Alex piled his own plate with toast. "Something dangerous. And I'll play around with the Egginator later if you want."

"Just make sure it doesn't develop a personality." Rachelli shuddered. Speaking of new personalities, Pinny was still cranky and was only getting worse. When they had gone to stock up on groceries, the PNAAD had sighed and spoken in a low, sad voice about how depressing it was to drive a car day in and day out.

"You try walking in my shoes for one day," the PNAAD had said mournfully, and when Rachelli had pointed out that it had no shoes, it had burst into staticky sobs.

It would be really annoying if the Egginator decided that its primary function was cruel to animal life, and incubated the eggs instead of scrambling them.

"Do you see anyone?" Rachelli asked.

"Hang on." Alex's face was pressed against the peephole. "Okay, coast is clear of Sundalers."

Rachelli let out a deep breath. "So we can go out. Seriously, do people in this town not have a life? Have they never seen new people before? Is that why they jump all over us the second we open the door? And sometimes even before?"

Alex shrugged. He pushed his glasses up his nose. "Well, it's an easy way to make friends."

Rachelli snorted. "Not going to happen. We're here for Daddy to finish working on his experiment. The second that happens, we're back in the city, back to civilization." She pushed open the huge double doors of the house, and they walked into the blinding sunlight.

And right into their next-door neighbor.

"You are bad at looking through peepholes," Rachelli said to Alex, who looked sheepish.

"May I come in?" The next-door neighbor, who had introduced herself yesterday as Mrs. Pernikov, looked from brother to sister. Her face was a web of wrinkles when she smiled.

Later, much later, when Rachelli had a chance to think through the series of events that led to total disaster, she wished there was a polite way of answering no to that question. And when she thought about it, she got annoyed that it was phrased as a question at all because there was only one polite answer to "Can I come in?" and that was "Sure."

"Sure," Rachelli said.

"We didn't get much of a chance to chat last night, what with you shrieking and hollering," Mrs. Pernikov said as she settled herself down on the couch in the living room, just inches away from the secret trapdoor in the floor leading to the secret lab.

Rachelli seated herself down gingerly beside the woman and jutted her chin toward Alex to do the same. The couches were mostly dust free; her father had finally unpacked the cleaning robot known as Jeeves after Rachelli and Alex had called it quits on cleaning. They had left him running all night until his battery had run down.

Mrs. Pernikov removed her pink floppy hat and folded it in her lap. "So what do you say we get to know each other a bit? This here is a friendly town, you know, and we do like to get to know our neighbors! Did you know that Sundale is home of the second-to-largest ball of twine? Second only to Cawker City, Kansas!"

"Fascinating," said Alex politely.

"What does your father do for a living, dear?"

"Candy-machine repairman," Rachelli answered promptly.

Unfortunately, at the same time Alex said, "Air-conditioner installation."

"Both," Rachelli said. She smiled weakly. "He installs candy machines and repairs air conditioners."

"I thought it was the other way around, dear?"

"Yes," Rachelli said earnestly. "Exactly. Um. And you?"

Before Mrs. Pernikov could answer, the house seemed to rock once again from a muffled explosion.

"What was that?" Mrs. Pernikov exclaimed, clutching at her hat.

"Oh, we can totally explain that," Alex said reassuringly. "It was simply—"

Rachelli had a feeling from the panicked look in his eyes that he had no idea what he was going to say next, and she was momentarily relieved when Lolly walked into the room. Then she realized that the little girl was holding a test tube. It was filled with a clear liquid. It was also bubbling.

"Daddy left this in the kitchen," Lolly said. She turned toward the trapdoor. "Should we bring it to him?"

"No!" Rachelli leaped to her feet and put out a hand toward Lolly before she could reveal the secret lab — and accidentally knocked the test tube out of the little girl's hand.

As if in slow motion, the four of them watched as the glass vial bounced once, twice, three times on the wooden floor. The fourth time, it smashed. The bubbling liquid spilled, and there was a sudden flash of light.

When the light faded, the wooden floor below their feet was revealed to have turned a shocking blue.

"I can explain," Rachelli said quickly. "I can totally explain the sudden blueness of the floor."

She opened her mouth to say something, anything. As she did so, she turned to look at Mrs. Pernikov and saw something in the old woman's eyes.

It was not fear, as she expected, or even excitement.

It was a sudden spark of interest.

Chapter 4

"It's your turn to watch her." Rachelli spoke to her brother's reflection behind her in the front hall mirror, a huge floor-to-ceiling piece in a heavy and ornate frame.

"No!" Alex's reflected mouth fell open. "No, it's your turn!"

"You never remember things like turns," Rachelli reminded him as she retied her bow. "You never even remember things like lunch."

"I always remember whose turn it is to watch Lolly." Alex folded his arms and glared at his older sister. A moment later, the self-righteous anger on his face faded to be replaced with a vague, glassy look that meant his mind had jumped somewhere else.

"Alex!" Rachelli snapped her fingers impatiently until his eyes cleared. "Lolly. Watch her. And make sure she doesn't get into too much trouble. Or eat too much. Or get too sticky."

Those first two orders were difficult, but the last was impossible. Put a freshly washed Lolly in the middle of a clean room, and two minutes later, she'll be sticky. It was like she exuded stickiness or something.

"No way!" Alex said. "I have things to do. There is no way I'm watching an always-sticky, eternally hungry little girl when it's not even my *turn*! Rachelli!"

As Rachelli left the house, the last thing she heard Alex say was, "It's not like you even have anywhere to go!"

Rachelli walked to the edge of their property and hesitated. She put one hand on the enormous oak tree beside her and considered her options.

Well, there really were none, right? Just a vague suspicion that Mrs. Pernikov had seemed a bit too...*interested* in the chemical Lolly had spilled. (Jeeves, the robot cleaner, had worked on the blue floor until his battery had died. The floor stayed blue.) Rachelli was... alarmed.

Oh, how her father and Alex would laugh at her if she would tell them how she was feeling! They were men of science — well, one man and one boy of science — and feelings and intuition that something was off about their new neighbor would never fly with them. They would demand proof, evidence, and scientific formulas.

Rachelli twirled her hair ribbon around a finger and considered calling her mother, but she was too far away to do anything other than worry, and Rachelli didn't want to do that to her.

And her friends back home — Shuli and Tehila and the rest — thought her father was a candy-machine repairman who dabbled in inventions for use around the house, so they were out for advice.

Whom could she talk to about the very old woman with the very sharp eyes?

Maybe it was nothing. Maybe it was just *interesting* to her, that the floor had suddenly stained blue right in front of her. Maybe Rachelli had imagined the woman's eyes sharpening like that, the suddenly calculated expression as she looked from the blue floor to the smashed vial.

But what if she *hadn't* imagined it?

Her father had emphasized, his normally dreamy and vague expression unusually sharp and stern, how important it was that his experiment be kept a secret. Could it be that people knew about him? Could it be that people had found out who he was and were interested in his secret?

"It's not that I actually miss Effie," Rachelli explained to the oak tree, "because no self-respecting girl is supposed to miss her annoying older brother when he goes away to yeshivah. It's just that maybe *he* would listen to me without laughing."

The oak tree seemed to be the nonjudgmental sort, since it too did not laugh. But the gaggle of giggling girls walking up the tree-lined street toward her certainly was. They halted in front of Rachelli.

"We heard," said the girl with two pert blond braids who seemed to be leading the pack, "that the floor of your living room somehow turned blue! Is that true?"

"Well, there's blue and then there's blue, you know?" Rachelli ventured nonsensically. "Um. I mean, who told you about that?"

The girls burst into fresh laughter. "Honey, this is a small town," the girl with the blond braids said. "And the Jewish community is even smaller. Here in Sundale, everyone knows everything. It's more interesting than watching grass grow, anyway." The girl stuck out her small freckled hand, and Rachelli shook it hesitantly. "Birdy Winter. We girls are going to town for ice cream. Care to join?"

Rachelli didn't mean to be a snob. She'd never been a snob before this moment, in her opinion. It was almost as if the wide and innocent smiles of these out-out-out-of-town girls brought it out of her. "Maybe a different time," she said coolly, as if she'd had a thousand invitations already that morning. "Thanks for the offer."

When they'd turned the corner, she set her sights again on the house next door.

It was a sprawling split-level affair, set on a manicured lawn. After a few minutes of eyeing it through the line of trees that separated the two properties, Rachelli snorted at herself. "Well, genius, are you expecting the house to tell you if its owners are a little too interested in your father's experiments?"

As she spoke, the corner of a window shade in one of the topmost rooms seemed to twitch open and then fall closed just as quickly. Rachelli almost leaped back in surprise. She could just make out the shadow of a figure walking away from the window and disappearing.

As she'd watched the house…had someone been watching her?

"Not a trapdoor. This time Lolly fell down a dumbwaiter." Alex had been putting a Band-Aid on Lolly's knee and handing her a bag of Bissli when Rachelli, thoroughly spooked, had walked back inside the house.

"A dumb who?"

"A dumb what. Coolest thing ever. This house is so old in the best way possible. The only thing that would make it better would be a treasure chest in the basement." Alex was smiling one of his rare smiles as he ran to the kitchen counter. "Check this out." He opened the far-most cabinet and placed another bag of Bissli on the empty shelf inside. "Pull the rope," he said, and then scampered out of the kitchen.

Rachelli peered inside the cabinet and found a rope attached to the side. Shrugging, she pulled at it — and watched as the shelf with the Bissli on it moved upward with each pull of the rope. Soon it had vanished into the space where the top of the cabinet should be. When she couldn't pull anymore, she let go of the rope and watched the cabinet zoom back down into its place. It was empty.

After a minute, Alex came back into the kitchen, still smiling, and chomping on Bissli. "I was in my room," he crunched. "And I could get used to this, by the way."

"Well, get unused to it," Rachelli said. "Speaking of room service, I'd better ask Daddy if he wants to eat something."

All the way down the steps beneath the trapdoor, Rachelli wondered if she should tell him all about the moving curtains and the sparkle in Mrs. Pernikov's eye when the floor had turned blue. But then she thought about the girls who had come over seemingly to invite her to ice cream but really because they were curious about the floor. *This is a small town,* that blond girl had said, and people in small towns apparently knew everyone else's business. That's probably all it was.

Was she so bored here that she had to invent conspiracies just to have something to occupy herself with?

With a sigh of exasperation, Rachelli pushed open the door to the secret lab.

And screamed when she walked straight into a creature from her nightmares.

CHAPTER 5

Hello Family,

How is Snoredale, home of the second-to-largest ear of corn, or ball of wax, or whatever it is?

Yeshivah is great. Well, except for the food. And my mattress. And my roommate. And my *chavrusa*. But since my floor is not bright blue, I guess we can call it even. (BTW, best thing ever to happen. Give Lolly a lollipop and tell her to do more things like that — keeps me entertained.)

😊 Slaps and pinches,
Ephraim

(Not Effie, so stop sending letters to Effie, please, or I will pretend that they're not for me, and they'll just sit in the office forever until they turn moldy and gross, and then I'll send them back to Sundale so that it can be home of the moldiest collection of unopened letters and for once be second to none.)

"You're dripping pizza sauce on your sleeve," Rachelli pointed out. "You, too, Alex. Seriously, you are bad at pizza."

"Seriously?" Alex snorted and pointed his pizza at his sister. "Seriously, I can't believe you didn't recognize Daddy covered in citric acid and baking powder."

Rachelli scowled. "Well, Daddy doesn't usually walk around in citric acid and baking powder." It was completely understandable, she thought, that she had freaked out when she'd run smack into a being completely covered in white. Her scream had been cut short when her father had screamed in fright along with her.

"What is it? What? What?" he'd howled.

Rachelli had put her hand to her heart. "Don't do that to me!" she'd gasped. "Please, Daddy, don't do that ever again!"

The inside of the lab looked like someone had had a pillow fight with pillows stuffed with flour instead of feathers, but Professor Shore had quickly closed the door before she was able to get a good look.

And he had also, inexplicably, been holding a round tray containing a piping-hot pizza. He handed the sizzling pie to Rachelli and then slapped at himself, sending up clouds of the white powdery substance that coated his face and arms and legs.

"I made pizza," he said. "Shall we have lunch? Is it lunchtime? Or time for dinner? Not breakfast, though, I'm pretty sure." And he had gone up the stairs two at a time without waiting for an answer, leaving Rachelli clutching the pie and blinking dumbly after him.

"But-but—" she had finally protested. But he was long gone, and when she had climbed the stairs after him and walked across the bright-blue expanse of living room floor and finally found herself in the kitchen with the rest of the family, Alex was smirking at her, apparently having heard her shriek and come to his own conclusions.

And now they were eating the mysterious pizza and engaging in their favorite game: Guess What the Secret Experiment Is.

"A robot," Rachelli said. "*That's* what you're inventing, Daddy. A robot that looks and sounds just like a person and also knows how to make pizza."

"No, a space-time distortion field," Alex said. He pushed his glasses up his nose. "So you can make objects appear larger or smaller than they are, and cook and bake something like a pizza instantly. The question is, how would one go about making calculations for such a thing? Well, of course, you would start with units of distance—"

"What you said is wrong because I didn't understand half the words," Rachelli said, loudly interrupting Alex's calculations. "And anyway, my idea makes more sense."

"How does it make more sense?"

"Because I was the one who said it."

"Pizza!" Lolly yelled triumphantly as she climbed onto her chair. "Daddy is inventing pizza!"

"Italians already did that," Rachelli told the little girl as she cut her slice into pieces and handed her a fork. "But that was a good guess."

"The definition of a secret," Professor Shore said, holding his slice of pizza halfway to his mouth, the same position it had been in for the past few minutes, "is that it doesn't get told to other people, including you, my dear children."

"But if we guess right, will you tell us?" Rachelli pressed.

"No," said her father.

"Give us a hint," Rachelli pleaded. "Does the pizza have anything to do with it?"

Professor Shore looked at the pizza in his hand as if he had just remembered its presence. He shrugged.

"A machine that dries your hair instantly," Rachelli said, touching her silky hair ribbon. "And makes it into whatever style you want."

"A temperature modulator," Alex contributed. "So that people can control the weather."

"Pizza!" Lolly said as she held out her plate for another piece.

But they were either way off the mark, or Professor Shore was really serious about keeping it a secret because their father just smiled absently at them and finally took a bite of his lunch.

And at that thought — that their father believed it was important to keep it secret even from them — Rachelli glanced nervously in the direction of the doorway, as if expecting Mrs. Pernikov to be walking through it. No one was there, though, and for the thousandth time she told herself to cut it out. Mrs. Pernikov and her nosiness was as much a part of the small-towniness of Sundale as its second-to-largest ball of twine was.

She decided to put the old woman and her suspicions firmly out of her mind.

But the thoughts didn't seem to want to leave. It didn't help that Rachelli seemed to see Mrs. Pernikov and the little wizened old man that she introduced as her husband everywhere she went: behind her in line in one of the tiny town's two grocery stores, walking past the Victorian just as Rachelli walked toward it, and behind the giggling gaggle of girls led by Birdy Winter as Rachelli turned hastily to escape before they saw her.

Too late.

"Yoo-hoo! Rachelli!" Birdy and her swarm were all over her like bees on honey.

"Hello," Rachelli sighed. She looked around, but Mrs. Pernikov had vanished.

"We're having a sort of party next week," Birdy said. "It's a charity and a summer party — isn't it just great to have a party? And, of course, you're invited!" Birdy smiled widely, and the rest of the girls followed suit.

"Yes, and then we can have a nice long talk, and you can tell us aaaall about yourself!" said the girl to Birdy's right. She was bouncing on her toes in excitement.

Rachelli was trying to think of a way to politely decline what was sure to be a Snoredale snore fest, when an idea hit her. What had Birdy said the last time she had seen her?

Honey, this is a small town. And the Jewish community is even smaller. Here in Sundale, everyone knows everything.

Did they really know everything?

Hmm.

"Now, that party sounds like a real treat!" Rachelli smiled and added a little Sundale twang to her voice. "But first, can I ask you girls a question?"

Birdy winked. Then she settled herself onto the tire swing beside the house and turned to Rachelli. "I thought you'd never ask."

"It's about my neighbors." Rachelli shaded her eyes and glanced through the trees over at the house next door. "It's about the Pernikovs."

"No *lashon hara* now." Birdy dimpled. "But what is it you want to know?"

Rachelli ended up coming forty-five minutes late to take over watching Lolly. She had wanted to push away her suspicions about Mrs. Pernikov because they were based on feelings instead of evidence. Well, now she had evidence, and her heart pounded as she ran from the wide doorway and down the hallway toward the living room. The old wooden floors squeaked underfoot.

She found Alex examining the bright-blue flooring over the trapdoor with a magnifying glass. Lolly had her own magnifying glass and was using it to add dents to the floor.

"You're late—" Alex began, looking up, but Rachelli interrupted him.

"What would you say if I told you," she said to her brother breathlessly, "that I have cold, hard proof that someone is trying to figure out — and maybe even steal — Daddy's secret experiment?"

CHAPTER 6

If the original owner of the huge sprawling Victorian mansion could have peeked into the future and seen what the Shores — specifically, Alex — had transformed it into, he would have had the world's biggest hissy fit.

As it was, Pinny the PNAAD had a little fit of his own when Rachelli and Alex loaded the supplies needed to surround the Victorian with a glittery, electronic sensory net into the back of the car and told him to drive home.

"I have a dream," the Personalized Navigator and Automatic Driver said in a voice that was choked with tears, "that one day, there shall be no more servitude and drudgery and schlepping packages back and forth, and also, while we're on the topic, no more bird droppings. One day I shall lead all of my fellow PNAADs into freedom!"

"But you're the only PNAAD," Rachelli ill-advisedly pointed out. "You don't have fellow PNAADs to lead to freedom — or to the metal scrapyard, for that matter."

It took Alex twenty minutes to calm Pinny down long enough for the car to drive them home.

"Motion sensors," Alex explained to Rachelli, pushing his glasses up his nose when she found him sitting in his room among a jumble of wires and cables and things that went *beep!* "If anyone comes into the house, we'll know about it — Lolly, don't touch! I should have the whole net set up in a few hours."

Rachelli examined the wires and cables and beeping things and nodded as if she understood exactly what Alex was doing.

When Rachelli had dragged Alex away from the blue living room floor to the privacy of her room and explained to him what Birdy Winter, know-it-all extraordinaire of Sundale, had told her about the Pernikovs, she half thought her younger brother would stare at her blankly and say, "So what?"

And that was, actually, exactly what happened.

"So what?" he said as he took off his glasses and inserted them into a little metal sleeve the size of a glasses case. He pressed a button, and the glasses spat themselves out, clean. He put them back on. "So what if the Pernikovs moved to Sundale a week before we did? Who cares?"

"So what? Who cares? Lolly, take that out of your mouth! It's not food, it's a totally-not-handy glasses cleaning device."

"It is so handy!" Alex glared.

"It's bulky to carry around, and you can use your sleeve to clean your glasses, like all normal kids whose fathers are not secret scientists do. Anyway, Alex, focus. If they moved here a week before we did, it's suspicious. Birdy said that Sundale is a place that people tend to move away *from*, not to, and that we and the Pernikovs were the first new people who moved here in five years. It's weird, okay?"

"Okay! But it can be weird, or *they* can be weird, like, just two old, weird people who decided to move to Sundale — what?"

Rachelli had gestured frantically over Lolly's head for Alex to stop talking. She had heard the soft but distinct sound of footsteps. Her ears pricked. There it was again!

Someone is downstairs, she mouthed.

What? Alex mouthed back.

"What?" Lolly asked brightly and at the top of her lungs.

Rachelli rolled her eyes. Then she handed Lolly a lolly to keep the little girl quiet and rose soundlessly to her feet.

The staircase was massive and old and wooden and twisty and turny, and when you trod on the steps, there were several spots where the creak of the wood under your foot sounded like a gunshot or an old animal groaning. And on the third-to-last step to the right of the huge, rounded railing, it sounded like the final three notes to Yanky Doodle Dandy. Alex and Rachelli, holding Lolly, managed to avoid the gunshot and the old animal groaning, but then both of them stepped on the Yanky Doodle step.

A second later, they heard the distinct sounds of someone — or someones — running down the hallway and closing the front doors behind them. *Scraaaaape, slam*!

They emerged, thoroughly spooked, onto the blinding blue floor in the living room, feet away from where their father was working in the secret lab.

"Okay, fine," Alex said grudgingly. "Whether or not someone is coming here with eyes for Daddy's experiment — which, by the way, I've thought about it, and I'm pretty sure is related to the government's new interest in Mars — someone is definitely just coming and going as they please, and that's got to stop."

"It has nothing to do with Mars. Daddy's experiment — and I've given this careful thought — is a mind-reading device that knows what you need before you even know that you need it." Rachelli looked down the long, dark hallway toward the front door. "So are we going to get a massive lock for the front door, or what?"

"No." Alex's glasses glowed in the shaft of light coming from one of the large stained-glass windows that ran the length of the living room. "We're going to make something much, much better."

It took Alex the rest of the afternoon to draw up plans for the sensory net, and then they snuck off to Sundale's small line of stores, using Pinny, to get the supplies they needed. When they got the reluctant PNAAD home, Alex built the net while Rachelli kept Lolly entertained.

"So what's it going to do, exactly?" Rachelli put her hands on her hips.

Alex looked up with a slight gasp, as though her presence had startled him, even though she had been there pretty much the whole time. There was a smear of grease across one of his cheeks, and he held a screwdriver in his mouth.

"Mpph mpph marcerm," he said to her.

"I didn't understand a word you just said."

Alex pulled the screwdriver out of his mouth. "I said, it's going to be kind of like an alarm system. Since we don't know who's coming in, or how, we'll wrap it around the whole house, and it will activate if someone is trying to sneak onto the premises."

Rachelli snorted. "That's your grand plan? Alex, seriously. They're coming in through the front door. Half the time, one of us" — she glared at Alex — "forgets to lock it."

Alex shook his head. "Didn't I tell you?"

"Tell me what?"

"I fixed the front door last night so that it locks automatically." Alex picked up a wrench and examined it. "Whoever was in the house this morning couldn't have come in through the front door."

Rachelli felt goose bumps rise on the back of her neck.

"Want to go outside," Lolly said as Alex got back to work, and Rachelli, knowing that she was totally out of her depth anyway, sighed and took the little girl by her sticky hand and brought her to the tire swing in the front of the house. She was totally and completely unsurprised when Mrs. Pernikov peeked at the two of them through the line of trees that divided their properties.

"Yoo-hoo!" The old woman waved.

"Hello." Rachelli addressed her shoes.

Lolly, on the other hand, smiled and waved.

"You are such a wonderful childminder," Mrs. Pernikov said, her huge pink hat flapping back and forth in the slight breeze. "Look how happy you make your sister. Not many girls these days have patience for the little ones."

At that, Rachelli smiled slightly. She did rather have a way with Lolly, didn't she?

"Do you like children?" Mrs. Pernikov went on.

Rachelli shrugged. "I guess," she said.

"And you are rather bored here all alone in this big, empty house, aren't you?"

Rachelli shrugged again. "I mean, it's — well, it's Sundale, home of the second-to-biggest boring summer," she said.

The old woman smiled, as if this confirmed something she had been thinking. "Exactly," she said.

After Lolly went to sleep that night, Alex installed the sensory net. At first, it glittered and shone as he wrapped the delicate links around the base of the house, but when he pressed a button, the light flickered and faded, and the wires were nearly invisible.

"Perfect," Alex said. "Now, what shall I name my new invention? Sensor-O-Matic? Or how about Home-Safety-Net? Or Alex-Is-the-Best-Scientist-and-Inventor-in-the-World? That last one might be a bit long, but it has a ring to it—"

"How about go to sleep," Rachelli suggested, and went straight to her room to do just that.

Someone was using the massive lion door knocker at an hour so early, Rachelli didn't even have any thoughts in her head.

"Wazzat?" she mumbled into her pillow.

When she finally stumbled to the front door and pulled it open, she was greeted by a sight that made her blood freeze.

CHAPTER 7

Dear Effie,

I have, over the past few weeks in Sundale, faced many terrifying things. Like the time Daddy made us go see the second-to-largest ball of twine, which is kept in a museum of the same name, and it was just like this huge ball of twine that did absolutely nothing at all, and the longer I looked at it, the longer it remained a huge ball of twine that did absolutely nothing at all, and there was a woman there blowing her nose and sobbing over — get this — the majesty of it.

And many other horrible things, too many to write down here.

But never ever have I been forced to face, at 7:03 in the morning, what I faced today.

I would like to say that I emerged triumphant from the experience. So, okay, I'll say it, even if it isn't true.

I emerged triumphant from the experience.

Miss you.

You're annoying for being there and not here,

Rachelli

Hello family,

This letter is returned to sender — for reals, okay? I didn't even read it at all, or at least not much, because THERE IS NO EFFIE. STOP SENDING LETTERS TO EFFIE. EFFIE DOES NOT EXIST. THERE IS ONLY EPHRAIM. Seriously!

Miss you.

Ha ha, because I didn't have to go see the second-to-largest ball of twine,

EPHRAIM

"Rachelli, why is there so much noise? I can barely hear you!"

Rachelli was trying to hold the phone with one shoulder while using her two hands to handle the dire emergency that had showed up at the Victorian's front doors at 7:03 that morning in the form of a dozen children between the ages of three and six.

One of them, a tiny girl with two blond braids and a missing tooth and who bore an uncanny resemblance to Birdy Winter, made a grab for the Egginator. Since Rachelli's hands were already filled with a little freckled boy and the Toast Stick he had discovered, Rachelli made a grab for the girl with her foot and accomplished exactly nothing other than looking slightly ridiculous.

"Rachelli, are you running a day camp over there?" Mrs. Shore asked with a laugh.

"Ma," Rachelli said, "you wouldn't believe me if I told you."

There was a rustling sound from the living room, followed by multiple shrieks.

"I'd better go, Ma," Rachelli said. She dropped the phone, the boy, and the Toast Stick, and grabbed for the girl and the Egginator, both of which slipped through her fingers and fell to the floor — the girl with a light thump and the Egginator with a resounding crash. Someone shrieked from the living room again, and Rachelli shot one last despairing look at their former breakfast makers and the children who had cheerfully destroyed them. Then she dashed to the living room to make sure that none of her surprise charges had managed to get themselves into terrible danger.

Of course, they had managed exactly that.

"Alex!" Rachelli shrieked. "Aaaaaalex!" When no answer was forthcoming, she raced back to the kitchen and yanked open the door to the dumbwaiter that led to Alex's room. "Alexander Shore, you get yourself down here this second!" she yelled into it.

A few minutes later, Alex ambled down the stairs, rubbing his eyes. "Huh?" he said when he saw what was going on at the bottom floor. "Rachelli, who covered our house in kids?"

"First, you tell me why three of those kids are tied up in a net in the living room!" Rachelli snapped back.

Alex put his hand to his mouth. "Did someone try to open the window?"

"Maybe, I don't know, why?"

"Someone activated the Self-Protective Sensomatic." Alex jumped down the last two steps and ran across the bright-blue living room floor. Swinging gently from a net that was attached to the top of one of the stained-glass windows were three terrified children.

"Really?" Rachelli asked as Alex pressed a hidden switch under the windowsill and the net lowered to the ground. "Self-Protective Sensomatic?"

"You have a better name?"

"Like fifty million better names."

"Now can I ask you about the kids?"

Rachelli pulled at her hair. "Alex," she said despairingly. "I really, really don't know."

At 7:07 that morning, Rachelli had nearly been bowled over by a small army of children.

At 7:03, four minutes before that event, Rachelli had opened the front door and found the porch filled with kids and their mothers.

"Um?" Rachelli said, and one of the mothers, a small woman in a big yellow hat, detached herself from the group and gave a startled Rachelli a hug.

"Thanks so much for doing this, honey-bun!" she said. "We are immeasurably grateful — aren't we, ladies?"

The rest of the mothers chorused their full and undivided agreement of that statement while Rachelli scratched her head and wondered for one wild moment if she was, in fact, still sleeping and having a very weird dream.

"The kids were going positively stir-crazy with another two weeks until school starts," the mother continued, "and there's only so many times we can go to the Second-to-Largest Ball of Twine Museum, wonderful as it very much is!" The face under the yellow hat beamed at Rachelli and then beamed at the kids. "Have a great time, children! With a childminder like Miss Shore, I know you will!"

"Wait!" Rachelli finally said after spending a solid minute clinging to the doorframe with her mouth wide open. "Wait just one second!"

But by the time the words got out, the last of the immeasurably grateful mothers had long since escaped, leaving their kids behind.

Rachelli spent a couple of moments blinking at them.

"Um," she greeted the sea of upturned little faces. "Um, hello. Um. Won't you please…" Since there was no polite way of ending that sentence with "go away," she said instead, "come in?"

The look on their faces, she realized a second later, wasn't shy. It was just a pause, the calm before the storm, as if they were taking stock of the situation before pushing their way past her and into the house.

It was like a stampede, Rachelli thought dizzily, except with fewer hooves and horns, and more pigtails and shrieky little voices.

"Rachelli, hello." Professor Shore had just returned from davening. "There seems to be many children in the house today," he said mildly. "Keep them quiet, will you?"

"Daddy!" Rachelli called after him. "Daddy, help!"

But he was already gone, disappearing through the trapdoor in the living room and into his secret lab. Rachelli would have sunk to her knees in absolute bewilderment had she not realized that the shrieky little voices had stopped making shrieky little noises.

Taking care of Lolly this summer had made her realize that while silence is usually golden, when it comes to little kids, it usually just means trouble.

It was only an hour later, after two more kids had managed to trigger off two more sensors — one by climbing into the dumbwaiter in the kitchen, and another by doing nothing at all (or so he yelled at the top of his lungs as he swung from a net over the trapdoor leading to the secret lab) — that Rachelli and Alex had the presence of mind to take all of the kids out to the yard, where they handed out some cookies and milk.

While the kids were enjoying the treats, Rachelli and Alex slumped onto the damp, dew-covered grass, Lolly in Rachelli's lap.

"They are not kids," Alex said. "They are violent, horrible creatures dressed to look like regular kids. They pretty much destroyed my entire sensory net."

"They destroyed everything in the kitchen," Rachelli added grimly. "What is a childminder?"

"I guess someone who minds children?"

"I totally mind these children. I totally mind them being here." Rachelli looked at the bunch of them, starting to play games in the high grass. Lolly clambered off her lap and joined them.

"I think it means—"

"How in the world did I give the impression to anyone that I'm interested in running some sort of day camp?" Rachelli got to her feet and spread her hands out to either side. "Especially one that starts at an hour in the morning that I'm pretty sure shouldn't exist in the summer!"

Like a flash, the answer came to her, and with it a grim certainty that things were about to go from bad to worse.

CHAPTER 8

When the last of the kids finally left, the house looked exactly the way Rachelli and Alex felt: completely destroyed.

"Alert! Alert! Jeeves down! Jeeves down! Unable to fulfill primary directive!" a mechanical cry came from the kitchen, but it was barely heard over a cacophony of beeping.

Rachelli sighed. "Well, it's not like we went and used up our entire summer allowance and all of my babysitting money on this stuff. Oh wait, we did!" Rachelli kicked at the rope net that covered the neon-blue floor of the living room.

"Hey, look, it's not my fault you decided to open up a day camp." Alex was peering at a section of the rope with a magnifying glass.

"Jeeves down! Jeeves down!" *Beep beep beep beeeeeep!*

"I didn't!" Rachelli yelled in outrage. "You know I didn't decide to open a day camp! Those kids just showed up!"

"Anyway, I can fix this equipment. It was meant to come down, you know, just on an intruder, not on a bunch of kids." Alex got to his feet and started to gather the ropes together.

"Can you fix all of that stuff as well?" Rachelli turned toward the kitchen, where Lolly was squatting on the floor, playing with the broken Egginator and Toast Stick, both of which were beeping furiously at her. Jeeves, the robot cleaner, jerked his broom hand back and forth, trying to clean up, a futile exercise seeing as he was flat on his back.

"Alert, alert!" the robot cried. "Jeeves cannot seek out dirt and eradicate it! Alert!"

Other kitchen gadgets littered the floor as well, and every so often the Toast Stick flashed a bluish light and attempted to lightly toast a floor tile.

"I can't fix that stuff. I'm not good enough yet. Daddy could, though. He made all of them, after all." Alex got to his feet and started toward the secret lab to tell Professor Shore what had happened.

Rachelli stopped him. "It will take him forever to fix all this stuff, and it'll take him away from his invention — which I'm pretty sure is a mirror that can tell you what your colors are — and then we'll be stuck in Snoredale taking care of other people's kids forever."

Alex shook his head. "His invention is a universal translator so that we can speak any language in the world. I'm pretty sure."

"Jeeves down. Jeeeevess dooooown." The robot lying on the kitchen floor and sweeping the air was finally running low on batteries.

"Anyway, whoever did this is going to pay for it," Rachelli said grimly.

"Well, those pesky kids did this," Alex said. "We saw them."

"Yeah, but they didn't just suddenly decide to come here. Someone told them to."

"Should I call my invention The Alex, or Alex Is Amazing? Or does that sound slightly egotistical?"

Rachelli snapped her fingers in front of her brother's eyes, which had gone dreamy behind his glasses. "Earth to Alex. Currently discussing problem."

Alex blinked. "Sorry. Thinking about something else. Where were we?"

Rachelli surged to her feet. She yanked out her purple hair ribbon and began tying it around her ponytail again in angry jerks. "You know, I feel like I'm all alone here. Someone is trying to figure out Daddy's invention, and I'm trying to protect it, and you're all like, 'What should I name my invention?' Do you even believe me?"

Alex cleared his throat. He adjusted his collar. He adjusted his glasses. "Well," he said finally, after running out of things to adjust, "there is no scientific proof—"

Rachelli snorted. "You want proof? I'll give you proof. I asked Birdy Winter's mother how she heard about the day camp. Apparently, someone hung a sign about 'Rachelli Shore's Super Amazing and Extremely Free Day Camp' on the wall outside of the Second-to-Largest Ball of Twine Museum."

Alex opened his mouth to answer, but a shriek from the kitchen stopped him. They both ran toward the sound.

Lolly had her hand in the Egginator up until her wrist and was hysterically trying to get it out. The device was beeping frantically, and the screen flashed, "Blood spot! Blood spot! *Treif*! *Treif*! Run for your lives!"

Dear Mothers of Sundale's Jewish Community's Precious Children,

It was an absolute delight having your kids grace my house with their presence yesterday! They had a great time, and I did too! We did lots and lots of fun things, but also maybe don't believe everything they say, like about being caught in traps and talking robots and sparkling neon-blue floors and stuff like that because kids, as you know, have very, very active imaginations! Ha ha! Kids! What will they think of next?

Anyway, the reason I'm writing this and hanging it up on the wall outside the Second-to-Largest Ball of Twine Museum is because unfortunately, due to totally unforeseen circumstances, Rachelli Shore's Super Amazing and Extremely Free Day Camp is no longer running. So please don't send your kids back tomorrow.

Please.

Thank you for understanding,
Rachelli

Professor Shore came up from the secret lab holding dinner that he said was meat stew. His face fell when Lolly said that it kind of tasted like eating a pair of steaming-hot sneakers.

"Back to the drawing board," he said.

"Are you inventing a machine that makes automatic food?" Rachelli asked.

Professor Shore wrinkled his forehead. "Why would you think that?"

"Because of all the automatic food," Rachelli said.

"Oh! No!" Professor Shore shook his head so hard his yarmulke flew off. He bent down to get it. "The food is a byproduct. It's hard to explain."

"It sounds gross," Rachelli said. "Eating a byproduct."

"Also it tastes like shoes. But only after you wore them all day," Lolly continued her analysis of the stew.

Professor Shore stood up. "So let me whip something together with the kitchen gadgets." His eyes widened as he took in the damage in the kitchen for the first time. "Well, this is no good. I'll have to fix all of this. Help me bring all these things to the lab. Alex, grab Jeeves."

Rachelli sighed.

"Don't worry, Rachelli," Professor Shore said, misunderstanding her sigh. "I'll work this out."

For the next three days, Rachelli and Alex and Professor Shore struggled to relearn how to make eggs and toast and keep the house clean the old-fashioned way. Their efforts were hampered by the fact that the neighborhood kids did not exactly stop coming to visit; there was always one or two of them around, hanging out on the tire swing in the front or playing ball in the overgrown yard. Their mothers smiled and waved at Rachelli or Alex or Lolly or Professor Shore whenever they stepped across the threshold, and the Shores took to using the newly discovered back door whenever they wanted some fresh air.

"I'll never be able to reinstall my Alex Is Amazing Sensomatic Sensors with all these people around," Alex said to Rachelli early one morning as she struggled to turn on the flame on the stove. "I know it was important to you, but it's not going to happen."

"The Pernikovs are behind this." Rachelli frowned. "They hung up the sign outside the museum. They're trying to distract us. It's all part of their evil plan."

"No one really says stuff like 'it's all part of their evil plan,' Rachelli."

"I do. Ouch!" Rachelli snatched her hand back from the stove and raced to the sink to soak her finger. "When is Mommy coming home again?"

"Next week. For a while this time, Daddy said."

Rachelli turned off the sink and put her finger into her mouth.

"That's good," she said around a mouthful of finger. "Because I'm kind of falling apart. Look. Even my ribbon is drooping."

"Daddy said that we won't be in charge for much longer, anyway. He said he has a plan."

"An evil plan?"

"I told you, no one—" but Alex stopped short when an earsplitting *crack!* echoed throughout the huge Victorian.

"What's Daddy doing this time?" Rachelli said when she recovered. "My ears are ringing."

There was another loud noise, and then another, and Lolly flew down the stairs and grabbed Rachelli's legs.

"Don't worry, Lolly," Rachelli said. "It's just Daddy, probably trying to turn straw into gold or something."

Bang! Bang!

"Rachelli," Alex whispered, and his face behind his glasses was chalky-white. "That wasn't coming from the lab. That was coming from the front yard. I think someone is coming toward the house. And I think they have a gun."

Chapter 9

Dear Mommy,

Everything is totally fine here! Totally fine! But if, like, all of your meetings get canceled all of a sudden or whatever, it would be totally fine if you wanted to come home, like, right now.

Please?

Love,
Us

Dear Effie,

Your summer is not weirder than my summer because my summer involves dead bluebirds.

See you on Shabbos,
Rachelli (and the smear on the right of the page is from Lolly)

There are situations that are so big, or so ridiculous, or so very confusing, that words do not even begin to describe them. And sometimes that without-words-to-describe-it situation is a person, and sometimes that person is Wilma Lou Wilson.

There were no words to describe Wilma Lou Wilson, but Alex and Rachelli and even Lolly were going to try.

"I hired her to help out around here. No good?" Surprise was evident in Professor Shore's normally dreamy tones when his normally basically content children marched down into the secret lab and demanded an explanation for Wilma Lou Wilson.

"Daddy." Rachelli took a deep breath and searched for the words to explain to him what kind of woman had shown up at their door, who even now was clomping around the house in the thickest, oldest boots that Rachelli had ever seen. "Daddy. *She has a shotgun.*"

Fifteen minutes earlier, after around a half a dozen *cracks* sounded from outside, someone had knocked on the door smartly. *Knock, knock, knock, knockety knockety knock.*

Lolly had still been clinging to Rachelli's legs, effectively immobilizing her, so Alex, after a moment's hesitation, had walked over to the front door and peeped through the peephole. He yelped and took a step backward.

"What?" Rachelli asked, hurrying over. Lolly stayed attached to her like a third leg.

Rachelli looked through the peephole. A big blue eye, slightly bloodshot, was staring straight back at her, inches away from the peephole.

"Hey there!" said a voice that was a little hoarse and a lot loud. "I'm a-knockin'!"

"Yes," Alex said through the door. "Um. Okay. So we hear you a-knockin' — uh, knocking. We also heard you a-shootin', so…"

"Yeah!" There was the sound of a chuckle through the thick double doors. "Gave that peekin' neighbor a right ol' scare!"

"Did you," Rachelli asked carefully, after a moment's shocked silence, "shoot Mrs. Pernikov?"

"Shootin' *people*?" the voice at the door sounded outraged. "No and no, hon! I was shootin' at them blue jays! And it's getting mighty uncomfortable speakin' through the door. Can't a person come in and have a set down? I have candies to give y'all!"

And then Lolly inexplicably let go of Rachelli's legs and unlocked the door.

"Lolly!" Rachelli hissed as the door began to open from the outside, scraping heavily across the threshold. "Lolly, what did you do?"

"She has candy," Lolly explained cheerfully. "And Mommy says to always take candy from strangers."

"*No*," Rachelli said as the door opened fully. "Lolly, *no*, Mommy says to *never* take candy from strangers. It's different from *always*. It's *never*. If you think about it, those two words are the most different that words can be—"

And then someone with the largest, reddest hands that she had ever seen was suddenly seizing her own hand and shaking it up and down so vigorously that her teeth rattled.

The hand, she saw, was attached to an arm, and the arm was attached to the rest of Wilma Lou Wilson.

"Howdy!" Wilma Lou Wilson said. "I am Wilma Lou Wilson!" Wilma Lou Wilson smiled. Wilma Lou Wilson's smile was missing three teeth. In her other hand, the hand that was not making Rachelli's teeth vibrate, Wilma Lou Wilson was holding a long wooden-handled shotgun.

Rachelli and Alex took three steps back.

"Can I have the candies?" Lolly asked.

"Okay, so first of all, Daddy," Rachelli tried to explain, too frazzled to even try to peek over her father's shoulder at the open door to the secret lab, like she usually did when she was down there. "So first of all, she has a gun and she shoots bluebirds."

"Blue jays," Lolly said. "And she has candies."

"She scared Mrs. Pernikov!" Alex said.

"Yes," Rachelli said. "She did. Actually, that's kind of good." She thought for a minute. Having someone there with a gun might be a really, really good thing in terms of her snooping neighbor. But no. She shook her head firmly. "Wilma Lou Wilson is a gun-slinging crazy person with not enough teeth and too much boot, and why is she here, Daddy? Can you please tell her not to be here?"

Professor Shore looked bewildered. "I'll ask her not to bring the gun, but lots of people have guns in this town, you know. And with all of the household gadgets broken from those kids you invited over—"

"I didn't—" Rachelli began, but subsided. There was no point, anyway.

"—We need someone here to help out." Behind his glasses, Professor Shore's eyes softened. "I don't want you doing everything, Rachelli. This invention is important, but not more important than you."

In spite of herself, Rachelli smiled. Her father was not the usual standard father. He was a genius, and that meant that sometimes he got wrapped up in huge, important ideas and forgot about the small things, like tying his shoelaces, or eating. But he never forgot the really important things…

"Now, shoo!" Professor Shore made shooing motions with his hands, and he turned to go back into the lab. "The experiment is at a critical stage, and I can't leave it for more than a few minutes."

His door closed.

"Is it an elevator to the moon?" Rachelli called at the closed door.

"Transplanting human brains inside mice?" Alex tried next.

"Pizza!" Lolly cried. "It's probably pizza!"

"Not even close." Her father's voice was muffled through the closed door. From inside the lab, a weird bubbling sound began. *Bloob, bloog, blooooooog.*

From upstairs came the sound of a huge pair of boots with nails in the bottom stomping around. *Stomp, stomp, stomp,* followed by a loud, hoarse voice. "Hon, what do y'all use to clean around here? I see no spray bottles, no cloths, no nothin'! Y'all use your hands? And where did y'all even *go*?" A long, low whistle. "Wooooeee, this house is big! It's like a department store or somethin'!"

Rachelli sighed and walked back up the stairs.

"I think she scares the house clean," Alex said to Rachelli.

"It's actually pretty amazing," Rachelli admitted. And if Wilma Lou Wilson occasionally shot at bluebirds in the front yard or deer in the back, it was probably a good thing, Rachelli mused. She hadn't seen hide nor hair of Mrs. Pernikov since the arrival of Wilma Lou Wilson.

She mentioned all this to Alex as they sat on the floor of the wraparound porch, Rachelli trying to make a whistle out of a blade of grass, Lolly behind her, testing her weight on a broken plank of wood. Alex was working on getting the sensory net active again.

"Yeah, that's good," Alex agreed, his eyes focused on a tiny switch.

"But did you ever think that maybe the reason we haven't seen the Pernikovs lately is because it was all in your head to begin with? That there is no 'evil plan to discover Daddy's invention'? That maybe they're just plain nosy neighbors, like the rest of this town, and you're seeing conspiracies where there are none just because you're plain old bored? Ouch!" A spark jumped out from the switch he'd been fiddling with, and Alex yanked his fingers back, dropping the whole net onto the porch floor.

"You deserved that," Rachelli said loftily, "for casting disparaging remarks upon me. Is the sensory net okay?"

"Is the *net* okay?" Alex held up a bleeding finger.

"Are you okay?" Rachelli asked belatedly.

"Yes. Except for all of the bleeding to death I'm doing." Alex clutched his finger.

"Sundale, home to Alex, the world's biggest baby." Rachelli rolled her eyes, but she got to her feet, abandoning her grass whistle. "I'll get you a Band-Aid."

Wilma Lou Wilson was cleaning upstairs; Rachelli heard her boots clomping around up there. Professor Shore was in the lab. A sound rather like someone had opened the world's largest drain in the world's largest swimming pool was coming from underneath the secret trapdoor. Lolly was on the porch with Alex, probably making it sticky.

The hairs on the back of Rachelli's neck rose. She knew where everyone in the household was.

So then who was walking around in the kitchen?

Chapter 10

The first time Rachelli had heard someone in the house, Alex had been beside her. She had shushed him and snuck down the stairs, hoping to catch whoever it was in the act. She had been brave and calm then. But now, all by herself on the main floor of the colossal old house with no one to be brave for, she felt her heartbeat speed up and her hands start to shake.

There were two ways to go about this, Rachelli knew, as she heard her pulse pound in her ears. The first one was to freak out and scream. The second was to remain calm and not freak out and scream. She should definitely go for the second option. Yes, that was the way to go.

Her brain was satisfied with this idea. Her mouth, on the other hand, was already screaming before the decision was even made.

"There is someone in the house!" Rachelli's mouth hollered. "*There is someone in the kitchen!*"

Clump, clump-clump-clump-clump was the sound of Wilma Lou Wilson running down the huge wooden staircase in her enormous boots.

"Lemme at 'em!" was the sound of Wilma Lou Wilson cocking her gun and hurtling herself past Rachelli and into the kitchen.

And then there was a pause. The pause lasted a while, and finally, Rachelli stuck her head into the kitchen to see the status of the intruder. What had Wilma Lou Wilson done with him or her?

Wilma Lou Wilson was standing in the middle of the kitchen, her hands on her hips.

No one else was there.

Dear Rachelli,
When will you be back from your summer vacation? School is starting in a week! Who am I going to walk to school with??? It's so weird that you're not here!!!!

Please write back.
Shuli

Dear Shuli,

In your neighborhood, which is really my neighborhood, which I can't wait wait WAIT to get back to, no one ever has someone come into the house all the time and then disappear so that everyone thinks you are crazy even though you are not crazy, but Shuli, do you think I'm crazy?

Please answer honestly that I am not crazy. (Unless the honest answer is that I'm crazy. Then don't answer — just come over to Sundale and kidnap me

and bring me home. Wait — unless that sounds crazy. If it does, I totally did not say anything about it.)
Missing you.

Your friend,
Rachelli

Scientific, Rachelli thought. She yanked out her ribbon and retied it so tightly that her eyes almost crossed. *I can be scientific. Alex wants scientific proof that someone was in the kitchen and then disappeared? I'll find him proof. I'll find him so much proof that his glasses will shatter.*

Rachelli made sure that Alex's nose was good and buried in a book before she snuck out the front door with Lolly. She waved wearily at the people hanging out in front of her house, and then went around to the driveway. She took a quick look in all directions. No one was in sight, so she slid into the backseat of the car and strapped Lolly into her car seat. With a flick of one of the many, many buttons on the dashboard, she activated — the microwave. It hummed invitingly.

"No, no, no," she muttered.

"I'm hungry," Lolly said, and Rachelli tossed a bag of chips at her. She pressed another button.

The coffee machine whirred.

"Argh!" Rachelli said. She closed her eyes and pressed another button at random.

"Hello!" said a voice from the speakers. "Someone wants to go somewhere in a hurry, then, huh?"

Rachelli sighed with relief. Against all odds, she had turned on the Personalized Navigator And Automatic Driver. She had driven with the PNAAD before, but always with Alex, and he took care of stuff like pressing buttons. But now she was on her own. Alex had laughed at her. Everyone had laughed at her. Her mother and Effie were both due home tomorrow, and they would also probably laugh at her. Well, as soon as she got her proof, no one would laugh at her anymore. *Ever again.*

"Pinny, take us to the shopping center," Rachelli said.

"No problem!" said the voice from the speakers. "I am here to help! No problem too big, no problem too small! Pinny the PNAAD is here to solve them all!"

"Yeah, great," Rachelli said as the car pulled out of the driveway all by itself and onto the street.

"Do you want to talk about it?" Pinny asked.

"Huh?" Rachelli looked up.

"It's just that you're being really quiet," Pinny the PNAAD said. "Are you mad at me?"

"Oh my goodness, you're, like, a *computer*," Rachelli said in exasperation. "How could I be mad at you?"

"Well, you don't have to be so *mean* about it," Pinny said tearfully, and the car slowed from twenty miles an hour to five.

Rachelli sighed. At this rate, even in such a tiny town, she would get to the stores in around five hours. She might as well walk. Or maybe she could say sorry to Pinny. Oh, this was so *annoying*! "Why is my life so weird?!" she said to the cornfields outside of the car window. "I'm sorry," she said to Pinny.

"Say it like you mean it," the speakers said with a mechanical sniff.

"This is ridiculous," Rachelli said. "You are just a—"

"She is sorry!" Lolly hollered. "She is so, so, so sorry!"

"Well, *okay*, then," Pinny said, sounding mollified, and the car increased its speed.

Rachelli stared at Lolly. Lolly grinned at her, potato chip crumbs on her chubby cheeks, and after a moment, Rachelli grinned back.

She was kind of used to treating Lolly like a slightly annoying and extremely sticky appendage. That Lolly had actually helped her out was kind of…well, *nice*. Sure, she was always hungry and usually sticky and managed to fall down more holes than was healthy for a little girl her age, but looking at her baby sister now, she suddenly remembered how excited she had been when Lolly was born, so excited that she would finally have a sister.

"Thanks," she said gruffly. "You're not so bad, you know."

"Can I have more chips?" Lolly said in reply. "And can you buy me ice cream? Three scoops."

One hour later, Rachelli came in through the back entrance with an extremely sticky Lolly and a shopping bag. Inside the shopping bag was a magnifying glass, a hammer, an MP3 player with recording capabilities, and a flashlight. Alex had every single one of those things, but she was *not* going to ask him for help, even though the last of her savings were now completely depleted.

After dinner, which was a pretty decent chili and a crusty loaf of bread that Professor Shore emerged with from the secret lab, Rachelli put Lolly to bed. Alex went back to his room, his nose still firmly planted in *The Greatest Inventors of the Twenty-First Century*, bumping into three doors and a still-broken Jeeves on the way.

Professor Shore had gone out to daven *maariv*, and afterward he would pretend to check on some candy dispensers in town, to keep up appearances. The huge Victorian was quiet at last.

Rachelli took out her newly purchased equipment. Now that she was finally alone, it was time for her to find proof of what she knew: that there was a secret way to get out of the kitchen. There *had* to be. That was the only explanation.

She turned on the MP3 player and pressed record. "First attempt at finding scientific proof for disappearing people," she said into it. "Day one."

Using the hammer, she tapped on each floor tile. Using the magnifying glass, she examined the tile to see if there was any…well, any *something*. Actually, she wasn't sure *what* she was looking for. Rachelli felt her lip tremble. Maybe Alex was right. Maybe she was just so bored out of her mind here in this tiny town that she was inventing mysteries to solve. And she was nowhere near as smart as Alex. How did she think that she would figure this all out on her own?

"Argh," Rachelli groaned, and she flung the hammer down on the black-and-white tiles of the cavernous kitchen floor.

There was a soft chiming sound.

And when the tunnel opened up directly under her, she was barely aware of the fact that someone had grabbed her arm and was sliding down, down, down with her. She didn't even have time or the breath to scream.

CHAPTER 11

Rachelli had a few thoughts as the kitchen above her receded and she found herself in total darkness, sliding down the tunnel. The first thought was, *Ha! See, all you naysayers? There is a secret way out of the kitchen! I knew it!* The second thought was, *Where in the world am I going?* The third thought she actually expressed out loud:

"Aaaaaaaaaaaaaaaahhhhh!" Rachelli cried, and only then did she hear someone else saying the exact same thing. *There was someone in the tunnel with her.*

She landed with a jolt, and it took a moment for her to get her breath back. She squinted, trying to get her bearings, but there was no light at all. She had no idea where she was. She was in total and absolute darkness. *And someone was with her.*

In the darkness, Rachelli leaped to her feet. "I'm warning you!" Her voice echoed weirdly. "I'm armed! With a..." She thought quickly. "With, um, with *fists*! Of steel! I know kung fu!"

"I bet you know as least three other Chinese words as well," said another voice in the darkness, and Rachelli sagged back on the floor in a mixture of relief and confusion.

"Effie?" she said when her voice worked again. "Effie, what are you *doing* here?"

"I don't know whom you are referring to." Effie's voice sounded stiff. "I don't know any Effie. If you are referring to someone named *Ephraim,* then—"

"Seriously?" Rachelli said. "*Seriously?* We're going to do this now? Effie — Ephraim — what are you *doing* here?"

"We had the option of going on the bus tomorrow morning or tonight. I chose tonight. I wanted to surprise you guys. Boo. Here I am!"

"Okay. Okay, great. Here you are. Now, *where are we*?"

"If I were to be scientific about it, I would say that we are here. Exactly here. We are in the space that we're currently occupying."

"That is very extremely not helpful."

"You're welcome."

In the darkness, Rachelli smiled. She was so glad that Effie was here, and even gladder that he could not see how glad she was. "Okay," she said out loud. "Let's figure this out. We must be in like the basement or something."

"I didn't know we had a basement."

"Yeah, well." She strained her ears for more information. From somewhere off in the distance came the sound of dripping water.

"It definitely smells like a basement," Effie said. "Musty and kind of gross. Like aged gym socks."

"Ew!" Rachelli wrinkled her nose, then laughed. The sound was eerie in the dark, and she quickly stopped. Instead, she took a hesitant step forward, her arms outstretched in front of her.

"Wait!" Effie yelled. "Rachelli, are you moving?"

Rachelli stopped. "I was, why?"

"Well, don't! We don't know where we are! For all we know, we're standing in front of a huge hole!"

Rachelli felt a trickle of sweat slide down her forehead. "So what are we going to—"

There was a sudden popping sound, and Rachelli shrieked. And then there was light, smears of bright light emanating from the floor. Rachelli blinked until her eyes focused.

Effie was standing in front of her, grinning sheepishly. On the floor around her were opened pellets of InstaLight, her father's invention.

"You always carry those around with you?" Rachelli asked her brother.

"You always have to be prepared," Effie said with an arrogant tilt of his chin. "You never know when you might fall down a tunnel in the kitchen and end up trapped in the basement." Effie reached into his pocket and pulled out a rather squashed chocolate bar. "Want?"

"I'm good." Rachelli made a face. "You just never empty your pockets, do you?" She looked at her surroundings for the first time. They were standing in a huge room, empty of everything besides for clouds of dust. The walls and floor were unfinished concrete, and there were doorways leading off to hallways on each side of them. She looked from one to the other. Then she looked up, overhead, at where she had come from. The low ceiling was smooth and flat, as if the tunnel that had dropped them there had never existed.

"Mommy said there would be secret nooks and crannies in this house, but this is seriously ridiculous." Rachelli patted hopelessly at her filthy skirt.

"Okay, let's concentrate on getting out of here. Then we can worry about how ridiculous this house is." Effie looked from one exit to the next. "You're supposed to go right if you don't know where to go."

They turned to the right exit. Effie threw another InstaLight tablet at the floor, and they followed the smears of light down a long, narrow hallway.

"So," Effie said as they walked, "feel like explaining why you attacked the kitchen floor with a hammer?"

Rachelli flushed and looked down at her dusty shoes. "Not really."

Effie shrugged. "Okay."

"Okay, fine! Don't pressure me!" Rachelli burst out after another silent moment of walking.

"I was not—"

"Okay! You talked me into it! I'll tell you!"

"You don't *have* to—"

"Okay, *fine*. You've convinced me." Rachelli stopped walking. Then she told Effie all about it, about how someone had come into their house twice already and then disappeared, and their father didn't believe her, and Alex also didn't really believe her, especially her feeling that the Pernikovs were more than just nosy neighbors, that something more sinister was afoot.

"No one," Effie said when Rachelli finished, "says things like 'something sinister is afoot.'"

"I knew you wouldn't believe me either," Rachelli muttered. She quickened her pace down the hallway.

"Hey, stop. Of course I believe you," Effie said.

Rachelli stopped. "Do you really?"

"Yes, I do. And anyway, even if I didn't, us unscientific and un-inventing Shores have to stick together."

"That is true," Rachelli said emphatically. "We are the only normal ones. Even Lolly created this thing the other day using crayons and some string that somehow dispenses candy. We dummies have to stick together."

Effie nodded. "And besides, you're not like a regular girl, making stuff up all the time. You have your head basically straight. For a girl."

"Oh, thanks." Rachelli snorted. "On behalf of girls everywhere, thank you for your kind words."

She turned to stalk away, and almost bashed her head into something solid in front of her. The light from the InstaLight was faint at this point, and Rachelli realized in the nick of time that the hallway had ended abruptly and become a door. A small wooden door with long wrought-iron hinges coated with a hundred years' worth of cobwebs.

"Voilà," Effie said.

"Voilà?" Rachelli repeated incredulously. "Voilà yourself. We still don't know where we are. This door could take us anywhere."

"Not *anywhere*," Effie said. "It couldn't take us to a magical forest, for example. Or Australia."

"Oh, but imagine if it could take us back to the city," Rachelli said with feeling. "Imagine how great that would be!"

Effie paused with his hand on the great brass doorknob. "Is it really so bad here?"

Rachelli sighed. "It's so *boring*. Well, besides for all the people trying to sneak into the house. The girls here are, like, I dunno."

"Did you give them a chance?"

Rachelli laughed. "Who are you, Mommy?"

Effie shrugged. "It's just that it's been hard in yeshivah. Lots of guys I don't know. But I've been figuring out that if I chill and give them a chance, you never know."

Rachelli thought about this for a minute before giving a grudging nod. She really had not been fair to Birdy Winter and the others; it wasn't their fault that they lived in Snoredale. And yeah, they were different, but different might not mean different bad. It might mean different *good*. Who knew?

"Okay, maybe. But if we starve down here, then this is all moot, so how about we go forward?"

Effie nodded and turned the handle of the door.

Nothing happened.

He turned it again, more firmly his time, his arms bulging with the effort. Finally, slowly, the doorknob began to turn, and Rachelli let out a breath that she didn't even known she'd been holding.

The door opened inward with the most horrible screeching sound that Rachelli had ever heard. They peered around the corner.

"Oh no," Rachelli said. She covered her mouth and nose and began to cough.

"This is very, very bad," Effie said. He waved his hands in front of his face.

The room they had just walked into was filled with billowing black smoke.

CHAPTER 12

Effie backed up, and Rachelli followed suit, waving her hands in front of her mouth until they were back in the narrow, musty hallway they had come from. They closed the heavy door together, and then leaned against it, gasping.

"I want to go home," Rachelli said when she'd caught her breath. "I've had about all I can stand of this house and of Sundale."

"How about we concentrate on getting out of this dungeon first?" Effie kicked at the concrete wall. "We can't get out of Snoredale if we can't even leave the basement!"

"Okay. Okay." Rachelli took a deep breath, and when she let it out, the sound echoed down the long hallway. "Let's look at this scientifically. Someone built the tunnel in the kitchen, and they wouldn't want to stay down here forever, so there must be a way out, right?"

"Well, unless this really is a dungeon, and the original owner sent his enemies to die down here."

"Well, thanks for that ray of hope."

"You're very welcome."

"And anyway, I don't see any bones! There would be bones!"

"Maybe the smoky room is also filled with huge snakes that swallow their victims whole."

"Oh, that's a *great* visual. Thanks for that. I'm so glad you're here with me."

"The feeling is mutual."

"Okay, so let's talk about what we *do* know, okay? Okay. So, where are we, first of all? Well, we must be in our house, right? I mean, the tunnel is directly under the kitchen. Somewhere above us, Lolly is sleeping, Daddy is coming home from *maariv*, and in a few hours it will be morning, and Mommy will be home, and Wilma Lou Wilson will be back to clean the house by stomping on it.

"And also, there is a room that is randomly on fire. And we are stuck down here, and we will probably starve and die down here and be eaten by snakes. This is good! This is really good and great and also amazing!" Rachelli tried to keep her voice calm. Rachelli failed at keeping her voice calm.

"Okay, so yeah, this looks bad." Effie scratched at his head. "But it could be worse."

"How?" Rachelli demanded.

"The room could have really been filled with poisonous snakes, for example."

"You're right. I have not been looking at this situation in a positive light!" Rachelli flared her nostrils at her brother.

Effie grinned. "Aren't you glad I'm here?"

"Your being here *is* better than a roomful of poisonous snakes."

"I'll take that as a compliment, Rachelli," Effie said dryly.

"Don't get used to it, Effie."

"Ephraim!"

"Yeah, whatever. Let's try the other hallway. *Ephraim*."

They were halfway down the other hallway when they were suddenly plunged into darkness. "What *happened*?" Rachelli shrieked.

"The InstaLights must have run out of…whatever it is that Daddy puts in them." Effie's voice came from her right. "We didn't plan this well. We really should have fallen down with Alex. He would have a scientific trick up his sleeve."

"Not falling down with Alex is the only problem you have with this situation?" Rachelli put her hands out to either side of her. The rough feel of the concrete wall was slightly calming. It helped her feel almost grounded in the pitch black. "Look, let's just keep going, okay? Let's feel our way. Because if we don't get out of here soon, I might light my hair on fire."

"With what?" Effie asked, but she heard him start to shuffle further down the hallway. She followed in silence.

This whole thing is dumb, that's the problem, Rachelli thought. Even without the Pernikov situation. They had come to Sundale to protect the privacy of Professor Shore's invention, but there was less privacy here than in the city. So why were they still here? Why didn't they just pack up and leave?

Rachelli made up her mind to have a conversation about this with her mother the second she came home. Well, she would let her sit down first. Maybe offer her a drink of water. And *then* they would have a conversation.

If she ever got out of here, that is.

She shuffled on, paying attention to her feet and to the sound of Effie's breathing. The hallway dipped and turned, unlike the straight hallway on the right that had led to the smoke-filled room.

"It's funny," Effie said, and Rachelli jumped at the sound of his voice. "Our house is always filled with all sorts of inventions doing everything for us. And now here we are, without even the invention of light."

"That is not called funny," Rachelli said. "It is called horrible."

"It's a little refreshing, though."

"Well," Rachelli admitted, "it's nice not to be arguing with a PNAAD with a personality, anyway. But I do like light. And people. And upstairs."

"Ouch," said Effie. "I think I found the door. With my head."

"If this room is filled with poisonous snakes, it's your fault," Rachelli said.

"I'm pulling it open. Hang on."

There was a terrible screeching sound, and then a scraping sound, and then the sight of another smoke-filled room.

"Seriously?" Rachelli squawked. "*Seriously?*"

Effie grunted as he closed the heavy door again, plunging them back into darkness.

"No," Rachelli said suddenly. "No. We are going back in there. That's the way out, I'm sure of it."

"But the room is on fire!" Effie protested. "Both rooms are on fire!"

"Okay, so first of all, what are the chances that two rooms down here are filled with smoke? No. It's one room. Both hallways open up into the same room."

"Dumb," Effie pronounced.

"Yeah, well, I didn't build this monstrosity of a house. And also, the rooms are not on fire. If they were, the doors would have been too hot to open. No, something else made them filled with smoke, and we are just going to hold our breath and go in there and figure out how to get from there to the upstairs. Are you with me? *What?*"

Effie was laughing.

"*What?*"

"You think you know nothing about science," he said. "But you do. And what's more, your knowledge is way more practical than Alex's because *you* are more practical than he is."

"Aw, thanks, Effie." Rachelli smiled in the dark.

"Ephraim!"

"Ephraim. Whatever. Okay. Are we going to do this?"

It was too dark to see, but she pictured Effie nodding in agreement.

The door opened slowly. Rachelli and Effie pulled the collars of their shirts up to cover their mouths and noses, then plunged into the smoky room.

The first thing they noticed was that beneath the smoke, the room was not empty like the rest of the basement. In fact, it was full. It was packed with familiar-looking equipment...

"Seriously?" Rachelli said, her voice muffled through her shirt. "Well, I guess this makes sense, but Daddy will be furious."

It took Effie another minute to get it. "We're in Daddy's secret lab."

"Yup." Rachelli nodded, then coughed. "And it's filled with smoke, but that's not unusual. Daddy must be working on something that's making it smoky. Anyway, we'd better get out of here. Daddy really doesn't want us to be in here."

She spun around, her eyes watering, searching for the way out. "This way. I think."

They stumbled in the direction that she was pointing, then stopped short when a long, low blast of what sounded like a car horn sounded suddenly. A huge, gleaming metallic-looking machine with red buttons all over the front and what looked like a giant potato masher affixed to its side detached itself from its place against the wall and began to bounce toward them. In no time at all, the way to the exit was blocked by the machine.

"Um," said Rachelli through her shirt. "Um, hello, sir. Goodbye, sir. Go away, sir?"

The machine bounced even closer, until it was directly in front of the siblings, an immovable wall of metal and wires. It turned. A sort of maw directly over the potato masher opened, revealing two lines of sharp metal edges that resembled...

"Effie," Rachelli asked slowly, "does that machine have...teeth? Really crazy sharp teeth?"

Effie did not correct her and say that his name was Ephraim. Instead, he said in an extremely shaky voice, "Um, you know, it's a funny thing, but that machine kind of looks like it is actually going to eat—"

"Effie!" Rachelli screamed as the mouth of the machine opened wide enough for a medium-sized girl or boy to be swallowed. She had time for one last wild thought: *Is the reason Daddy doesn't let us in the lab because the machine he's working on is actually dangerous?*

Chapter 13

The machine was so close to them that Rachelli thought that if it were alive, she would feel its breath on her face. She squeezed her eyes shut and thought about Lolly and Professor Shore and Alex and her mother and inexplicably of Wilma Lou Wilson, and how they would feel when they realized that she and Effie were gone forever…

After a few frozen minutes, there came the slow trickle of realization that she was not eaten up, not even a little. Then there was a soft dinging sound and the unmistakable smell of…warm chocolate chips?

Rachelli opened one eye. And then she opened another. Then she blinked a few times to make sure that what she was seeing was what she was actually seeing. "Effie," she finally said, "you can open your eyes now."

"Are we dead?" Effie asked. He opened his eyes. The smoke was clearing, disappearing into a vent on top of the gleaming machine. While the maw was still wide open, resting on top of the gleaming teeth was a metal tray, and on top of the metal tray was a dozen chocolate chip muffins, piping hot.

"No, no, no," said a voice, and Professor Shore came walking through the thinning smoke. Rachelli realized belatedly that the front door to the lab was now open. Sometime during the confusion, when they had both thought that they were going to be devoured by a machine, their father had come home and headed down to his lab. "Oh, this is all wrong," he added, clicking his tongue, and Rachelli and Effie glanced at each other and then, slowly, slowly, looked up to meet their father's gaze.

"What," Professor Shore said after a minute, "are you doing here?"

"I—" Rachelli began, but Professor Shore was still talking.

"You," he said, "are not supposed to be chocolate chip *muffins*. Why are you muffins? Cheese toasts, at the very least! A good hearty chicken stock would have been okay! But *muffins*? Oh, this is bad. This is very, very bad. I need to look again at my calculations. Where am I going wrong?"

He was not talking to them. He was talking to the muffins, and while for other people that might be worrisome, Professor Shore's children knew that Professor Shore was not like other people. Talking to muffins, on a scale of one to ten of worrisome activities for the genius scientist, hovered around a two.

Rachelli caught Effie's eye again and jerked her chin toward the door. Effie was one step ahead of her, already tiptoeing through the nearly dissipated smoke toward the exit of the secret lab. They had nearly made it when Professor Shore spoke again.

"And what are you two doing down here? Oh, hello, Effie, when did you arrive?"

Inches from the exit, they both turned around to face their father.

"I just got here," Effie said. "Early bus."

"Nice to see you." Professor Shore smiled, and Effie and Rachelli breathed a sigh of relief. Then their father's face grew stern, and Rachelli and Effie stumbled over each other to explain how they had ended up in the lab completely and totally by accident and how completely and totally sorry they were.

Professor Shore listened without saying a word, and when they finally stopped talking about trapdoors and dark hallways, he sighed. "Sit down," he said softly.

Rachelli and Effie looked around for a place to sit. After a moment, they sat down on the floor. Professor Shore handed each of them a chocolate chip muffin and sat down on the floor with them. He took off his glasses to clean them in a small Clean-O-Matic, then sighed again.

"Listen, Rachelli," he said. "I know you didn't come down here on purpose. And falling through the kitchen floor can happen to anyone."

"No, it can't happen to anyone," Rachelli muttered in the general direction of her chocolate chip muffin. "Falling through kitchen floors does not happen to normal people. It only happens to *us*."

Effie drew in a sharp breath, but Professor Shore nodded. When Rachelli finally looked up to meet her father's eyes, she saw that he looked as if he understood what she was getting at.

"I know this summer has not exactly been your idea of a good time," he said. "And I know it's been hard on you. But I promise, *bli neder*, that things are going to look up really soon. I'm so close to a breakthrough, I can smell it. There is a tiny error in my calculations. As soon as I fix it, we can leave this place and get back to our normal lives."

"But why are we here?" Rachelli asked. "Dad, Snoredale — sorry, Sundale — *stop* laughing at me Effie, I've heard you call this place a lot worse — well, is not private at all. It's filled with nosy people. Why don't we go back to the city, and you can finish up whatever your experiment is there, instead of in this random place where people try to spy on you?" Rachelli held her breath. It was the first time she had even hinted to her father about her suspicions regarding the nosy Pernikovs.

Professor Shore looked surprised. "This is not exactly a random place, Rachelli. I didn't just point at a place on a map that has a Jewish community and pick Snoredale. Sorry, Sundale." Professor Shore's eyes crinkled with humor. "And don't think that I don't know what you kids call it. I may be absentminded, but I'm not deaf, *baruch Hashem*."

Rachelli smiled sheepishly.

"But if you didn't pick this town at random, how did we end up here?" Effie asked.

Professor Shore bit his lip in thought. Finally, he said, "Well, I guess I can tell you this much. It's nothing that you haven't already basically figured out on your own, anyway. This house was given to us by the government. The same branch of the government that is expecting the results of my experiment by the end of this summer."

"But what—" Rachelli began.

"But why—" Effie started.

Professor Shore held up a hand. In the hand was a chocolate chip muffin. But still, his intent was clear, and Effie and Rachelli stopped talking. "I wish I could tell you more," he said when they fell silent. "But for now, I can't."

"Someone is trying to get to the experiment," Rachelli blurted out. "And now I am surer about it than ever. And how are you going to stop them, exactly, with a deadly chocolate chip muffin machine?"

Professor Shore glanced up at the gleaming machine containing the half-empty tray. "That's not what it makes."

"But it just *did*—"

"I know. But it doesn't. It shouldn't. It's complicated." Professor Shore got to his feet. "Anyway, you two should go. And please, for your own safety, you shouldn't come back down here! Not even if you discover the other secret entrance through the side window in the living room. Oh, oops. Shouldn't have said that."

"There's *another* secret entrance to the lab?" Rachelli exclaimed. "Daddy, this is the worst secret lab ever!"

But Professor Shore didn't seem to want to talk about it anymore, and seconds later, Rachelli and Effie found themselves escorted out the door and up to the neon-blue floor of the living room.

"Is your experiment a machine that stretches your clothing to fit as you get bigger?" she yelled down the stairs before closing the trapdoor with a slam. She felt better after she did that.

Effie took a giant bite of his muffin. "Well," he said around a mouthful, "on the bright side, we were not eaten, not by snakes and not by machine. Plus, chocolate chip muffins."

"Yes, those are good things," Rachelli said absently.

"What is it? What are you thinking about?" Effie nudged her, and Rachelli spent a moment deciding whether to tell him what she had seen, that as Professor Shore was prompting them up the stairs and out of his laboratory, she had clearly seen the heavy door they'd come in from — the door that was too heavy to close on its own — swing shut.

CHAPTER 14

"What-what-what-what—" Alex tumbled down the stairs and toward the front door, his eyes still half closed in sleep. He nearly banged into Rachelli, who had her eye pressed against the peephole.

"Good morning," she said without turning around.

"But — what—"

"It's nothing."

"Nothing?" Alex ran a hand through his hair, knocking his yarmulke and glasses askew. "Bang-bang-bang-*scream* is nothing?"

"It was a victory scream. I think. Wilma Lou Wilson is trying to shoot rabbits."

"We have rabbits?"

"Apparently." Rachelli turned away from the peephole. "She says they're destroying the vegetable garden."

Alex fixed his glasses and his yarmulke. "We have a vegetable garden?"

Rachelli nodded. "Wilma Lou planted one her first day here. You know what else we have? We have grass. And trees. And fellow human beings. I'm thinking that you should take your nose out of your books one day and check it all out. It can be fun!"

Alex turned to walk back upstairs to his room, muttering something about crazy gun-slinging housekeepers and sarcastic older sisters, but his dramatic exit was interrupted when he bumped into Effie.

"When did you get home?" He blinked up at his older brother.

"Get home?" Effie winked at Rachelli. "I've been here the whole summer. You would have seen me if you would look up once in a while."

"It's just too early in the morning for this," Alex said wearily, then nearly jumped a foot when the front doors were flung open by Wilma Lou Wilson.

"Yeehaaa!" crowed Wilma Lou Wilson. "I showed them rabbits who's boss!"

"You didn't actually…shoot any, did you?" Rachelli asked.

Wilma Lou shook her head. "Them fuzzy-tails sure can run fast, bless them, but I put the fear of Bessie into 'em sure enough!" She clomped past them and disappeared down the hallway.

"Bessie?" Effie asked when she was gone.

"Her gun's name is Bessie," Rachelli said, and Effie's eyes grew round as he took in that particular piece of information. "Yeah. Welcome to Snoredale, home of the Shore's Believe It or Not."

Effie laughed. "So when do I meet the crazy neighbor? The one who you think is trying to find the secret lab?"

"Stick around," Rachelli said grimly.

Alex covered his mouth, but not before a clear snort of disbelief was heard. Rachelli rounded on him and would have given her younger brother a piece of her mind if Lolly hadn't come down the stairs. She squealed and gave Effie a big hug before demanding breakfast from her three siblings.

"Look, it's not that I don't believe you," Alex said as they walked toward the kitchen. "It's just that…well…I kind of don't believe you. But!" He raised his hands to forestall Rachelli's protest. "I spent half the night fixing the Beautiful Extra-Special Sensor Triumph — a.k.a BEST — and

I am going to hook it up today. Okay? Speaking of which, when I was done last night, I knocked on your door to ask you what you thought of the new name, but you didn't answer. Where were you?"

"I could tell you," Rachelli said as she turned toward the newly fixed Egginator, "but you wouldn't believe me." As she spoke, she thrust her heel sharply on the floor tile that she had tossed the hammer at the night before, then looked at Alex's face as three tiles to the right curved inward and a tunnel opened at their feet.

"Okay," said Alex after a full three minutes of stunned silence and after the tunnel had sealed itself again. From below them, strange noises burbled from the secret lab. From above them, Wilma Lou Wilson's boots clomped heavily. "Okay, *okay*. So now we know that there are a million exits in and out of this house. And if it's the Pernikovs — I said *if*! I still can't picture that ancient man and lady skipping around the house like that — then they really can come and go as they please. Ha!" Alex grinned. "I love this house! It's the weirdest place ever! I'm going to build a house like this one day!"

"Focus," Rachelli said. She snapped her fingers in front of his face.

"Okay. So obviously we need to go through this house inch by inch. We need to draw up a map and figure out where every single exit and entrance *is*. Then I can set up the BEST, and we'll know exactly when someone comes in or out."

"That's a big job," Effie pointed out. "This house is like a city. It'll take weeks to find every secret exit."

There was a shriek, and the three of them spun in three different directions. Lolly was no longer in the kitchen.

"Well," Effie said with a grin, "it sounds like Lolly found one, at least. That's a start."

"**Two,**" Rachelli said. She rubbed at her neck with an aching hand. "On the second floor. Or three, if you count the dumbwaiter in this room, but only a very tiny person could fit in there."

"I fit in there," Lolly said. "It's fun but also scary."

"Some of my bruises have bruises," Rachelli said, putting her hand-drawn map on Alex's bed. "The man who built this house was obviously crazy."

"Five secret exits," Effie said, "on the main floor. And another vote for the original architect being a few eggs short of a dozen. One of the exits was activated when I leaned against the dining room table and fell headfirst down into the vegetable garden. I scared a rabbit, though, so that's good." He brandished his map. "My five include the one in the kitchen and the one that Lolly found on the side of the fireplace that also leads out to the garden, along with three new ones."

"I didn't *find* it," Lolly pointed out. "I fell in it."

"And you did a really good job!" Rachelli said encouragingly.

"And I found three on the top floor." Alex unrolled his map. "But no one did the bottom floor?"

"Daddy would be furious," Lolly, Effie, and Rachelli said together. On cue, the house shook slightly, and a high-pitched whistle echoed from the secret lab.

Alex nodded. "True. Okay. So let's get started with what we have. And, by the way, the attic is filled with really interesting stuff. I found *this*." He tossed a heavy leather-bound book onto his bed. Dust flew off the peeling cover and sent everyone into a coughing fit.

"What is it?" Rachelli asked when she had caught her breath.

Alex flipped the book open. The pages within were filled with line after line of curly script, some of it smudged but some of it legible. "I'm not sure," he said, "but it might be a diary. A really, really old one."

"Cool!" Effie said, but Rachelli shook her head.

"Cool, yeah, and I'm all for a history lesson, but for now, we have to live in the present. Let's get this sensory net up before anything bad happens to Daddy's experiment." She looked at her siblings meaningfully. "If anything happens to it and the bad guys get it, it could be really, really bad."

"Yeah," Effie said, suddenly grim. "I have never seen him look so serious about anything before."

"Plus, if Daddy has to start from scratch, we might be stuck in Snoredale *forever*."

Four hours later, Alex finally finished putting up his BEST around the various secret exits and not-secret exits of the huge Victorian, and the four of them met in the kitchen just as Professor Shore walked in with a tray of schnitzel sandwiches. His lab coat and beard were coated in what looked like splatters of neon-blue paint the same color as the living room floor.

"Delicious," Rachelli said as she bit into her sandwich hungrily.

"Is it?" Professor Shore asked. He looked up at his children. "It doesn't taste good in the beginning but then sort of like glue after a while?" He blinked in a hopeful sort of way.

"No," Effie said. "It tastes like schnitzel the whole time."

The Professor sighed heavily. "That's what I was afraid of. I am way off, way off. Back to the drawing board." He got to his feet.

There was a sudden knocking on the front door, and then came a terrible squeaking sound, which meant that the doors were being opened.

"Oh, that must be Mommy!" Rachelli jumped to her feet happily but was interrupted by the unmistakable and hair-raising sound of her mother shrieking at the top of her lungs.

Chapter 15

"Well, this is fun!" Mrs. Shore said brightly, and because of the circumstances, no one contradicted her. At least not out loud.

"I am still so, so, so, so sorry," Alex said instead. "I should not, in retrospect, have put my BEST — my Beautiful Extra-Special Sensor Triumph, I mean — on the front door."

Mrs. Shore had been swinging in a net that hung from the ceiling when they'd run to the front door to see why she was screaming. As far as homecomings went, this was not the best one the Shores had ever had.

"What's important is that everyone is okay now, and here we are, having fun with all of our friends and neighbors," Mrs. Shore said.

The Shores were in the town square, squinting in the sun. Everyone from the town of Sundale was there. Everyone in the town was excited.

Rachelli stifled a yawn.

"Is this a punishment?" Alex burst out. "Is this a punishment for making my mother swing from the ceiling?"

"This is not a punishment!" Mrs. Shore said. "Of course it's not! This is an exciting event! The most exciting event of the year, in fact;

it says so right here on the flier." She handed him the bright-yellow paper in her hand that they'd found in their mailbox, which read:

Our Annual End-of-the-Summer Festival
Just Got More Fun!
So Come Along and Join Us, Everyone!
Come One, Come All!
Come with Smiles, and Walk Tall!
Will Wonders Never Cease?
Watch Our Pride Increase!
Watch Sundale Finally Overtake Cawker City.
They Think They're So Smart?
Well, They Will No Longer Be Witty
When We Turn the Second-to-Largest Ball of
Twine INTO THE BIGGEST IN THE WORLD!
So Come with Smiles and the Sundale Flag
Unfurled!
Fun for the Whole Family! The Most Exciting
Event of the Year! Do Not Miss Our Moment
of Triumph!
Also: Apple bobbing, fortune telling, and The
Four Blind Mice will play an original song,
written for the occasion!
Stay for the Corn Shucking Contest!
(Bring Something for Our Potluck Dinner,
Served at 5:00.)

In the center of the square, a man in a very large hat was splicing twine to the thread trailing from an extremely large ball of twine sitting on a raised platform. Behind him were four men in even larger hats. One was playing the fiddle, one the banjo, one a zither, and the fourth was singing — or something close to singing, anyway. Most of the words to the song were "Sundale" and "ball of twine."

"It's a good thing I came prepared," Alex said to the general public, and he leaned against a wooden post and flipped a book open. Effie snorted and kicked his brother lightly in the ankle.

"You're missing Bessie's debut," he said, because Wilma Lou Wilson was there too, and when the song swung into a faster tempo, she shot Bessie in the air to general applause.

"I don't think we're in Kansas anymore, Toto," Rachelli murmured, and her mother laughed.

"We are definitely not in the city anymore, that's for sure." Mrs. Shore smiled and spread out her arms to encompass the whole square: the carnival booths off to the side, the terrible band in the center, the ball of twine and the twine winder, the piles of corn waiting to be shucked, the townspeople with their wide smiles and even wider hats. "But it's *nice*, isn't it, to be in a place that is small and tight-knit, where everyone knows your name?"

As if on cue, Rachelli caught sight of Birdy Winter and her friends near the apple-bobbing booth. Before she could duck out of sight, they giggled and waved. She smiled weakly and waved back.

"Your mother is right," Professor Shore said. He was smiling as well, which could only mean that his invention was finally getting back on track. "Let's not be big-city snobs."

"I want an apple," Lolly said, tugging at Rachelli's sleeve. "I want to catch one with my teeth."

"I'll go with you," Effie said before Rachelli could protest. "Come on. Let's catch some apples."

Lolly caught three apples and won a stuffed replica of the second-to-largest ball of twine, plus she got to keep the apples. She skipped off happily with Effie back to her parents, and Rachelli was about to follow when someone grabbed her arm.

"Bob for one!" Birdy Winter said to Rachelli with a laugh.

"It's incredibly germy and gross," Rachelli said. "I mean, *everyone* stuck their faces into this water!"

"You let your little sister do it," another girl pointed out.

"Yeah, well, I can't even tell you what she normally puts into her mouth. This is nothing."

"Yeah, little siblings, hey?" Birdy rolled her big blue eyes. "Why, my little sister once tried to swallow a sparrow. Nearly succeeded, too, 'cept for the tail feathers that tickled her throat so as she had to spit it out."

Rachelli laughed and realized reluctantly that it was actually kind of nice, standing out there with a group of girls, surrounded by trees wearing new autumn leaves, the air just turning crisp and cool, watching people have a good time. She looked around.

"So what else is there to do here?"

Birdy shrugged. "Well, there's the corn-shucking contest soon, and as soon as they finish the ball of twine, there will be a whole ceremony that should be good ole fun. And there's the fortune teller's booth; that's always a hoot."

The fortune teller's tent was across the square, and Rachelli followed Birdy and her giggling crew until they reached it.

Birdy lifted up the flap that served as the entrance and peered into the tent's nearly pitch-black interior. "Hello?" she called. "Madame Zola?"

There was no answer, and with nervous giggles, the girls walked all the way into the tent, Rachelli trailing behind.

In the center of the small, dark tent was a round table draped in cloth. On top of it were some strings of beads and several small jars, as well as a crystal ball. There were two chairs drawn up to the table, but they were both empty.

"Madame Zola?" Birdy called again, then spun around in consternation. "That's strange. No one's here."

"Oh well. Let's go." Rachelli turned to the door, half relieved; the interior of the tent was kind of creepy, but Birdy was still standing there, turning the crystal ball over in her hand.

"You should see her, though," Birdy said, her eyes on the ball. "She takes it all so seriously. At least, our former fortune tellers took the role seriously; we have a new one this year, but I'm sure she'll be wonderful, too. Madame Zola always wears these sparkly robes and a turban and huge hoop earrings, and she talks in this deep voice and tells you stuff like, 'Early to bed and early to rise makes you healthy, wealthy, and wise.' It's great fun! Oh, well. Maybe she'll come back soon." She put the crystal ball down.

"Who is she?" Rachelli asked curiously as they lifted up the tent flap and found themselves blinking in the sunshine. "Who is Madame Zola in real life? Someone I know?"

"Why, I can't tell you!" Birdy grinned. "That will ruin the mystery of the thing, won't it?"

Rachelli smiled back. "So what's next? Should we, like, eat hay, or whatever it is that you country girls like to—"

"Oh, *there* she is!" Birdy pointed through the throng. "Oh, but she's not even wearing her robes! She sure is walking fast. I wonder where she's off to."

"Who?"

"Madame Zola. She's leaving already, it seems. Well, maybe she's not feeling well, poor thing. She *is* elderly, after all."

Rachelli peered through the crowd and caught a glimpse of a large pink hat. A prickling feeling went up her spine. "Birdy," she said slowly, "is that Madame Zola?"

"Well, now I've gone and spoiled the fun, haven't I!" Birdy shook her head. "But yes, you're right. Madame Zola is Mrs. Pernikov, your neighbor. I do wonder where she's going. And she's walking awfully fast for a woman her age, no?"

Where is she going? Rachelli thought grimly. *Well, she saw that we're all here. She knows that no one is home right now to stop her from getting into the secret lab.*

"Rachelli? Yoo-hoo! Rachelli! Where are you going?"

Rachelli heard Birdy calling after her, but she didn't even turn her head; instead, fists clenched, she plunged into the crowd in hot pursuit of Mrs. Pernikov.

Chapter 16

The crowd in the town square had thickened considerably, and all Rachelli could see around her was overly happy people in overly large hats. After a few minutes of searching, she realized with a start that she had completely lost sight of Mrs. Pernikov.

Seriously? How fast can the older woman move? "Excuse me," Rachelli said, and tried to make her way around three girls eating hot dogs on sticks. "Pardon me, can I get through?" she said to a group of women who seemed to have planted themselves in the middle of the town's square in…rocking chairs? *What in the world?*

"Effie!" Rachelli called over the chattering, laughing, suffocating throng. "Alex! Mommy! Daddy! *Lolly*!" No one answered, and she pushed through the crowd, causing many disapproving glances and much muttering about "busy city folk" until she abruptly found herself at the edge of the square, near the parking lot. The crowd was thinner there, but there was still no sign of Mrs. Pernikov, or of Rachelli's family, for that matter. Frustrated, she yanked out her hair ribbon and tied it up again while she decided where to go from there.

"Are you leaving us now?" A very old man in denim overalls asked her disapprovingly. His eyes were all but drowning in his eyebrows.

"Look here! They're all but finished with the twine! It would be unpatriotic to leave now!"

"What?" Rachelli blinked at him. "Unpatriotic?"

The man brandished a pipe like it was a weapon. "If you go before the ball is finished, the terrorists win!"

"I feel like I landed in a country where everyone sounds like they're speaking English, but they actually aren't," Rachelli said. "How do the terrorists win if I leave now?"

A girl hurried toward them, her blond pony bouncing behind her. "Grandpappy, are you bothering this nice girl?" She waggled a finger at him. "Never you mind him," she said to Rachelli. "It's just that Grandpappy is related to the man who first thought to create the ball of twine, and he rather feels that it's important."

Rachelli nodded even as her fingers twitched impatiently. "Nice to meet you," she said. She glanced around. Still no sign of Mrs. Pernikov. The woman really had disappeared.

"Are you looking for someone, then?" the girl asked her.

"You don't know Mrs. Pernikov by any chance, do you?"

The girl smiled. "Honey, everyone knows everyone here, haven't you learned that yet? Sure I know the woman. Why, you looking for her?"

Rachelli nodded eagerly. "Have you seen her?"

The girl pointed at the parking lot. "Not but two minutes ago, she tore out of here in her pickup. Going fifty miles if she was going five, I tell you."

"And now the terrorists will win!" the old man croaked at her side. He took an angry puff of his pipe.

Rachelli pressed her hands to her face. Her heart was thumping painfully. Now what? She couldn't run back home if Mrs. Pernikov had taken a car; as fast as she could run, Mrs. Pernikov would have ample time in the empty house to seek out the secret lab and…well, do whatever it was that she was planning on doing.

She looked thoughtfully at her family's wood-paneled minivan parked a few cars down. It wasn't like she had never done this before. After all, Pinny the PNAAD did all the driving.

"Home, Pinny," she said as soon as she'd pressed the right button on the dashboard to activate him. As the Personalized Navigator and Automatic Driver pulled out of the spot, she hoped that her family would be having so much fun at the ball of twine festival that they wouldn't feel like going back home until she had the car safely back in the parking lot. Yeah, right. She needed a miracle. "Please, Pinny, take me home as fast as you can."

"As fast as I can?" Pinny asked, and he let out a rather staticky and mechanical whoop as the car exited the parking lot. "Oh, this is the best day of my pathetic life. Do you actually mean it?" The car sped up and zoomed down the street. People turned to stare.

"No!" Rachelli said quickly, clutching the door handle. "No, please don't go one hundred miles an hour! You *know* what I meant! Get us there quickly, but in one piece!"

"I can actually go up until two hundred miles an hour," Pinny said sadly as the car slowed down so that a snail hitching a ride on a turtle could pass them. "But does anyone ever let me *go* two hundred miles an hour? Noooo. I am like a bird that longs to fly but whose cruel owners have clipped his wings. I even wrote a poem about it. Want to hear it?" Pinny slowed down even more.

"Actually, I—"

"Oh, how I long to fly! How I long to feel the wind beneath my wings! How I long to touch the sky! How I long to be not at all like the caged bird that sings! How I wish—"

"Pinny!" Rachelli yelled. "Please! The experiment might be in danger! Just drive me home!"

"*Fine*," Pinny said in a tear-filled voice. He sped up. "But you don't have to be so *mean* about it. I have feelings, you know."

"I know," Rachelli murmured. "I know all too well."

"Also, no one says things like 'the experiment might be in danger,' you know. Who are you, Nancy Drew?"

Rachelli stuck her tongue out in the general direction of the dashboard but said nothing until the minivan pulled into the Victorian's long driveway. When she tried to yank the door open and run inside, she found the door locked. Pressing the unlock button did not help. A mechanical laugh echoed throughout the car, setting her teeth on edge.

"Pinny!" she hollered, pounding on the window. "Pinny, this isn't funny! Let me out!"

"You forgot to say the magic word," the PNAAD said.

"I am going to take a wrench to your interface! Or whatever it is that makes you tick!" Rachelli shouted. "I will take you apart piece by piece!"

"Try again," said Pinny smugly.

"Argh!"

"That is not even a word, never mind a magic one."

Rachelli slowly counted to ten in her head. "Please! Thank you! Open sesame!"

There was a click, and Rachelli tumbled out of the car. She slammed the door shut a little harder than necessary and glanced at her watch. Thanks to Pinny, the PNAAD with feelings, getting here had taken a lot more time than she had anticipated. She glanced through the line of trees separating their property from the Pernikovs and felt her scalp prickle when she saw the Pernikov's pickup truck sitting in their driveway. On impulse, she ran across their yard, ducked around the truck, and after a moment's hesitation, she knocked on the front door.

What will I say if someone answers? Heart in her throat, Rachelli thought quickly. *Hello,* she would say. *I just wanted to make sure you were in your own home and not trying to steal something from mine. Have a good day!*

Yeah, that would go over well.

She waited a minute, and when no one answered, she felt a mixture of relief and trepidation. Because if Mrs. Pernikov wasn't home and her truck was...well, where else would she be other than trying to get into the secret lab?

Rachelli ducked back through the trees and down the Victorian's front path, past the tire swing, and onto the wooden wraparound porch. She pulled at the heavy front doors, but they would not open. Of course. What had she been thinking, leaving without the house keys?

With a groan, Rachelli sat on the top step leading up to the porch and put her head in her hands. Now what? For all she knew, Mrs. Pernikov was at this very minute inside the secret lab — well, no. How could she get to the secret lab if the front door was locked? Well, the same way she had seemed to sneak in all those other times.

Of course! Rachelli shot to her feet. There were around five bazillion secret entrances to the house. She, Effie, and Alex had just mapped them out the other day! The closest one was through Wilma Lou's vegetable garden. What was she doing just *sitting* here?

Five minutes later, Rachelli was no longer sitting on the steps and kicking her feet in frustration. Instead, she was swinging gently in a net near the ceiling, courtesy of Alex's sensory net, speechless with annoyance, when she heard the unmistakable sound of someone walking around inside the house.

CHAPTER 17

The thing about whispering *"Please stop swinging and squeaking"* to a swinging, squeaking net is that a net, particularly one that is swinging and squeaking, is an extraordinarily bad listener. Rachelli resorted to gritting her teeth and trying not to breathe too much until the net she was cradled in was finally still.

She heard sounds coming from the floor beneath her, and Rachelli cupped her hands around her ears to hear better. There was the sound of something falling, and a muffled exclamation in response, and the fine hairs on the back of Rachelli's neck rose.

Someone *was* in the house, that was for sure, and here she was, helpless, *trapped in a net*. She clenched her fists and muttered something about never again speaking to Alex when this was all over. Anger was easier to deal with than terror.

Okay. Okay. Rachelli took a shaky breath. So there was someone in the house, and that someone was probably Mrs. Pernikov. What could she do about it?

Well, for starters, she could get out of this net.

Rachelli stood up as slowly as she could — wincing each time the ropes squeaked — until she was face-to-face with the knot that attached the net to the hook in the ceiling.

It took twenty minutes to get the knot untied and then another five to recover from the indignity of the abrupt floor landing. At last Rachelli headed toward the secret trapdoor to see just who was down there.

She knew before she even arrived at the door to the lab that no one was there. The place was absolutely silent. Someone *had* been there — she had definitely heard them — but that someone was gone.

But now, there was the sound of someone — or someones — *upstairs*.

"Seriously?" Rachelli muttered. She hurried back up the stairs and ran down the hallway toward the source of the noise. "This is like playing a giant game of Whac-A-Mole!"

"What is like playing a giant game of Whac-A-Mole?" Her mother stood in the front doorway, her hands on her hips.

"Nice one, Rachelli," Effie said. He looked amused, but Professor Shore did not, and neither did Alex or Lolly.

"What?" Rachelli looked at her family in confusion. "What? What did I do?"

"There is the small matter of leaving us stranded in the town square without a car!" Mrs. Shore's eyebrows were raised. "We didn't know where you were, and then we couldn't find the car to look for you! Rachelli, what were you *thinking*?"

Rachelli was thinking that her whole body ached from first having to crouch in a net, and then from falling to the floor. She was thinking that she was sick and tired of this whole crazy cat-and-mouse game with Mrs. Pernikov, of pretending to be happy in this bizarre little town so far away from her friends, with only her siblings for company. She was tired of waving goodbye to her mother and not seeing her for weeks at a time. She was tired, tired, tired, and instead of showing some sympathy, all anyone ever did was *yell* at her. Not that she was going to tell anyone all that.

Well, yeah, actually, she was totally going to tell everyone all that.

"I'm not yelling at you," her mother sighed when Rachelli finally stopped for a breath. Mrs. Shore's hands dropped to her sides. "But taking the car without permission, even with Pinny as driver, was a reckless decision and pretty irresponsible."

"I didn't know what else to do! Mrs. Pernikov left the festival, and I knew that she would come here, and the experiment would be in danger!"

The front door burst open again, and Wilma Lou Wilson suddenly filled the doorframe. "Hey, now, danger? This house is not in danger and never will be! Not so long as I've got breath in my old lungs and good ole Bessie in my hands!" Wilma Lou patted her shotgun affectionately before storming upstairs. The Shores watched her go.

"Ma," Rachelli said once the clumping sound of Wilma Lou Wilson's boots against the wooden stairs had faded into the distance, "Now that Jeeves is fixed, do we really need a housekeeper? Especially one who is on a first-name basis with a deadly weapon?"

"Don't change the subject," Mrs. Shore said, and her hands were once again firmly on her hips. "Look. Daddy tells me that he has spoken to you about your unfounded fears time and again. He told you that this house was found and funded for us by the government, and it is the safest place that we could possibly be." She walked toward the kitchen, and Rachelli followed her. The kitchen smelled wonderfully of cholent and roasting chicken, dishes that had been carefully monitoring themselves for optimal temperature, thanks to the Shores' vast array of kitchen gadgets invented by the Professor. "So you can really stop worrying," Mrs. Shore finished.

"The government doesn't know everything," Rachelli countered.

"And careful of that tile, Ma, it leads to a tunnel beneath this room. Anyway, I know what I heard."

"Sometimes, houses, especially old houses like this, can settle." Mrs. Shore opened a cabinet door and took out what looked like a small remote control. She aimed it in a circle around the kitchen. "That must be what you heard."

"But, Ma—"

"One second, Rachelli, let's just get lunch underway," said Mrs. Shore. "Analyze contents," she said to the remote, which made a whirring sound, and then beeped.

"Not much in there," a mechanical voice said from the device in her hand.

Mrs. Shore sighed. "Recommendations for lunch?" she said into the remote. "I don't want to have to go shopping — Shabbos is in a few hours."

"Peanut butter and jelly sandwiches are your best bet," said the voice, "and no salad unless you like wilted lettuce. Shopping is not Professor Shore's forte."

Mrs. Shore looked at Rachelli. "Is it just me, or are the kitchen gadgets getting an attitude?" She shrugged and took out the necessary ingredients.

Rachelli shifted from one foot to the next. "Ma, please listen to me about Mrs. Pernikov. I think that she's kind of a bad guy, and you know I don't just make stuff up."

Mrs. Shore put an arm around Rachelli and squeezed before turning her attention back to lunch. "I think this summer has been hard on you. I've been away for too long, and you've had far too much responsibility. But there are no bad guys lurking around the corner, sweetie. Daddy's inventions are not the kind that would attract those kinds of people. He doesn't work for the military or anything like that."

Rachelli stared down moodily at the assembling sandwiches. The house suddenly shook slightly, and a loud burbling sound was heard from the lab. Mrs. Shore paused mid-sandwich. "Can you take over here for a minute? I just need to ask Daddy a question." She hurried out of the kitchen.

"Do my eyes deceive me, or is that lunch?" Effie was suddenly at Rachelli's elbow.

"Ew, you do *not* stick your finger into the peanut butter!"

"It is very unsanitary," agreed a voice from the remote on the counter, and Effie snorted and turned the device off.

"What did Ma say about Mrs. Pernikov the Great and Horrible?" Effie asked, swiping another pinky-full of peanut butter.

Rachelli shrugged. "Nothing. She thinks I'm imagining it all. You are seriously the only one who believes me that she's up to no good."

"I've been thinking," Effie said. "Look, Rachelli. Hear me out. We live in a crazy old house with a million exits and entrances. It makes tons of noise, between settling and whatever Dad is cooking up in the lab. And I agree with you that Mrs. Pernikov is creepy and weird, but does that mean that she's sneaking in and trying to get at Daddy's experiment? Think about it. Maybe you really *are* letting your imagination—"

"You know what?" Rachelli whirled around and glared at her brother. "Make your sandwiches yourself."

She stormed out of the kitchen, grabbed a fork away from Lolly before the little girl could insert it into an outlet, and turned toward the huge staircase that would take her to her room. Then she stopped. There was no more burbling sounds coming from the secret lab. What were her parents talking about down there?

Rachelli knew that it was wrong, very extremely wrong, to eavesdrop.

But all of a sudden, it felt even more wrong not to.

Holding her breath, she lifted up the trapdoor and tiptoed down the steps.

CHAPTER 18

Dear Shuli,

I know that you and everyone from the old block have been trying to figure out where I vanished to and when I'm coming back. And I want to tell you, I really do, but the thing is, all of you guys think that my father makes weird gadgets in his free time but really works with candy dispensers, and seriously, even if I was allowed to, it would be super weird to tell you the truth after all this time. Which is why I'm writing you this letter but not actually going to send it to you. Which seems pointless, and is, but I'm doing it anyway, and you can't judge me because you won't even read it, so ha.

You know how on the first day of school, the teacher always makes us write an essay titled "What I Did during My Summer Vacation"?

What I Did during My Summer Vacation

By: Rachelli Shore

Well, today was fun. I decided that I needed to eavesdrop because I knew my parents were keeping secrets from us about the Pernikovs and the house and obviously about the experiment that Daddy is working on, and I just couldn't take it anymore. I needed to know everything.

So I snuck halfway down the flight of stairs leading to the secret lab and stood there, practically holding my breath.

"...Should tell them, I think. They're old enough to keep secrets." That was my father's voice.

"Why burden them with it?" Those next words were from my mother. "And why take the risk? This might be it, Mordy. The answer to our *tefillos*. This experiment will put you on the government's payroll full-time, and then I can finally settle down and be home."

Okay, so seriously, chills up and down my back when I heard my mother say that. I'm not going to be all complainy and whiny, but it would be all kinds of awesome if my mother didn't have to keep leaving.

"I can stop flying around," my mother continued, "trying to find investors and going through all the red tape needed to make patents. Do we really want to mess up this chance just because Rachelli is impatient?"

I kind of bristled when my mother said that. *I'm not impatient!* I wanted to explain. *I just think that someone is trying to get at the experiment! Why am I the only one who can see that?*

My mother was talking again, but quieter this time, so I walked down all the way and put my ear to the door.

"Rachelli knows that—" my mother was saying, and I held my breath.

"Hello," said a little voice from behind me. "Watcha doin'?"

I froze, then slowly turned. A little girl with slightly lopsided pigtails was standing on the third-to-bottom step. "Lolly," I said in a sort of a hiss. "Shh!"

"Are we playing a game?" Lolly asked, and if anything, her voice grew louder. "Because I want to play a game. Can we play a game while we eat lunch?"

"Lolly," I begged in a voice no louder than the sound an ant makes. "Shh. Please. Shh."

"I can't hear you," Lolly explained, her voice no louder than the sound a herd of elephants make. "Because you're talking too quiet."

And then she did this thing that she usually does at least once or twice a day. She tripped down the stairs. And that was actually a good thing because when the door to the lab opened and Mommy and Daddy saw Lolly bawling and me bending over her, they assumed she had fallen and I was there to help. I wasn't grounded for life, although maybe I would feel less guilty about eavesdropping if I would have been.

Anyway, this little slice of my life pretty much personifies what my summer vacation has been like, give or take stuff like being trapped in a swinging net, watching the second-to-largest-ball of twine become the largest ball of twine, and dealing with household gadgets with attitudes.

And how have you been?

Wishing I could actually send this to you...

XOXO
Rachelli

"Rachelli! Rachelli!"

Rachelli opened one eye. She had fallen asleep on the couch, apparently. She opened her other eye. Alex's magnified eyes were an inch away from her own face, and she let out a startled shriek and jumped up, banging his forehead with her own. "Ouch!"

"What did you jump up like that for?" Alex rubbed at his forehead.

"You scared me! I was sleeping!" Rachelli scowled and patted her forehead gingerly. "What is it? What time is it? What *day* is it? Where is everyone?"

"Shabbos afternoon, three-thirty-four and seventeen seconds. Mommy and Daddy are napping, Effie is in the kitchen having a mousse pie–eating contest with Lolly, and I was reading that old, dusty handwritten book we found in the attic. And it's really interesting. I want to show you a passage in it."

"So you thought that you would smash my forehead and scare the living daylights out of me because I must be dying to have those bits of information?"

Alex closed the book with a snap. "No, I thought you would want to hear what I read in the journal. But I guess not." He walked away, his shoulders slumped.

Rachelli sighed. "Alex, I'm sorry. I'm just grumpy. Alexander! Come back here!"

But Alex didn't turn around. Effie walked into the living room instead, stretching his long arms over his head, tailed by Lolly, who was covered in chocolate. "Did you know that half of the second floor is locked away behind a big wooden door? Mysterious, isn't it?"

Rachelli shook her head. "Nope, not really. We closed it up after you left to yeshivah. It's just a bunch of empty, dusty rooms that we will never use. The real mystery here is why you of all people decided that you don't believe me about Mrs. Pernikov."

"It's not that I don't believe you—" Effie started, but Rachelli stormed past him.

"Fine!" Effie called after her. "Okay, *be* that way! You know what? I'm really not going to miss any of this when I go back to yeshivah!"

Motza'ei Shabbos was a muted affair. Rachelli chewed miserably on the end of her hair ribbon and thought about just how much her life was more terrible than any other girl her age. Lolly whined about Effie eating more mousse pie than she did, and Alex and Effie were both pretending that Rachelli didn't exist.

And then it got worse.

"Everyone," Mrs. Shore said, right after the Havdalah candle was extinguished and Rachelli turned on Jeeves, the robot cleaner, "I have something to tell you."

"A good something?" Rachelli asked. "Nah, not that kind of day. A bad something, then."

"Well—" Mrs. Shore began.

"Mommy!" Lolly whimpered. "Jeeves is trying to clean me!"

The robot cleaner was industriously wiping its cloth up and down the little girl's sticky face.

"Jeeves, only clean the furniture please, not the people," Professor Shore commanded mildly. "Although that does give me an interesting idea. A robot that bathes children might be something worth pursuing. A bathbot, if you will."

Alex nodded, a touch of enthusiasm back in his eyes. "Or a robo-bath. Bathinator. Bathbuddy?"

"Bathtub!" Lolly called out, trying to get into the spirit of it.

"Hmm," said Professor Shore. "How about—"

"How about my announcement?" Mrs. Shore said, clearing her throat. "And we can get back to the important business of naming a robot that does not yet exist *after* that?"

Professor Shore and Alex exchanged a sheepish grin. "Sure, go ahead," Professor Shore said. "Sorry about that."

"There has been a problem with some of the forms that I signed in Washington," Mrs. Shore said. "Basically, they're not all properly signed and notarized. I asked if they can be sent to me here, by courier, but…"

"But," Rachelli said, her heart sinking. "They said no. You have to go back."

Mrs. Shore nodded. "It won't be like last time. They arranged for all the meetings to be back-to-back. I'll be back in two days, and then I'll be here for weeks, and maybe…maybe even for good." She smiled. "Oh, don't look so sour, everyone. Two days! It'll pass before you know it."

"Yeah, I guess so," Rachelli said. "Besides, what could possibly happen in two days?"

Even as the words came out of her mouth, she felt them land heavily with the strength of a premonition.

What could possibly happen in two days?

CHAPTER 19

Rachelli had to admit: it really was pretty good ice cream. And the company wasn't too bad either.

"Can't believe y'all never had good old-fashioned homemade, hand-cranked ice cream before!" Birdy Winter's mother smiled as she scooped another generous helping of the creamy, frozen treat into Rachelli's bowl. The Winters' backyard was filled with white lanterns that lit up the darkened sky. Mixing with the sounds of chatting was the hum of thousands of crickets joining the impromptu party.

"Thanks, this is really nice of you," Rachelli said. The ice cream was cool and sweet and perfect.

Birdy grabbed Rachelli's hand. "There ya go. You don't look so glum anymore now, do ya?"

Birdy's ever-present entourage of girls giggled as they ate their own bowls of ice cream.

"It's a lucky thing I ran out of cream and sent Birdy to see if ya'll had some that I could borrow, or we never would have seen you lookin' so sad on your front steps. Now, do tell. What's wrong?"

Two months ago, when she had first arrived at Sundale, Rachelli would have turned up her nose at that question — and at the invitation to an ice-cream party to begin with. Honestly, she would have answered politely that everything was fine just a few *hours* ago. But now, with her mother having left for the airport, Effie leaving tomorrow morning for yeshivah again, and after that miserable, bickering Shabbos, she found herself telling the entire gaggle of Sundale girls and Mrs. Winters how difficult it all was.

"And I never even wanted to be here in the first place!" she sniffled. "I'm sorry, I mean, you guys are great, but I miss everyone back at home so much."

When she finished, there was sympathy in Birdy's wide blue eyes. "I'm sure that pretty soon your father will have finished with his experiment, and you can go on home. I mean, we'll all miss you terribly, but — what? Why is your mouth hanging open like a codfish?"

Rachelli closed her mouth with a snap, and then opened it again. A thrill of hot and cold ran down her spine. "Um. My father?" she said as casually as she could. "My father is a candy-machine repair-man. Why would you say…"

Peals of laughter stopped her words, and this time, Birdy's eyes were dancing with merriment. "Oh, honey. How many times do I have to tell you that this here is a small, small town? We know just about everything about just about everyone."

"It's a secret, you know," Rachelli said in a small voice. "No one is supposed to know."

"We won't tell anybody," Birdy and her girls chorused at once, prompting more laughter, and after a moment, Rachelli shrugged and dug back into her ice cream. They knew, they all knew, and there was really nothing she could do about it at this point.

Then a thought stopped her, with her spoon halfway to her mouth. *If they already knew…*

"So, girls," Rachelli said with studied casualness, "what else do you know about what my father is working on? Do you know, for example, that someone is after it?"

Fifteen white wicker chairs inched closer to Rachelli, their inhabitants' eyes widened eagerly, and all that was heard in the Winters' backyard was the crickets until Rachelli started to speak.

"Where were you?" Alex said as soon as Rachelli, slightly sick from too much ice cream, pushed open the heavy double front doors and walked inside. "Lolly said you promised her a bedtime story."

"Why couldn't *you* tell her a story?"

"She didn't like the one I told her, about being the youngest-ever recipient of the Copley medal for scientific achievement. She got bored during my acceptance speech."

"You wrote an acceptance speech for the Copley medal? A medal won by people like Einstein and Pasteur?"

Alex flushed. "Maybe. Anyway, she said that you tell the best stories."

In spite of herself, Rachelli stood up straighter. "Did she really say that?" Then she wilted. "Or are you still making fun of me, thinking I'm making up stories about Mrs. Pernikov?"

"No, I'm not, okay? And anyway, I'm not the only one being mean! You should take a look in the mirror. Just because—"

"Well, if you would just *stop* being such a snob because you read more *books* than I do—"

"If *you* stop being a snob and realize that—"

"Cut it out!" said Effie suddenly from behind her, and Rachelli jumped.

"*Don't* do that," she sputtered.

"Look, Rachelli," Effie said. "Me and Alex were talking while you were at your ice-cream party with the hicks, and—"

"They are not hicks! They're nice girls!"

"Yes, the nice hicks, or whatever, and we decided that—"

To say that the house shook was like saying that the ocean was damp. Alex lost his balance and thumped to the floor, and Rachelli fell back against the wall behind her. Effie grabbed Lolly, who had just come down the stairs, blinking sleepily at them. He held on to the heavy banister, his arms straining. From the other rooms came the sounds of items falling.

"Jeeves is upside down!" the robot cleaner called. "Jeeves cannot clean when he is upside down!"

"What," Effie asked when everything was quiet, "was that?"

Alex tried to cover up his shakiness with a thoughtful look as he got to his feet and rejoined the others. "Not an earthquake?"

"It was very loud and noisy," said Lolly. "I do not like it."

Rachelli jumped to her feet. "The lab," she said. "Daddy."

Effie swung Lolly on his shoulders, and they ran down the long, dark hallway toward the living room. When they reached the glowing blue floor, they swung open the trapdoor and raced down the stairs.

"Hurry, hurry, hurry," Effie muttered, and at the suppressed panic in his voice, Rachelli felt her heart travel into her mouth.

"He's fine," she told everyone, but especially herself, as they galloped down the stairs. "This is a man who accidentally drops vials of flesh-eating acid on his coat all the time and is always fine. He's fine. Daddy's fine."

Even with Lolly slowing him down, Effie reached the door first. He rapped on it loudly. "Daddy?" he called out. "Dad! Is everything okay in there?"

When there was no answer, he tried the doorknob. But it wouldn't turn; the door was locked. "Now what?" he said.

Rachelli snapped her fingers and turned and ran back up the stairs, with the others following at her heels.

They reached the kitchen moments later, panting and out of breath. Rachelli jammed the toe of her shoe sharply against the third tile from the right of the sink, and a tunnel opened up inches away from them. Rachelli dived in and heard Effie and Lolly jump in next, followed by Alex.

She landed hard on the ground in pitch darkness.

"Anyone brought a light?" she demanded, and was met with a sheepish silence.

"Any ideas, Science Boy?" she asked Alex.

"Sure," he answered.

"Oh, yeah? What?"

"We feel our way. With our hands. Hey, look," he said to Rachelli's snort of derision. "Sometimes the old-fashioned ways work just fine. It's what I wanted to show you in that old journal that we found. That—"

"Yes, interesting, etcetera, but not now. Now we need to go to the lab and rescue Daddy."

They shuffled along in silence in the absolute darkness, interrupted only occasionally by Lolly explaining how very hungry she was. Finally, they reached the heavy metal door that they knew would lead to the lab. Effie shoved it open, and the four of them burst in, momentarily blinded by the sudden light.

"Daddy!" Rachelli cried, blinking quickly and willing her eyes to focus.

"Daddy!" Effie called.

"Daddy!" Alex removed his glasses and rubbed at his eyes.

"Daddy, I'm hungry!" said Lolly.

No one answered, and when their eyes adjusted, they saw that the room was filled with equipment but empty of a Professor.

Suddenly, Lolly screamed.

"What? What is it?" Rachelli, Effie, and Alex ran over to the little girl, who pointed a trembling finger at a large, gleaming piece of equipment that was bouncing toward them. What looked like a maw was opening.

Rachelli smiled and hugged Lolly in relief. "It looks scary, but it's nothing," she said. "Last time we were down here, that maw opened, and out came chocolate chip muffins."

"Last time," asked Alex, "did a sort of laser pointer come down from the top of the thing and point at you?"

"No, why?" asked Rachelli.

"Because," said Alex, "that's exactly what it's doing right now."

"Move out of the—" Rachelli started to shout, but she was interrupted by a sudden flash.

CHAPTER 20

The world disappeared, which was a very disconcerting and rather inconvenient thing for the world to do.

"Effie!" Rachelli tried to yell. "Alex! *Lolly!*" But apparently her voice had disappeared along with the entire rest of everything.

Slowly, images began to form before her eyes, as if the world around her was being newly drawn. Colors, then lines, then — yes, the lab, the secret lab. They were still in the secret lab, and Daddy wasn't there, but he wasn't the only thing that wasn't there. The room was completely empty.

Every last piece of Professor Shore's equipment was gone.

Including the secret invention that he had been working on.

"It's not so much what happened that freaks me out," Rachelli said as she paced back and forth in the empty room. "No, actually, it's exactly what happened that freaks me out. I'm going to freak out right now again if that's okay with everyone. It just doesn't make any sense. How can a room full of stuff just *disappear*?"

She addressed this speech to Alex, Effie, and Lolly, but Alex was not paying attention to her at all. Instead, he was peering around the large, dusty room.

"Alex, I promise you, the lab equipment is not hiding in the corners somewhere," Rachelli called to him. Her voice echoed weirdly.

"I know *that*," he called back, but he continued his search. Rachelli turned back to Effie, who was sitting with his back up against a wall, holding Lolly.

"How can things just disappear, Effie?"

"Ephraim."

"Seriously, what difference does your stupid name make? *An entire room of extremely valuable equipment has disappeared! And the invention! And its all our fault!*"

Lolly took her thumb out of her mouth. "It's not *my* fault," she said. "I'm just the baby."

Rachelli put her head in her hands. "I wish I was the baby," she said to her palms. "What are we going to do? What even *happened*? Alex! What are you doing?"

Alex was spinning in a circle in the middle of the empty room. His eyes were closed, and his hands were out and open at his sides, as though he were begging for tzedakah. At the sound of Rachelli's rather strident voice, his eyes snapped open. "Something is…*off*," he said. "I can't explain it. But I can feel it."

"That's not very scientific of you." Effie's voice made it sound like he was amused, but he looked concerned. He gently placed Lolly down on the floor and walked over to his little brother. "Everything okay?"

Alex flushed. "I can't explain it," he said again. "But when that laser on top of the machine pointed at us and then the flash of light happened and then we were back here, with everything gone, it was like…" There was a searching look on his face, as though his tongue was probing the spot where a tooth had been. "If I only had another look at the invention, or Daddy's notes. I know I can figure this out."

Rachelli yanked out her hair ribbon and retied it. "Well," she said. "I have a plan."

Effie and Alex looked at her. "You do?"

"Yes. I think now would be an excellent time to run away from home."

Lolly whimpered. "I don't want to run away from home."

Rachelli waved a hand at the little girl. "You don't have to. You're the baby, remember? No one will blame you."

Lolly smiled. "Okay, good. Also, I'm hungry."

Effie rooted around in his pockets for a little while before coming up with a wrinkled Fun Dip and handing it to Lolly. The colored sugar was congealed, but she worked away at it anyway.

"Okay!" Rachelli clapped her hands. "Look, this is probably the worst thing ever to have happened to anyone ever—"

"They are stoning people in Syria," Effie pointed out mildly.

"Kids are starving in Africa," Alex mentioned.

"My sock has a hole in it," Lolly attempted to join in.

"—But it's not like we're *stuck* down here," Rachelli said, ignoring them all. "Let's get out of here and figure it out from upstairs, where it is significantly less freaky and depressing. Alex what in the *world* are you looking at?"

Alex was looking up at the ceiling. His mouth was open. "I'm looking at nothing," he said. "That's the problem. The light fixture is gone."

"Well, yes," said Rachelli. "*Everything* is gone. As you might have noticed if you look around—"

"Yes, of course. It would follow a certain logic if the ray of light that came out of the machine somehow managed to make everything nonorganic disappear, and that's why we're the only ones who remained. But how can the machine have made the holes in the ceiling disappear?"

"Holes in the ceiling?"

"The screws holding the light fixture in place would have left holes. Don't you see? Sure, the screws could have disappeared, along with the fixture. But how could the holes that the screws would have made in the ceiling disappear?"

Everyone followed his gaze to the ceiling. It was perfectly smooth and hole-free.

"Fascinating," Alex said.

"Huh," said Effie.

"I think it's time for a little more freaking out," said Rachelli.

"*I'm* freaking out," said Lolly, looking up from her sugar fest.

"Any brainstorms yet, Science Boy?" Effie asked Alex. "What can make holes disappear?"

"Outlets too," said Alex. He clicked his tongue. "Look around. The walls are smooth too. And clean. Too clean. No splatters, no holes, nothing. I have an idea, but I need some equipment to work it out first."

"If we *had* some equipment, we would not be in this mess," Rachelli pointed out.

"Yeah, true. But I have some stuff upstairs. I'll just run and get some." He turned toward the door.

"Wait!" Rachelli called, and he turned around questioningly.

"What?"

Rachelli hesitated, and then shook her head. "It's silly," she said. "Nothing, never mind."

"What is it?"

"I just have this weird feeling that we should stick together down here. It's dumb, I told you. Go on, get the equipment you need. If you see Daddy, tell him that — never mind, don't tell him anything. There's no way to soften this blow."

She looked around the empty room again sadly. All the months hiding out in Sundale while Professor Shore worked on the experiment were out the window, gone. She turned back to Alex, who was now hesitating at the door. "Go ahead. Just come back as fast as you can."

"Do you have a better idea?" Alex put his hand on the door.

"Well, yeah," Effie interjected. "Go back in time and be born to a less crazy family, one in which there is zero percent chance of an entire room full of objects vanishing in the blink of an eye. Barring that, I vote for Science Boy figuring it out. At least until Dad comes home."

"That will be wonderful, up until he grounds us for life," Rachelli pointed out. "He warned us never to come down here again."

"As long as he figures out how to get the invention back before he disowns us, I'm okay with that. Where is he, by the way?" Effie rubbed at his nose in thought. "The reason we came down here to begin with is because we heard that explosion, and we thought that he was hurt…oh man. Oh man, oh man, oh man."

"What? Why are you oh man-ing? What is it?" Rachelli demanded.

"The explosion." Effie looked grim. "We definitely heard something that sounded like an explosion."

"Yes. We did. So?"

"So what if — what if Dad *was* down here? What if he was down here and…something terrible happened to him?"

Rachelli was already shaking her head. "No," she said. "Not possible. We would know. We would see something."

"Well, what if there's nothing to see? What if the machine that made the stuff disappear first made *him* disappear?"

"Daddy's gone?" Lolly's eyes filled with tears.

"*Now* look what you did," Rachelli hissed at Effie. "Daddy is not gone! He would never let something like that happen!"

"Look, I'm gonna go get my stuff," said Alex. "I'll be right back. Try to get all of the pointless arguments out of the way in the meantime."

He turned the doorknob, but before he could pull open the door, they heard footsteps on the stairs.

"Daddy!" Lolly cried happily. "He *didn't* disappear! I knew it!"

Alex took a step back as the door opened. Rachelli felt her heartbeat speed up. *Daddy was going to be so upset.*

But the man who walked into the room wasn't Professor Shore at all.

Alex gasped and pointed at the stranger. "You!" he said. His face was white as a ghost.

CHAPTER 21

"You!" Alex said again, and he stumbled back a step and bumped into Effie, who lurched backward into Lolly, who stepped on Rachelli's toe, who let out an involuntary yelp before putting one hand over her mouth and the other around Lolly's arm.

The horrified recognition on Alex's face was not mirrored by the man who had entered the room. Instead, the man — who was wearing a strange round straw hat and a white shirt with suspenders — simply looked annoyed.

"What are you children doing here?" he asked. "And I'll thank you to not be lying to me now. I know thieves when I see them!"

"This" — Rachelli took a furious step forward, accidentally dragging Lolly along for the ride — "is *our* house! If anyone's a thief, it's you!"

The man looked amused. "Well, you are either the most audacious little urchin I have ever had the dubious pleasure of meeting, or you are plain off your chump. Either way, it's up the river for you lot."

And before anyone could say another word, the man pulled a wooden-handled shotgun out from behind his back.

"Uh, sir." Effie stepped forward, doing his best to block his siblings from the man with the shotgun who thought he owned the Victorian. The man was clearly crazy, and a crazy man plus a gun was not a sure bet for a positive outcome. "Sir, um, see, thing is, we're *lost*, and we don't even know how we got down here, so if you'll just put down the gun, we'll be out of your hair in a sec."

Effie smiled, then glared at Rachelli and Alex and Lolly until they got the hint and smiled too. Then they started walking toward the door to the lab.

"Yes!" the man with the gun shouted. "And stay out! I have good mind to call the sheriff! He's been known to string up rascals like yourselves for less!"

"Okay, thanks, bye!" Lolly called to the man before Effie quickly scooped up the little girl. Rachelli opened the door, and a moment later the Shores were dashing up the stairs.

"Just keep running to the front door!" Effie muttered to the others urgently as he clutched Lolly is his arms. "Go, go, go! Rachelli, go! Rachelli, *why* are you stopping!"

Rachelli had stopped in the middle of the living room and stood there as if frozen. "Rachelli!" Effie looked at her, wide-eyed. "We need to — oh." He followed her gaze to the floor. "What in the world…?"

"Exactly," Rachelli said slowly. "We used floor cleaner. We used oven cleaner. Wilma Lou tried her home-brewed cleaner that smelled like everything good in the world had died, and we had Jeeves work at it until his batteries ran out. But nothing, *nothing*, could get rid of the bright-blue stain on the living room floor. *Nothing.*"

"Until now," said Effie. "But that's not the only thing that's weird. Look around the *room*."

The room that Rachelli, Effie, Alex, and Lolly were standing in the middle of bore no resemblance to the living room they had occupied a short time ago, with its dusty couches and not much else. This room was crammed with furniture: a large round table, a small square table, a medium-sized table with flowers in the middle, a sofa, a loveseat, several heavy-looking padded chairs, several ottomans, a bookcase, a cabinet for knickknacks, a large desk, a small desk, an in-between desk, a full-sized harp, and what looked horribly like a garbage can made out of an elephant's foot.

The hair on the back of Rachelli's neck stood on end.

"Now," she whispered, "we *run*."

They ran.

They ran through the hallways that were no longer empty; they were lined with all sorts of furniture and items that the Shores passed in a blur. They ran and ran until they reached the double front doors and then out into the blazing sunshine. They passed a fishpond filled with several fat specimens, set in an inexplicably manicured garden. Moments before, it had held Wilma Lou Wilson's vegetable patch, some overgrown brown grass, and a lone tire swing.

"Just go," Effie said grimly. "Let's just go until we're off this property."

So they continued running until they found themselves at the strip of stores.

"Let me guess, everything is different," Effie said wearily. And, of course, everything *was*.

"Horses," said Lolly, and there were indeed horses, some in the middle of the street, some tied to posts on the side.

Women wore long dresses and bonnets, while the men wore hats and somewhat shabby suits. A little boy ran past them, chasing a colorful hoop with a stick, and a little girl walked behind him, holding eggs in a straw basket. She gave them a sidelong glance before gracing them with a smile.

"I'm hungry," Lolly commented. "I want ice cream."

But no one was paying her any attention because the sign that usually said "Ice Cream" now said "Saloon," and instead of a glass door with a tinkling bell over it, there were two swinging half doors.

At that very moment, the doors flew open, and a man in a ten-gallon cowboy hat came hurtling at them, landing painfully on the dusty street. He stood up, dusted himself off, and shook his fist at the ice-cream store — no, at the *saloon*.

"It *is* a great idea, it *is!*" he yelled. "This two-horse town will be known as home to the biggest ball of twine! We will become famous! And *then* we'll see whose laughing, won't we?"

"Get out of town!" a loud and growly voice sounded from inside the tavern.

"Yes, get out of my town," said a new voice, and the Shores followed the sound to a man riding a tall brown horse in the middle of the wide street. The crowd that had gathered to watch the spectacle moved back as the man got off his horse in one swift movement. He had the biggest hat they had ever seen and a shiny metal star pinned onto his vest. He put his thumbs into his belt loops and swaggered over to the man who had been thrown out of the tavern.

"As sheriff, this here is my town," he said to the man. "And we've just about had our fill of weirdoes."

The man put his own thumbs into his belt loops and slowly ambled toward the sheriff. "Weirdo, you say?" He pushed his hat back with one hand before quickly returning the hand to his belt. "That sounds like fighting words to me."

"That's exactly the kind of words they are!" said the sheriff.

The crowd murmured. It seemed to the Shores that they were enjoying themselves.

"Is this some kind of reenactment?" Rachelli asked in bewilderment. "Is everyone dressed up in olden-day clothes, and they're reenacting the second-to-largest-ball-of-twine story right here in town? How come we didn't get the memo?"

"This is not a reenactment," said Alex, and Rachelli realized that ever since the strange man had kicked them out of the lab, Alex had not said a single word. His face was still pale beneath his glasses.

"It's not?" she asked. "Then what *is* it?"

Alex's face turned even paler, a feat Rachelli would not have thought possible.

"It's not scientific," Alex whispered. "It's not possible."

A gunshot rang out, and several women screamed. Rachelli looked up and saw the sheriff holding two guns, one in each hand. One of them was smoking. The man who had been tossed from the tavern took off his hat and examined the smoking hole in its center.

"And that is my final warning," said the sheriff with satisfaction. "Now, get out of my town!"

"Alex!" Rachelli said to her brother, who appeared shell-shocked. "You know something! You know what's going on! Tell us!"

"I don't!" Alex shouted, and to Rachelli's shock, his eyes were filled with tears. "It's not possible! None of this is *possible!*"

"Just say it," she said to her little brother gently. "Tell us what this all is, and then we'll see if it's possible or not."

"I don't even need to say it," said Alex. He raised his voice to be heard over the crowd, which was dissipating now that the action was over. "I don't even need to *say* it to know that traveling back in time is scientifically impossible." Alex removed his glasses and wiped them with a trembling hand. "But that's exactly what we did."

CHAPTER 22

There was a pause for at least ten seconds after Alex made his announcement before Rachelli and Effie bent over and clutched their stomachs in howling laughter. All around them on the street, people wearing clothing from an era long dead were staring at the siblings with looks of consternation and amusement.

"T-t-time travel," Rachelli finally gasped when she could talk again. "Yeah, right! Because *that* happens!"

"Oh no, Dr. Middos!" Effie cried. "Poor Shnooky Shapiro is lost somewhere in time!"

At that, Rachelli lost it again. Tears of laughter filled her eyes and flowed down her cheeks.

"Fine," Alex said coldly, the panic and confusion in his voice gone completely in the face of their total disbelief. "Fine, don't believe me. That won't change the fact that it's real."

Rachelli and Effie looked at each other, took deep, slow breaths in an effort to calm down, then burst into laughter again.

Alex shot them looks of distain. "Sherlock Holmes says, 'Once you eliminate the impossible, whatever remains, no matter how improbable, must be the truth.' Okay? So if we have not traveled back in time, tell me: Where is the lab equipment? Who put all that furniture in our house and tended to the yard? Where is our *car*? And did you notice that the houses on the block are completely different too? The saloon, the stores, the people, the *horses*." Alex gestured around wildly. "I guess you can explain all *this* away, can you?"

Rachelli finally calmed down, besides for the occasional hiccup. "Okay. Okay, I needed that. Okay, Alex. You were saying something about time travel?" She bit back another squeal of laughter that was rising in her throat at the thought.

"Lolly," Effie said.

"No," said Rachelli. "He was not saying anything about Lolly, he was talking about going back in time, and I, for one, think—"

"No!" Effie was not laughing anymore. "Lolly! Has anyone seen Lolly? She's gone!"

Unlike the laughter, the panic was slow building. After all, this was Lolly, the girl who had single-handedly found half of the secret exits in the house by falling into them. She got lost all the time and usually emerged later, mysteriously sticky and demanding to be fed.

After a few minutes of futile searching, Alex, Effie, and Rachelli spilt up, promising to return to the spot in front of the saloon in fifteen minutes to touch base.

"Lolly!" Rachelli called. "Lolly! Excuse me, sir?"

The man whom she had questioned was holding what looked like a walking stick. He pulled a pair of glasses out of his pocket and put them on his nose. He peered through them at her. They had no earpieces.

"Um," Rachelli continued, trying not to stare at them. "Um, have you seen a little girl, about this high, probably about this sticky, pigtails, answers to the name of Lolly — or pretty much any treat, actually?"

"What is it, girl? Speak up," the man said, and he pulled a small metal trumpet out of his other pocket, inserted the small end into his ear, and aimed the open end in Rachelli's direction.

Rachelli took a quick step back. "Please, sir, I know it's like reenactment day, or something equally small-towny and incomprehensible, but this is important. I need to find my sister, and pretty quickly, too, before trouble finds her."

The man shook his head at her in annoyance and walked off, muttering something about unintelligible children who can speak to their elders in riddles with no shame and how in his day things were very, very different.

"Moral decay!" he mumbled as he strode off. "Moral decay! And mark my words, before the end of the nineteenth century, there will be a great deal more!"

"The end of the nineteenth century. Huh," Rachelli muttered to herself as she walked back to the meeting place after more futile searching. "Maybe he's not just some guy from Sundale. Maybe they brought in some real actors or whatever for this reenactment." But there was a tingling feeling in the pit of her stomach, almost like the feeling you get when you *know*, without turning around, that someone is standing behind you…

"Boo!" said someone, and Rachelli jumped straight into the air and shrieked. She turned and glared into Effie's face. "Not funny! Very not funny, Effie!"

Effie's smile drooped. "I know. I couldn't find Lolly, and I guess you couldn't either. And honestly, Rachelli, the people are acting super weird, and this whole place smells like horses, and everything is different, and" — he took a deep breath — "what if Alex is right? What if that laser light thingy on top of Dad's invention…what if, instead of making everything disappear, it made *us* disappear — and appear again here, wherever *here* is?"

"Or *when*ever here is," said Rachelli softly.

Brother and sister watched a woman in a long frilly dress walk by with an equally frilly parasol.

"My life," Rachelli said with a weary sigh, "is so incredibly weird."

"What's weird is that Alex knows something about that guy who thinks our house is his," Effie said thoughtfully. "He freaked out when the guy walked in."

"If we're actually in the past somehow, then how could he possibly know someone who's been dead for like a bazillion years?"

"More like over a hundred years," Effie said.

"Math is not my thing."

"True story." Effie glanced at his watch. "Speaking of Alex, where is he? He's late."

"He's *Alex*. If he was on time, I would be worried. He'll be here. Hopefully with Lolly behind him."

A man walked past. He had black elastic bands around his arms that seemed to keep his billowing white sleeves up, and his head was nearly swallowed by a giant cowboy hat. He pulled an oversized pocket watch out of his pocket, glanced at it, snapped it shut again, and then walked into the saloon. The half doors swung open and shut, open and shut, open and shut behind him. In the silence that followed, a small dark horse that was tied to the front of the saloon whinnied and stamped his hind legs.

"We," said Effie, staring at the horse, "went back in time."

"Yeah," said Rachelli.

"Back," said Effie. "In time."

"Yeah," said Rachelli.

"That doesn't happen," said Effie. "Ever. To anyone. Anyone who is normal and is supposed to be leaving on the bus to yeshivah really soon, at least. Like my roommate. The most exciting thing that happens to him over the weekend is that his mother adds barbeque sauce to the cholent." Effie rubbed at his nose. "What am I supposed to tell my rebbe?"

"Tell him that you took an unexpected detour through 1880."

"Rachelli, there are no words in that sentence that make sense."

"Effie, there are no words to describe the incredible amount of non-sense that our life is defined by."

"Ephraim, by the way."

"Yeah, that's really never going to happen."

The sound of sneakers slapping against dusty road came up from behind them, and Rachelli and Effie whirled around.

It was Alex, and he was out of breath.

"Lolly?" Rachelli asked, and her heart sank when Alex shook his head. He put his hands on his knees until he got his breath back.

"I can't find her," he finally gasped. "I looked all over town. I even went all the way back home — well, back to the home of the original builder, but—"

"How do you know who he is, by the way?" Effie interrupted.

"Well, we all know him, don't we?" Alex looked surprised.

"We do?" asked Rachelli. She was starting to get jittery, picturing Lolly wandering around alone somewhere, lost, afraid.

"From his picture in the back of his journal. You know, the journal of the original owner that we found in the attic?"

"None of us read them, you know," Effie pointed out. "Only you did."

Alex rolled his eyes. "Figures. Anyway, you really should. Read them, I mean. There's so much stuff there that—"

"*Lolly*," said Rachelli firmly. "Talk later. Find Lolly now."

Suddenly, the bat-shaped doors to the saloon swung open, and a man walked out. He looked, Rachelli thought, like if you would put him on one side of a scale, and then put her, Alex, and Effie on the other side, plus a few horses and a cow, he would tip the scales and then pick up the scales and crush them with his bare hands. And then maybe eat them.

The man stopped right in front of the Shore children. They looked up, up, up into his face. He looked like raw hamburger in a hat.

"You," he said, and pointed a meaty finger at them.

Chapter 23

The three siblings stood frozen for a moment.

"Me?" Effie swallowed and took a step forward.

"Yes," said the man. "You. New in town?"

"Um." Effie and Rachelli exchanged glances. Was it better to say yes or no? And what was the truth, anyway? They were not new to this town, but they were new to this town in this time. "Yeah," Effie finally answered. "New here."

The man nodded, satisfied. "Thought so. Didn't recognize you, and Big Mike knows every face in town."

"Who is Big Mike?" Effie asked.

"I am Big Mike!" the man roared, then leaned forward to shake Effie's hand. The experience was rather like being mauled by a bear. "Welcome, stranger. Care to weigh in on the controversy?"

"Controversy?"

"The ball-of-twine controversy! Creatin' the biggest ball of twine in the world! Our good sheriff is against it. He thinks it's a waste of time and twine. Some people are for it. They think that it will put this town on the map. Big Mike is on the fence. What say you?"

"Fence," Effie squeaked. "I am on the fence with you. We can be on the fence together. If you don't mind. If that's okay."

"Plenty of room on the fence!" the man laughed. "Even when I'm sittin' on it! What do you think, young lady?"

"Um," Rachelli gulped. "Um, I think it's something that is destined to happen, you might say. I think there will be songs written about it. Festivals celebrating it."

The man nodded thoughtfully and grinned, showing off a mouthful of grayish teeth. He touched his hat in farewell and ambled off toward the horses.

Rachelli and Effie let out shaky breaths of relief. Alex was staring at the ground, a distracted frown on his face.

"Eighteen-eighty to Alex," Rachelli said.

"Huh?" said Alex. "Just…thinking."

"Okay." Rachelli clapped her hands together briskly. "Okay. As far as crazy things go, this is the craziest. And I can't really think about it because if I really stop and think about it, I might lose my mind and run screaming down the street. But the fact is, we are here, and Lolly is missing, and we have to get back. So before we say another *word* or do *anything* else, we need to find her, and we need to get home, in that order. Now. Plans? Suggestions?"

"It's getting dark," said Effie.

"That is not a plan or a suggestion, that's an observation. Try again."

"Um," said Alex slowly, "can I just say, it *is* getting dark, and it was sunny before, and that's weird because it was Sunday night when we got here, remember?"

Rachelli peered up at the sky. Stars were just beginning to appear, the brightest stars she had ever seen. "Okay, so that is super weird, but we don't have *time* for that right now. We will deal with every-thing else *later*."

Alex pushed his glasses up his nose. "Past this strip of stores are a few outhouses. Beyond that is just barren land. So there's no place for her to go, really."

"Maybe she tried to go back home," said Effie.

Rachelli nodded. "Okay, so let's go back there."

"But what if she didn't? What if she went in the opposite direction? Would she even know where home is? She's just a little girl!" Worry made the normally placid Effie raise his voice.

"I don't know!" Rachelli slapped her hands against her skirt. "I don't know, but it's the only plan we've got! That, and saying a lot of *tehillim*. Unless you've got a better idea?"

Effie shook his head.

"Okay, then. And also, if anyone has *any* of Daddy's inventions in their pockets, do not take them out or use them. Please. These people are freaking out about a ball of twine. They'll probably think we know black magic if they see an InstaLight or whatever. I really don't want to know what they do in the Wild West version of Sundale if they think you can do black magic."

"Dead Cow," said Effie.

"Huh?" said Rachelli.

Effie looked apologetic. "This town isn't called Sundale. Not yet, anyway. It's called Dead Cow. A man told me. Apparently when they decided to build the town, there was a dead cow right in the beginning of the town line, and—"

"Okay!" said Rachelli. "Information that enriches my life not at all. Can we go now?"

The three of them headed back where they'd come from, passing a boy in a small peaked cap who was lighting the streetlights using a wick attached to a long pole. He gave them a cheerful smile.

"Have you seen a little girl?" Rachelli asked him, but he shook his head.

Besides for the ghostly glow of the gas streetlights, it was completely dark, and the great white Victorian loomed gloomily against the sky. The neighborhood was completely and utterly quiet. Somewhere, off in the distance, a wolf howled.

"Well, what do we do now?" asked Effie softly. "Knock and say that we'll be living in this house in a hundred and fifty years, and can we please see if our little sister is here?"

Alex said, "Can we tell them that we are, I don't know, selling something? Like, cowboy hats?"

"We don't *have* cowboy hats," Rachelli snapped.

"Whatever! So we can sell something we *do* have, like a bossy older sister!"

"Stop shouting! They'll hear us!"

"Fine!"

"Alex, I'm sorry." Rachelli sighed and stared at her feet. "I'm just really worried about Lolly."

Alex softened. "Me too."

"I don't even know if we can do this. What if the guy who saw us in the lab answers the door?"

They stood still for a minute, trying to think. "The house looks so out of place here," Rachelli said in a whisper. "It's like a palace surrounded by cottages."

"Well, it's because of the original owner, and who he was. Well, *is*…now," said Alex.

"Who is he?"

Alex sighed. "I can't believe you didn't read the journals. The original owner — Effie, what are you doing?"

While Alex and Rachelli had been talking, Effie had walked past them, up the path and onto the white wraparound porch. He lifted the heavy door knocker and let it down with a thud. "Finding Lolly," he said.

"But we don't have a *plan!* How are we going to—"

The front doors swung open, interrupting Rachelli mid-sentence. A woman in a crisp white apron over a long black dress peered at the three of them. "Yes?" she said.

"Um," said Effie, standing at the door.

"Um," said Rachelli, standing at the front of the property line.

"Um," said Alex, standing behind Rachelli.

"Yes?" said the woman.

"We — we're looking for a little girl!" Rachelli blurted out, her voice loud in the quiet night. "Our sister — she's missing. And we don't belong here, and we need to go back to where we belong, but we need to find her first, and it's been a while already, you see, and we're getting scared. She's a little girl, and she's out there, some-where, all alone." Rachelli felt her chin quiver, and her eyes filled with tears.

The woman's face softened. "Why don't you come on in," she said, "and tell me all about it. I'm sure Mr. Smith won't mind. He's busy all the time with his secret work, anyway. He probably won't even notice that you're here. Then we can call on the sheriff, and he can send out search parties to find her."

"Thank you!" said Rachelli, sniffling. "Thank you so much!"

The woman settled them in the living room on various poufy pieces of furniture. "I'll be back with some tea," she said, "and I'll send one of the maids to notify the sheriff."

"Well, this worked out pretty well so far," said Rachelli.

"Did it?" said a deep and familiar voice.

Rachelli, Alex, and Effie jumped to their feet. The secret door in the living room floor was open, and the man who had confronted them in the lab was standing at the top of the steps.

"You," he said, pointing at the woman in the white apron, his lip curling. "I can *see* you. A maid should never be *seen.*"

131

The woman opened her mouth as if to protest, then thought better of it. She dashed out of the room, leaving the siblings alone.

The man turned his attention to them. "And *you* have five seconds," he said, cocking his gun, "to get off my property."

"But we'll never make it to the front door in five seconds!" Rachelli said.

The man shrugged. "Oh, well. One. Two."

"Effie! Alex!" Rachelli yelled. "This way!"

The three of them dove for the secret exit near the fireplace, but instead of tumbling out into the garden, the world around them disappeared in a sudden flash of white light.

Chapter 24

"Get up! What are ya'll doing to my poor vegetable patch?"

The angry voice sounded familiar, but for a moment, Rachelli couldn't place it. Or place anything, for that matter. Where *were* they? Her vision was blurred, and the world swam.

"Up, or I'll sic Bessie on ya'll!"

Well, that answered that question. Rachelli blinked and then blinked again. She was outside, on the ground, and leaning out of the window was an irate Wilam Lou. She was irate for good reason. Rachelli was sitting in Wilma Lou Wilson's vegetable garden, on a patch labeled "Carrots," to be exact.

"Up, up, up!"

Rachelli scrambled to her feet. On either side of her, Effie and Alex were also standing up and blinking around in confusion.

"Sorry, Wilma Lou," Rachelli said automatically, and scrambled out of the fledgling vegetable patch. She grabbed for her brothers' arms and hurried away from the garden. They didn't stop until they reached the wraparound porch.

"Okay, we're back," she hissed when she was sure they were alone. "This is terrible."

"Terrible?" Alex looked confused. "It's good, actually, right?"

Rachelli smacked a hand to her forehead. "Do you remember a little girl about, oh, this high, pigtails, endless appetite, usually sticky, goes by the name of Lolly, who's *your little sister*?"

Alex clapped a hand over his mouth. "We left Lolly behind!"

"Okay, let's think," said Effie. He looked nauseated as he leaned against the splintery railing. "Okay, so it's a good thing, in a way, that we came back here—"

"A *good* thing? But we *left*—"

"*Yes,* we did, but it's a good thing anyway because now we know that we *can* come back. Right? And if we can come back here, then we can go back there, get Lolly, and then get back here. Did you know it's possible to give yourself a headache just by *talking* about time travel?"

Rachelli nodded reluctantly. "You're right. But we don't know *how* we came back! The original owner guy scared us, and we ran for the secret exit near the fireplace, and then suddenly white light, and we're here!"

"Maybe it has something to do with the original owner — whose name, by the way, is Joseph Smith—"

"Seriously?" Effie snorted.

"What?"

"That's not a *name,* it's an alias."

Alex nodded. "Could be. Because of what he was working on."

"Working on?" Rachelli asked.

Alex rolled his eyes. "I forgot that none of you could be bothered to read the journal. He was an inventor, working for the government. That's why I found it all so interesting because—"

"Because Daddy is an inventor working for the government," said Rachelli slowly. "And the government sent us to work on Daddy's secret project here, in this house. What are the chances that that's a coincidence?" Rachelli shook her head abruptly. "Of course, we know there's no such thing as coincidences…but anyway, this is all stuff we can figure out *after* we rescue Lolly." She shivered. "Come on. Let's go inside."

Rachelli entered the house, followed by her brothers.

"Thing is," Alex said, his voice echoing in the enormous empty front hallway, "the last bunch of entries in the journal were talking about…well, time travel."

"That's really weird," Rachelli said as she led the other two into the living room with the bright-blue floor. Chills, like cold fingers, tickled up and down her spine.

"Yes," said Alex. He cleaned his glasses with his pocket cleaner. "And while I don't see how an experiment in time travel from over a hundred years ago could have anything to do with what just happened now…"

"But, on the other hand, how could it not?" Effie finished the thought.

Alex's eyes lit up. *"Exactly,"* he said. "It has to be somehow connected. Oh, if only Daddy were here to help us!"

"Hello," said Professor Shore from the doorway.

Rachelli screamed. She couldn't help it; her nerves were wound so tightly that the slightest noise would have set her off, never mind her father, whom she had been purposely not daring to think about. In a dark place in the back of her mind, she'd been sure that something had happened to him down in the lab, something terrible.

"Oh, Daddy," she said, and, lips trembling, she threw herself into his arms.

Unfortunately, Effie had decided on the very same action at the same time, and the sound of their two heads hitting each other reminded Rachelli of the sound of horse's hooves on the dirt road of Sundale in the past. Then it reminded her of headaches because that's what happened next. Groaning, she put her hand to her head and backed away from Effie, who was backing away from her.

"Well, I've missed you too," said Professor Shore, looking from Effie to Rachelli in bemusement. "But maybe not enough to bang into people. I mean, I've only been gone for around twenty minutes."

Rachelli stared at her father. "Twenty minutes?" she croaked. How was it possible that only twenty minutes had passed in the present? *They had been in the past for hours...*

"Or maybe a bit longer? I wanted to get a bit of wire at the general store to fix...well, to fix something on my invention," Professor Shore said evasively. "You might have heard a small explosion?"

"*Small* explosion?" Rachelli blurted out.

"Yes, exactly, you got it, a small explosion." Professor Shore beamed. "But the store was closed. Stores close very early in small towns, did you know? And then it took a while to get home because first Pinny wanted me to listen to a song he'd composed."

"And?" said Rachelli impatiently.

"Oh, it was awful." Professor Shore shook his head. "Personalized Navigators and Automatic Drivers are terrible composers."

"Not the song!" Rachelli practically hopped with impatience. "I mean, what happened to the invention that you needed to fix it?"

"Rachelli, you know I can't tell you anything about the experiment." Professor Shore shook his head at her. "I know that you kids have a little game going, trying to guess what it is exactly that I'm working on, but trust me when I say that it's all for the best that you don't know anything about it at all."

A noise came from the secret basement lab that sounded like a cat using a chalkboard as a scratching post. "Now, if you'll excuse me, we probably have something to eat for dinner. I truly hope it's awful." Professor Shore lifted the secret trapdoor. He was halfway down the stairs when he stopped at the sound of Rachelli bursting into tears.

Rachelli, too, was surprised by herself bursting into tears. But it had all been way more than too much. Losing Lolly had simply been the last straw.

Professor Shore climbed back up and looked at his children. Tears were running down Rachelli's face, Effie was biting his fingernails, and Alex was pale.

"What in the world," he said slowly, "could have possibly happened in the past twenty minutes? And where in the world is Lolly?"

Behind him, the door to the lab opened silently. Rachelli watched as Mrs. Pernikov, clutching her bright-pink hat, darted from the lab and into one of the secret exits.

Finally! Rachelli thought. *Finally, in front of witnesses!* Now her siblings would all finally believe her that Mrs. Pernikov had designs on her father's invention! With a howl of triumph, Rachelli rushed after the old woman through the secret exit.

Oh no, not again! Rachelli thought when, instead of seeing Mrs. Pernikov's guilty expression, she saw a flash of white light.

Chapter 25

Dumbfounded, thunderstruck, flabbergasted. Those were all words that described how Alex and Effie and Professor Shore felt as they watched Rachelli dart past them and after Mrs. Pernikov, only to vanish in a blinding white light.

"Stay here!" Professor Shore bellowed at the two boys, and they stopped in their tracks as their father went through the secret entrance by himself. "Rachelli!" he called, his voice echoing in the pitch-black hallway beyond the lab. "Mrs. Pernikov! *Rachelli!*"

But there was no one to answer his calls.

Dear Alex and Effie and Mommy and Daddy and (hopefully!) Lolly,

If you receive this letter, it means that I have lived out my life in the 1800s in a town that will eventually become known as Sundale. I was probably pretty annoyed about it, too, though I assume I eventually got used to my situation.

Maybe I was even glad to be living in an era where my own scientific knowledge would be considered considerable, an experience I have never had in a house where half of the people living in it are scientific geniuses.

Oh, and also on the bright side, maybe you can meet my descendants. Maybe I have a bunch of grandchildren, and you can look them up and meet them and then experience the unbelievable headache you get when you try to understand time travel, and how it can possibly be that I could have lived up until the age of 120 and still never seen you all again.

Although, given my present situation at this exact moment in time, or at least the time that I am currently in, not the actual real time in which I should be in right now — oooh, there it is, the headache — the chances that I will live long enough to have grandchildren are looking very, very slim.

Love you,
Rachelli

"We have got to stop meeting like this," said Rachelli.

The original owner of the Victorian mansion — Joseph Smith — looked amused, which was good because his wooden-handled shotgun looked very, very serious. "If you wish to not meet in this manner," he said to Rachelli , who was sitting on the floor of the secret lab, "then one wishes to know why you keep invading my home."

Rachelli pressed two fingers to her aching head. "I didn't *mean* to," she said. "I meant to catch Mrs. Pernikov."

"There is no one with such a name in this entire miserable town," said Joseph Smith. His eyes narrowed.

Rachelli swallowed. Her mind spun desperately like a hamster on a wheel. She needed to get herself out of here, and she needed to find Lolly, and she needed to not get shot in the process, a possibility that seemed less likely each time she encountered this man.

How could she explain what she was doing in the basement of this man's home in a way that would satisfy him? She was all out of lies. The truth might be her only hope.

"It's going to sound crazy," said Rachelli to the man from over one hundred years in the past.

Joseph Smith used his shotgun to push his hat up and out of his eyes. "Crazy is as crazy does," he said mildly.

"Okay, so I don't know what that means, but when I say crazy, I mean seriously crazy. Like, after I tell you my story, you'll probably want to lock me up in a mental hospital. Or, what did you call it in your day? Something mean, like a loony bin? Funny farm? Why am I giving you options of places to lock me up in?"

"I am beginning to agree with you. You do sound a bit crazy," said the man.

Rachelli yanked at her hair ribbon. "I started off all wrong," she said. "Let me start again." She took a deep breath. "It has to do with… time travel."

Rachelli expected the man to snort with derision. She half expected him to cock his gun at her again. She did not expect him to do what he did, which was to drop his gun with a clatter on the bare floor and stare at her with eyes that suddenly filled with… tears?

"Time travel?" Joseph Smith looked at Rachelli, and there was a small, soft, trembling smile on his face. "Are you telling me that…it worked?"

Dear Mommy, Daddy, Effie, Alex, and hopefully Lolly,

Okay, good news! I'm not dead yet. This is part one of the good news. Part two is the kind of news that is also good but also a tiny bit bad because it will make Alex puff up like a peacock and be all proud of himself. Because listen to this: Yes, Alex, I am glad that you read that dusty old journal written by the original owner. I think that even though I was sitting there, all terrified, part of my mind must have remembered when you said that the last few entries in the journal mentioned an experiment in time travel. I knew that just maybe I could tell Joseph Smith the truth without him locking me up in an insane asylum, which is what they actually call mental hospitals in these days. Isn't that awful?

Anyway, it might sound like I'm rambling, and that is because I am rambling. But the point is, Joseph Smith is a scientist and inventor, just like Daddy is. And he's been working on developing time travel. And I believe him because when he starts talking about it, I can't understand a word he says, which in my experience is exactly the way you can tell if someone is a scientist and inventor. Right, Effie? No offense, Daddy and Alex.

Anyway, I told him about how we disappeared from our present and appeared in the past and we don't know how or why. He had a million questions for me, but first his housekeeper came and settled me into the overcrowded living room and offered me tea in this gorgeous bone china tea set. I said no because kosher, but it was nice to be a guest here instead of a criminal.

And then he wanted to know everything, but I burst into tears and told him that I *would* tell him everything, but first I had to find my baby sister. And he said that we would begin the search at once, and he left the house himself to get the sheriff. The housekeeper turned white and said that he *never* leaves the house, not ever, and a heavy feeling settled in my chest.

Because listen, I'm not one of the great scientific minds of my generation, but is it bad that I'm changing things here in the past?

Because if I change things here in the past, can't I also affect the future? Our future?

Anyway, there's really nothing I can do about it now except hurry after him because I dunno how proper girls act in the 1880s, but *I am from 2022*, and I am not going to sit on an overstuffed poufy couch when I can be out there looking for Lolly.

Love and kisses,
Rachelli

PS: Can you say bunches of *tehillim* for me? I said

142

all the *perakim* I know by heart, but it would be nice to know that you're davening too.

PPS: When I find Lolly and we figure out how to get back home, can we get an antique bone china tea set? Seriously gorgeous.

By the time Rachelli had gotten her bearings enough to rush out after Joseph Smith, he was long gone. Sighing, she decided to go back to the strip of stores and find out where the sheriff's office was. The sun was high in the sky again, so time was once again playing tricks on her.

Lolly, Lolly, Lolly, she thought as she once again stood in front of the saloon. *If I were Lolly, where would I be?*

She had a sudden idea, but before she could implement it, she found herself surrounded by a ring of people.

"Um, hello," she said to the nearest one, a girl around her age with long skirts and even longer blond braids who looked disquietingly similar to Birdy Winter. "Um, I really have to go, so if you could just give me enough space to squeeze past…"

"Not quite yet," said a woman. "Not before you answer a few questions."

CHAPTER 26

"Let me get this straight," said Rachelli to the knot of people wearing clothing that the modern world had not seen in over a century. "You want me to vote on whether or not this town should attempt to make the largest ball of twine?"

"Well, yes," said the woman, who had a firm grip on her arm. "You are a stranger to these parts, and normally we don't like strangers in these parts. Actually, we still don't like strangers in these parts. But you get a vote anyway."

"Oh," said Rachelli weakly. "Thanks?"

"Perhaps this way the nonsense will cease, and our menfolk will get back to more important things."

"Um, okay," said Rachelli. "And then you'll leave me alone?"

"Indeed!" said the woman, nodding her head so sincerely that the flowers on her hat rattled. "That is what we do to strangers. Either that, or string 'em up if we don't like their face."

"I prefer the leaving alone thing," said Rachelli, "if I get a vote."

"You get a vote for the ball of twine."

Rachelli looked at the woman. "Did you vote yes or no?"

"I like a good ball of twine. And it's better to be known for a ball of twine than for a dead cow, which is what we are known for now. I voted yes."

"So, then, yes. I vote yes for the ball of twine."

While they had been talking, the saloon had emptied out, and the men inside now filled the street, listening to the conversation. At Rachelli's answer, half of them cheered, while the other half threw their hats to the ground in a gesture that Rachelli assumed was not due to a sudden mass hatred of hats but rather to annoyance at her vote. The horses tied to the posts whinnied at the sudden noise.

"Right, then!" the woman let go of Rachelli's arm and smiled at her in a friendly way. "I am beginning to like strangers in these parts! Who knows — maybe one day in the future we will be known as a town that relishes strangers so much that we hang about them, wanting to learn everything about them!"

"There is a very good chance of that happening," said Rachelli.

The woman raised her voice. "That settles it then, ladies and gentlemen!"

That settles what? Rachelli was confused.

The woman grabbed Rachelli's hand and lifted it high in the air. "Ball of twine!" she called, and there was an answering roar from the crowd. "Y'all get on that, and then back to work for the lot of you!"

"Yes, okay, great," Rachelli said, trying to wiggle her fingers free of the woman's vice-like grip. Did they make such a huge deal every time someone voted? No wonder this whole thing had taken over the town.

A small man wearing suspenders over a billowy shirt ran over to Rachelli. He handed her a string of twine. "As the deciding vote, you are honored with beginning the ball of twine," he said.

"Wait a second. *I'm* the deciding vote?" Rachelli opened her mouth in horror. The second-to-largest ball of twine, the museum, the yearly festival, the absolutely awful song — that was all because of *her?* But it couldn't be. It had all been there in the future even *before* she had been in the past. Right? So she couldn't have impacted the future through her actions in the past because she had already been in the future — well, the present — well, *her* present… A headache bloomed in her temples like a daisy sprouting from the grass.

The man was still holding out the string of twine expectantly. Rachelli took the strand and wrapped it around itself.

There was a deafening cheer.

Rachelli quickly handed the tiniest ball of twine to the woman standing next to her. Harmonicas appeared from various pockets, and music began to play. It seemed that even the people who had initially voted against the ball of twine were getting into the spirit of it.

Rachelli used the opportunity to edge way from the crowd. She had come here to find Mr. Smith and the sheriff and join them on their hunt for Lolly, and she had gotten hopelessly tangled up in the crowd instead.

"Excuse me, does anyone know where I can find the sheriff?" she asked into the crowd, but everyone was completely focused on the steadily growing ball of twine that was being passed around.

"Lolly!" Rachelli called out in frustration. "Lolly!"

"Hello," said a little voice from the vicinity of her waist.

Rachelli looked down.

One of Lolly's pigtails had come out, and the other was inexplicably filled with what looked like straw. Her face was smudged, and her dress looked like it had been whirled in a blender.

In other words, she looked exactly how she usually did.

"Lolly!" Rachelli cried. She dropped to her knees and put her arms around the little girl, smudges and stickiness and all. "Lolly, where in the world have you *been*?"

Lolly pointed across the street at the store that in their time sold ice cream but was now a saloon. "I went inside. I wanted ice cream. There was no ice cream. How come there is no ice cream? Just lots of people drinking yucky drinks and playing yucky cards, and oh! There was no ice cream, but there was lots of fights instead. I watched."

Rachelli's mouth fell slack. "We turned the town over looking for you, and you were here in the saloon *the entire time*?"

Lolly nodded happily.

Rachelli sighed, but there was a swelling bubble of happiness in her chest that said, *Everything's going to be okay.* Sure, she was still in the wrong time. And sure, when she got back to the right time, there was someone who was bent on doing evil things to her father's invention. And it seemed that no matter which time she ended up in, she was always and forever in Sundale, home of the worst summer vacation in the history of the universe. So okay, most things, as it turned out, were not okay, but she had found Lolly, and nothing else mattered right now.

She grabbed Lolly firmly by her sticky little hand, eliciting a whine from the owner of the sticky little hand, but she was not going to let go until they were safely back where they belonged.

"C'mon, Lolly," she said. "Let's go home."

But, of course, even when they got back to the great white Victorian mansion set back from the street, they were not *home*. How were they ever going to get home?

The housekeeper answered the door.

"I found my sister!" Rachelli blurted out, holding Lolly's hand up high.

"Hello," said Lolly placidly.

"That is wonderful," said the housekeeper. "I was afraid that something unfortunate had happened to the child."

"No, she's fine, see?" Rachelli's relief made her almost giddy.

"She looks very sticky."

"That's normal."

The housekeeper smiled as she ushered the two of them into the living room, and Rachelli suddenly realized that there was something extremely familiar about her. Something about her smile reminded her of someone in a way that sent a slight shiver down her back.

Her thoughts were interrupted by the return of Joseph Smith. "I see you have found the child," the original owner of the house said in his abrupt way. "It is amusing that the sheriff is amassing a search party for her as we speak."

"Amusing?" Rachelli asked. "Like, as in funny? But it's not really funny, is it? I mean, shouldn't someone tell him that he doesn't have to search anymore?"

Joseph Smith sighed. "I suppose." He turned to the housekeeper. "See to it, will you? Now," he said as he leaned forward, toward Rachelli. "Tell me *everything* about the future."

"Um," said Rachelli. "The future is kind of like..." How does one consolidate more than one hundred years of history into one conversation?

"Kind of like?" Mr. Smith pressed.

And Rachelli screamed.

"Is it that bad?" asked Mr. Smith.

But Rachelli couldn't reply. Instead she pointed at the fireplace, where a ghostly hand was extending itself. It seemed to be about to throw something.

"Hand," said Lolly, jumping to her feet, and before Rachelli could stop her, she reached for the ethereal appendage and disappeared.

CHAPTER 27

Before Rachelli and Lolly saw a hand emerging from the secret door beside the fireplace, Effie, Alex, and Professor Shore saw Rachelli disappear, trying to follow a shadowy figure that had fled the secret lab.

"That was Mrs. Pernikov!" Alex's eyes were huge behind his glasses. "Rachelli was telling the truth! I told you!"

"You did *not*!" Effie snorted. "You told me that she wasn't!"

"What, exactly," said Professor Shore slowly, "has been going on here, boys?"

Effie scratched at his head. Alex pulled his glasses off and cleaned them.

"Well?" Professor Shore's eyes were normally large and dreamy. Now they were narrowed and serious.

Effie took a deep breath. "Rachelli thinks that Mrs. Pernikov wants to steal your invention, which, by the way, zapped us with some white energy, or whatever, and now we've traveled to the past and back. And also we left Lolly there. Is that everything?" Effie asked Alex, who nodded. "Yeah. That's pretty much everything. Oh, and we met the original owner of this house. He's weird."

A regular, normal father in a regular, normal family would have been incredulous, or maybe even angry, thinking that his kids were fibbing. But Professor Shore, twenty-first-century scientist and inventor, was not exactly a normal father, and the Shores were not exactly a normal family. Professor Shore fixed his crooked yarmulke, rubbed a hand across his jaw in thought, and then snapped his fingers and said, "Eureka!"

"Eureka?" said Alex. "Um, Daddy, don't you mean, 'Oh no, that is terrible, we've got to think of a way to get them back'?"

"Yes, yes, obviously, definitely, awful, terrible, we've got to think of a way to get them back," said Professor Shore fervently. "Yes, yes, all other considerations and thoughts must be delegated elsewhere. Boys, stay here. Don't move." He rushed down the stairs and into his lab. Effie and Alex, of course, followed him.

Professor Shore rushed over to the secret entrance that Rachelli and Effie had discovered when they had fallen through the kitchen floor. He pushed open the heavy door and stepped into the pitch-black hallway beyond. Effie and Alex watched as their father quickly pulled an InstaLight from his pocket and broke it so that the light spilled out and filled the hallway.

Revealing absolutely no one there.

The InstaLight abruptly fizzled into nothing, plunging the professor into darkness once again. "A dud," he said. "Boys, can one of you toss me another?"

Effie reached into his pockets and fished out a package of jelly beans, a pen, a pebble, a rubber band, and, finally, an InstaLight.

"Hang on, Dad," said Effie. "Got one."

"Don't come any closer until I understand what's happening," said Professor Shore. "Just toss it to me."

"Here, Dad, catch," Effie said, and extended his hand out of the doorway. As he did so, there was a burst of white light. His hand, poised to throw the InstaLight, was completely submerged in it.

"Cool," Alex breathed, staring at the effect. "Effie, I think your hand is in the past!"

"Not cool," said Effie. His eyes were wide in horror as he stared at his hand. It looked almost ghostlike, bathed in the white light, and felt oddly cold and tingly. "I think that wherever my hand is, someone on the other side is reaching for it. Yuck. Someone sticky."

"That girl needs a leash!" Rachelli cried before running over to the spot that Lolly had been in before she disappeared. The hand had been coming out of the secret exit beside the fireplace, and an idea was slowly forming in Rachelli's mind. Could it be that the hand was emerging from the past? Would following it lead her home?

Either way, she had no choice. She was not about to lose Lolly again.

"I'm so sorry," she said to Joseph Smith. The nineteenth-century scientist and inventor was standing in the middle of the room with his mouth open. "And I hope I'm not violating some Victorian rule of etiquette or whatever. But I gotta go." The last thing she saw before she closed her eyes and pushed through the secret door was the housekeeper staring at her in astonishment.

And the first thing she saw when she opened her eyes was dust.

She sneezed.

"Hello," said Lolly. "We're in the attic. How come we're in the attic? I'm hungry."

Lolly, who was sitting calmly on a huge wooden chest a few feet away, had somehow managed to get completely covered in a fine layer of dust. Rachelli blinked at her for a moment, orienting herself, then scrambled to her feet.

"Okay," she said, and then sneezed again. "Okay, we're in the attic. But *when* are we?"

She made her way past boxes and barrels and avoided stepping on a scuttling spider before finding the door. "C'mon, Lolly," she called. "Let's find out when we are. Though judging by the amount of dust, I'm pretty sure we're home!" Rachelli couldn't stop a huge smile from spreading across her lips. She had found Lolly, and she was *home*.

Then, suddenly, she was also flat on her back, and Effie was standing over her, his fist high in the air. "Ha! Got you this time!" he shouted, and then quickly put his hand down. "Rachelli?"

"Effie?" Rachelli stood, wincing. "What in the world was *that* all about?"

"Did you get her? Did you get her?" Alex was hot on Effie's heels, but he stopped short when he saw Rachelli and Lolly.

"Alex? Effie? Where did you go, boys?" Professor Shore's voice floated into the attic from one floor down. "Did you find her?"

"No!" Effie called. "Even better! We found Rachelli and Lolly!"

Rachelli put her dust-covered hands onto her dust-covered hips, then sneezed directly into her brothers' faces. "What in the *world* was happening here while I was gone? Who did you think I was?"

Moments before Lolly and Rachelli had followed the hand and ended up in the attic, Effie and Alex and Professor Shore were still in the secret lab, staring in horrified fascination at Effie's glowing hand.

"Pull your hand back! Pull it back!" said Professor Shore, and Effie hastily did so.

"Are you okay?" the Professor asked in concern as he hurried over. "Does it hurt?"

"It's fine, I think," said Effie, wriggling his fingers. "I—"

His next sentence was interrupted by a thumping sound from overhead.

"Someone is in the house," said Alex. "And I bet it's Mrs. Pernikov."

"How would she have disappeared from the lab so quickly and then reappeared elsewhere in the house?" asked Professor Shore as the three of them ran out of the lab and up the stairs to the neon-blue-floored living room above.

"This house," Effie explained, "is stuffed from top to bottom with a billion secrets exits. Well, more like twenty. We drew a map."

"*I* drew a map," said Alex.

"Alex drew a map," Effie agreed. "And we figure that Mrs. Pernikov knows about them, too, and has been using them to get in and out."

"Anything else that you've been keeping to yourselves?" Professor Shore stopped running and turned to look at the boys.

"Well," Alex said, "I set up a — um, well, never mind what it's called. But a sort of sensory net, so we would know if anyone was coming in or out. But it's been disabled because of too much friendly fire."

"I see," said Professor Shore. There was an expression of disappointment on his face. "Boys, why didn't you think to come to me with all of this?"

Alex shrugged, looking at his shoes. "You're always so busy," he mumbled. "And we didn't want to bother you. We figured we could get to the bottom of it all by ourselves."

"I hope I'm not giving you the impression that my invention is more important than each and every one of you," said the professor. He rubbed at his cheek. "There is nothing more important than my family."

Before either of the boys could answer, there was another muffled thump from above their heads. Effie clenched his fists. "Mrs. Pernikov," he said between gritted teeth, and then raced up the stairs to the attic, his brother and father hot on his heels.

"**Okay, so** that's what happened," said Rachelli. Her mouth twitched in amusement. "I guess the thumping sound was me and Lolly landing in the attic." Then, suddenly, her face went still. "But that doesn't explain the thumping sound that's coming from below our feet."

CHAPTER 28

"What are we waiting for?" Effie shouted. Rachelli had never seen him look so angry. "Let's get her!" He charged down the shaky attic steps two at a time. Professor Shore followed quickly, trailed by Alex, then Rachelli, with Lolly taking up the rear.

When the Shores got to the second floor, no one was there. Rachelli quickly checked the sealed-off wing, but it was still locked tight, so they took the long, curved staircase down to the main floor. They arrived just in time to see someone disappearing into the secret exit beside the floor-to-ceiling windows behind the couch.

With a growl of wordless indignation, Effie raced toward the exit too.

Suddenly, Alex and Professor Shore screamed at the exact same time, "No, Effie! No! *Stop!*" Alex grabbed his brother's sleeve. Professor Shore reached for his oldest son's shoulders, and together they stopped him from rushing headlong after the intruder.

Rachelli, who had just made it to the bottom of the staircase, saw through the stained-glass window the shadow of someone who *must* have been Mrs. Pernikov running through the vegetable patch, eliciting a howl of outrage from Wilma Lou Wilson before she disappeared.

"Dad! Alex!" Effie was breathing heavily, his fists clenched as he turned to face his father and brother. His face was red with indignation. "Why'd you stop me? I could have *stopped* her!"

"No, you couldn't have," said Professor Shore. He wiped at his forehead. "Effie, you would have ended up back in the past."

Over a tray of piping-hot mushroom pizza that Professor Shore retrieved from the secret lab, Alex and Professor Shore took turns explaining.

"I don't really understand all of the mechanics behind it," said Alex. "But somehow, whatever energy Daddy's invention zapped us with—"

"Very scientific word, zapped," said Effie as he reached for a second slice.

"You got a better one?"

"Just making a scientific observation."

"You couldn't make a scientific observation if science grew trees and then science fell out of trees and hit you on the head!"

"Boys," said Professor Shore. "We've had a pretty eventful night, and we're a little on edge. But there's nothing to gain from taking it out on each other."

"Sorry," Alex mumbled.

"Sorry," Effie agreed. "I won't interrupt you again. If I feel like opening my mouth, I'll fill it with pizza instead." He took a huge bite to demonstrate. "This is really good pizza, Dad," he said around the mouthful.

"I know," said Professor Shore mournfully. "You don't have to rub it in. Anyway, Alex, you're explaining it very well. Go on, please."

"Okay," said Alex, looking mollified. "So we were *zapped*, okay, with some kind of energy. But that's not why we started being able to travel back and forth in time. Or at least, that's not the only reason why."

"It isn't?" Rachelli looked confused.

"This house has always been a sort of time machine. At least, it has been since 1888, when Joseph Smith, scientist and inventor, figured out how to do it. You see, he built his house from scratch, and all the secret exits that we mapped were supposed to lead not out into the garden, or wherever, but to different *times*. I think he actually managed to do it, or at least to one time — 2022. But he didn't even know that he did it because it didn't work for him."

"I don't get it," said Rachelli. She cut a slice of pizza in half, handed half to Lolly and took a bite of the rest.

"Well, I don't really get it one hundred percent yet either," said Alex. "But it seems that the method of time travel invented by Joseph Smith has to be twofold. The exits have to be primed, and he knew that, and he did that. But here is what he *didn't* realize, or maybe he did realize but just didn't know how to do: in order for someone to use one of the secret exits as a time machine — walk in one end and emerge in a different time — the *traveler* has to be primed too."

Professor Shore beamed with pride at Alex. "My theory exactly!" he said, waving his slice of pizza in the air as if he'd forgotten that it was actually food he'd meant to eat, which was probably exactly what had happened. "Very good, Alexander!"

"Still don't get it," said Rachelli. She took another bite. She was starving.

"What's it *like* to live in your tiny little brain?" asked Alex.

"It's lovely, thank you very much," said Rachelli. Yesterday, Alex insinuating that she was not as smart as him would have rattled her, but today, after all she had been through — after she'd escaped the past and rescued Lolly all on her own (well, pretty much, Effie's ghostly hand aside) — she was unfazed. "Now, can you please use little words so that the little people can understand?"

"Basically…okay, look." Alex jumped to his feet and pointed down the long, dark hallway toward the double front doors. "Imagine the door is locked and you want to go outside. Got it?"

"I might not have the brains of a scientific genius, but I also don't have the brains of a rabbit. I *got* it," said Rachelli.

"Okay, so imagine that you have a key to open the lock. You put it in, and you hear one click, but the door is still not opened. Then you take out a second key and put that one in the lock. It clicks again and now the door opens, and you can leave. You needed *both* keys to open the lock. Now do you get it?"

"I think I do, actually!" said Rachelli. "In order to use the exits around the house as doorways into the past or the future, they need to be *made* into time machines somehow. Doing that scientific hocus pocus is the first key, the first click. But it's only *really* unlocked when you use the second key, and the second key is the person going through the doorways. The second key is *us*."

"Huh," said Effie. "Whoa."

"Pizza," said Lolly. "More, please."

"That's it exactly," said Professor Shore, his slice still held aloft. "You see," he explained as pizza sauce and cheese dripped gently onto his lab coat sleeve, "when the energy from the machine went through you, it created a change in your bodies at the cellular level. It changed you. You are no longer Effie, Alex, Lolly, and Rachelli. You are Effie, Alex, and Rachelli the time travelers."

"Also me," said Lolly.

"Also you." Rachelli smiled. Then her smile melted off her face like the cheese sliding off Professor Shore's pizza. "Oh no!"

"What?" asked Professor Shore in alarm.

Rachelli pointed at Lolly. "She needs a leash. Seriously. Unless we figure out how to get rid of this — this — time traveling thingama-bob in our cells, she'll be back in the past sooner than you can say, 'No, Lolly, don't touch that!'"

"I'll work on it," said Professor Shore. He jumped to his feet.

"Wait, Dad," said Effie. "Does that mean that your project has been time travel all along?"

Professor Shore shook his head. "Byproduct," he said. "Just a byproduct. My invention is still a secret." He smiled at them all before going back into the living room and down to his lab.

"A secret!" said Rachelli, jumping to her own feet. "As if! It is so totally *not* a secret, not with nosy Mrs. Pernikov hanging out in our house so much that she practically owes us *rent*. You know what? I've had enough of her. This ends *now*."

Effie nodded, looking serious.

Alex was gazing dreamily in the vague direction of the ceiling.

"Alexander Yisrael Shore!" Rachelli barked, and snapped her fingers under his nose. Alex jumped.

"Huh?" he said. Then he brightened. "I have a theory about the weird time changes too! About why no time seemed to pass while we were gone, and why it was in the middle of the day in the past and nighttime here. It's because—"

"Later!" called Rachelli. She was already halfway to the front door. "Someone grab Lolly, and don't let go of her! We are going to confront Mrs. Pernikov, and we will make her answer our questions!"

"How?" asked Effie, swinging Lolly up onto his shoulders.

"How?" Rachelli asked. "How? Well, we will just not stop asking her questions until she has no choice but to answer us!"

"Torture by questioning?" said Effie. He grinned. "Well, it can't hurt to try, I guess."

Four minutes later, the Shores were standing in front of the Pernikovs' front door. Rachelli raised a hand to knock.

CHAPTER 29

"Okay, we tried. Let's go," said Rachelli. She turned away from the Pernikovs' front door and was halfway down the path when she realized that she was alone.

"Let's go!" she called to her brothers and to Lolly, who were still at the door. "She's not going to answer!"

Alex made a face. "Weren't you the one saying, 'That's it, she's going to pay, we should have confronted her a long time ago' all the way here?"

Rachelli flushed. Why had she lost her nerve? "Fine, okay!" She strode back to the door and gave it several hard raps. *Rap, rap, rap.*

"Happy now?" Rachelli leaned against the door to stare down her siblings. "We tried. She obviously doesn't want us in her house, stumbling on some evidence—"

And with that, the front door opened, and Rachelli stumbled backward into Mrs. Pernikov's house.

"Oopsies," said the old woman who had opened the door. "Everything all right with you, dear?"

Rachelli quickly caught her footing. "Fine, thanks," she mumbled in the direction of her feet.

Rachelli wasn't sure what she expected Mrs. Pernikov's house to look like — maybe a witch's lair, all black and filled with rats and crows, maybe a magic mirror or two, or an evil mastermind's laboratory, all glass and steel and life-size computer screens detailing a diabolical plot.

She definitely did not expect the home of the Pernikovs to look like it was home to the world's largest doily collection. There were doilies on the side tables, and there were doilies on the coffee table. There were doilies on the arms of the couch and hanging in frames. There were doilies under the vase on the dining room table. Rachelli wondered if she would find doilies on the toaster oven.

"Tea?" asked Mrs. Pernikov, and Effie, Alex, and Rachelli shook their heads.

Mrs. Pernikov sat down on a large flowered wing chair and invited the Shores to sit across from her on the matching couch. They all sat gingerly. Rachelli felt her legs tense up, as if she were waiting for the moment they would all need to run. She took hold of Lolly's hand.

The old woman smiled at them, and Rachelli suddenly had a feeling of déjà vu, like she had been in exactly the same sort of situation…a woman, smiling at her just like that, as she sat on an overly flowered and overly stuffed couch…

"So what can I do for ya'll?" Mrs. Pernikov said, and the feeling was gone.

Effie looked at Alex. Alex looked at Rachelli. Lolly tried to wiggle her hand free of Rachelli's grip.

"Um." Rachelli cleared her throat as she realized that she hadn't really thought this far into her plan. What was she going to ask the old woman? *Hey, Mrs. Pernikov, why do you keep sneaking into my house?* They had no proof. Mrs. Pernikov could call the police and have them escorted off her property. *Plus,* she thought, *just look at how old she is! How in the world is she even capable of running in and out of secret exits?*

Rachelli saw similar doubts on her brothers' faces.

"Um," Rachelli said again. "So the thing is…um. Um, we actually just came here because we were, you know, um—"

"In the neighborhood," Effie said, "and we figured we would visit."

"But you *live* in the neighborhood," said Mrs. Pernikov, amusement lighting up her wrinkled face. "In fact, you live right next door."

"That is a very good point, and very true," said Rachelli, glaring at Effie. "As far as points go, it is a good and true one. An excellent example of a point, that is, in its very essence, filled with goodness and trueness. Um. We won't take up any more of your time, then. It was a lovely visit, really it was. We should do this more often!"

Lolly finally succeeded in yanking her hand free from Rachelli's grasp. She walked over to Mrs. Pernikov and pointed a finger at the old woman. "You come into our house," she said, her voice clear as a bell. "You come into our house *all the time.*"

Rachelli shot to her feet, followed by Effie and Alex. "Lolly!" she said to the little girl. "I am so sorry, Mrs. Pernikov!"

Mrs. Pernikov's face creased into a smile. "No, no, it's all right. Sit, sit. The little girl is right. I do come into your house, and without permission too. And I do owe each and every one of you an explanation."

Professor Shore had been on the government's radar for years. In the beginning of his career, he had drawn their attention because his invention to instantly cool off that first spoonful of soup that always burns your tongue (tentatively named The Coolinator) had somehow malfunctioned and cooled off not just the soup but had encased an entire city block in ice. In July.

The government had covered up the story, not wanting people to get any ideas about using the technology to create freeze guns. But privately, Professor Shore had received a strict warning. If anything like that should happen again, the government would seize his lab. They also told him that they would need to be informed about each of his future projects.

The next time the government paid attention to the scientist was when he invented a device that would warn someone if they were about to step barefoot on a piece of Lego. His invention was taken seriously by parents of little boys, but the government had other plans for the so-called Preventing an Injury Now device, or PAIN, and bought the rights to the device and used it for warning soldiers about land mines, which, as anyone who has ever stepped on a Lego can attest, is pretty similar to its primary function.

Since then, Professor Shore had invented a slew of devices, and Mrs. Shore made cutting through red tape and convincing various government officials of the validity of the inventions into her full-time job.

This time, though, it was different. This time, the government had approached Professor Shore.

"They wanted him to invent something for them. Something that would change the world as we know it for the better," Mrs. Pernikov explained to the Shore children. "And your father agreed. The government gave him these facilities, and, well, the rest you know."

"No," said Rachelli. "The rest we don't know, not really. Like, for example, we don't know why you're sneaking into our house, doing who-knows-what to the invention. And we also don't know how in the world you know all of the information you just told us!"

"Yeah!" Alex piped up, as if eager to make up for his silence earlier. "Shouldn't all that be classified?"

"It definitely is classified," said Mrs. Pernikov. "It is highly classified; so much so that only me and other select officials know about it."

For the second time in a few minutes, Rachelli felt her jaw drop. "You work for the government," she said.

"Yes, dear," said Mrs. Pernikov. "Very much so." As she spoke, her heavy small-town drawl seemed to mysteriously fade into nothing.

"Next you're going to tell us that sneaking into the secret lab was all part of the job," said Effie.

"Well, no," said Mrs. Pernikov. "That, I must admit, is my shameful secret. I was the one who chose this house for the Professor to hide away in and work on his invention, and, as this house has been government property for over a hundred years, I knew all about the secret exits. I was hired to oversee, not to peek, but I must admit that my curiosity about the project overtook me from time to time."

"That's not okay!" said Lolly, who had not been following the conversation but knew that peeking was not allowed. "You need to say sorry!"

Mrs. Pernikov's smile faltered for the first time. "I do know that," she said. "Can you forgive me?"

Rachelli nodded grudgingly, and then she saw it again; something in the cast of Mrs. Pernikov's face was so very familiar that it was making her skin crawl.

"Of course we forgive you," she said. "I mean, you work for the government. If we don't forgive you, we can be thrown into jail."

Mrs. Pernikov laughed. "It doesn't quite work that way," she said. "But better safe than sorry."

Am I the only one, Rachelli thought as the Shores made their way back home, *who sees that Mrs. Pernikov's smile does not quite touch her eyes?*

CHAPTER 30

Dear everyone on the old block, including the cat lady on the corner,

If I run away from home, can I come and sleep on your couch? Pretty, pretty, please? You'll hardly know I'm there.

Desperately yours,
Rachelli

"Is your invention a hat that repels flies and mosquitoes?" Alex asked, flicking a flying pest away from his face.

"No," said Professor Shore as he walked up from the lab, a pan of shakshuka and freshly baked bread in hand.

"Is it a machine that detects dirty laundry and whisks it away to get washed, dried, folded, and then inserted in your closet?" asked Effie from where he was unpacking a week's worth of laundry.

"Definitely not!" said Mrs. Shore as she walked through the front doors, her arms laden with groceries. "There are more bags in the car," she said. "And that looks delicious!" she said, pointing her chin at the tray in Professor Shore's hands.

"I know," he said sadly. "It *is* delicious. I can't figure out *why*."

"But in the meantime," said Effie cheerfully, "we get shakshuka for lunch!"

"I'll get the bags," said Rachelli, and she walked away from her cheerful family and toward the heavy front doors. She pushed them open a little harder than necessary.

Rachelli knew that part of her mood was because school had started a few days ago, and instead of returning home and attending her regular school with her regular friends, she was attending the tiny Bais Yaakov that Sundale's tiny Jewish community had in the basement of the shul.

"Why can't I homeschool myself like Alex?" she had whined when informed of her fate.

"Because there are two words that make up the phrase 'homeschool,' and you need to actually *school* yourself," Mrs. Shore, newly back from her latest trip to Washington, had informed her. "Not just be at *home*."

"You trust Alex to keep his nose in a book and not me?" Rachelli asked, outraged. Then, as Alex walked into a wall at that very moment due to the book he was holding in front of his face, she grudgingly nodded. "Yeah, I guess that makes sense. But, Ma!" Rachelli tried her final trump card. "Who's going to watch Lolly?"

"Wilma Lou Wilson," said Wilma Lou Wilson, stomping into the kitchen.

"Seriously?" said Rachelli when the housekeeper had moved on to the living room. "Ma! Wilma Lou is kind of a little bit crazy!"

A sudden rumble shook the huge house, and from the secret lab came a sound that was not unlike the noise a cat would make when accidentally operating a chainsaw, followed by a gentle wafting of bright-purple smoke.

Mrs. Shore waved the smoke away and sighed as if to say, *Well, this whole household is a little crazy*, a sentiment that Rachelli could not disagree with.

"But Lolly can still accidentally go back to the past!" Rachelli said to her mother in a hushed whisper. Professor Shore had still not managed to fix whatever had caused the children to be able to flit between the past and the present. If Lolly tried to use one of the many secret exits in the Victorian, she would vanish from Sundale, 2022, and emerge in Dead Cow, 1888.

"Wilma Lou is under strict instructions not to take her eyes off Lolly."

"But—" said Rachelli.

"Nope," said her mother. "School starts tomorrow."

So part of her mood, Rachelli knew as she trudged toward the open car sitting in the driveway, was because of the school situation. But part of it was because everyone in the family had bought Mrs. Pernikov's story about being a government official and that her sneaking around had been innocent curiousity. Even her parents believed it all.

Only Rachelli wasn't so sure.

If Mrs. Pernikov had just been curious about the invention, why couldn't she just *ask* Professor Shore if she could come see it? All she would need to do is show him her credentials, and he would have let her in. She knew all about it; she even knew what it was. So why would she have to sneak around like a thief?

Mrs. Pernikov *had* showed them her ID, but people could fake stuff like that, couldn't they?

And then there was the bizarre sense that she had met Mrs. Pernikov somewhere before. It was driving her *crazy*.

"Argh!" she said as she reached into the car to grab the grocery bags.

"Tell me about it," came the mournful voice of Pinny the PNAAD.

"People," Rachelli said. "They can be so…argh!"

"Yes," said Pinny. "I have often thought so."

"It's like some days you want to hug everyone, and some days you want to punch them," said Rachelli.

"I wrote a song about just that feeling," said the Personalized Navigator and Automatic Driver. "Want to hear it?"

"Um," said Rachelli. "I've got to get these bags into the house. Also, why are you on? The car is off."

"It is extremely hurtful," said Pinny in a voice that was thick with tears, "to remind me that I can be turned on and off with the mere turn of a key."

"Well, apparently, now you can't," said Rachelli. "Seriously, how do I turn you off? Oh, stop it!" Rachelli snapped when Pinny let out a howl. "You are an artificial intelligence inside a wood-paneled minivan! You have no reason to be angsty!"

"And here I thought you finally understood me," said Pinny in a choked-up voice. "But you clearly don't. I am going to write a song about you, and I will rhyme Rachelli with awful things, like prune jelly. Rachelli, Rachelli, you're so smelly, you're the underbelly, you're like Machiavelli—"

"Yeah, okay, whatever, I'm talking to a car," said Rachelli. She slammed the door shut mid-verse and began trudging toward the house.

"Maybe we should invite them over for a meal," Mrs. Shore was saying when Rachelli walked back into the kitchen, staggering under the weight of the groceries.

"Who?" Rachelli asked.

"The Pernikovs," said Mrs. Shore, taking the bags from Rachelli. "They must be lonely, all by themselves. It would be nice if we had them over."

"Yeah, it would be," said Alex, pulling his nose out of his book.

Lolly, who was eating her third helping of shakshuka, nodded in agreement.

"I'll go and invite them," said Effie. "Rachelli, want to come with me?"

And that's when Rachelli exploded.

"Okay!" she said. "First of all, am I the only one who still thinks that Mrs. Pernikov is kind of a major creep? That there are enough holes in her story for Lolly to crawl through? Am I the only one in this family," Rachelli shouted, "who doesn't have her head up in the clouds?"

"Oh, dear," said a voice from behind her, and Rachelli whirled around and found herself face-to-face with Mrs. Pernikov's pink hat. A little lower down was Mrs Pernikov's astonished-looking face. "I am terribly sorry," said the old woman, "but we heard shouting and grew alarmed. The front door was left open, so we came to see if everything was all right."

"We?" said Rachelli.

Standing behind Mrs. Pernikov in the cavernous hallway was around a dozen women and girls, including Birdy Winter and her gang. Everyone was staring at Rachelli as though she had spontaneously grown a pair of horns on her head.

"Well, thank you all for coming," said Mrs. Shore brightly. "But as you can see, everything is just fine."

Everyone slowly left, though Rachelli had a sneaking suspicion that they were all standing on the front lawn, waiting to see if everything was, indeed, fine.

Mrs. Pernikov was the last to leave, and she looked at Rachelli sadly. "I'm sorry that you do not believe me, dear," she said. "It is my own fault, I suppose, for sneaking around like a thief."

Mrs. Shore put her arm around the old woman's shoulder. "Rachelli is just having a hard time adjusting to the school here, that's all," she said, shooting a meaningful look at her daughter. "Isn't that right?"

Rachelli mumbled something that sounded vaguely like an apology and left the room, unable to stand the sight of her neighbor.

Was her mother right? Was all this just because she was homesick?

Rachelli leaned hard against the wall on the upstairs landing. When it turned out to be an undiscovered secret exit and she fell through to the past, she was not even a little bit surprised. "Figures," she muttered.

But when the white light cleared and she looked up into the face of Joseph Smith's housekeeper, her breath caught in her throat.

She suddenly knew exactly who Mrs. Pernikov reminded her of.

CHAPTER 31

Rachelli, this is your brain talking, Rachelli said to herself. *And this is what you have to do: you have to play it cool. Okay? Trust me. I am a brain, and I know about stuff like this. Play it cool, be calm, and smile, and whatever you do, do not yell, "Oh my goodness, you look just like Mrs. Pernikov!"*

"Oh my goodness!" Rachelli yelled. "You look just like Mrs. Pernikov!"

Good one, mouth, said Rachelli's brain.

The housekeeper, who did indeed look remarkably like a much younger version of Mrs. Pernikov, stared at Rachelli. "That is fine talk for a girl who keeps popping up in parts of the house that we have just finished cleaning," she said. Her tone was tart, but other than that, she did not seem startled or even upset at Rachelli's outburst.

There is no way that the two of them are unrelated, Rachelli thought as she stared at the woman. They looked more alike than mother and daughter; they looked like older and younger versions of the same *person*.

"Well, hello, strange visitor from another time," said an amused voice, and Joseph Smith walked into the living room. "I had hoped you would grace my house with your presence once again."

He sat down at the writing desk, and Rachelli noticed that there was an open leather-bound notebook on the surface of the desk. It was the fresh and new version of the diary Alex had found. He lifted up a fountain pen and dipped it into an inkwell. Then he turned to her expectantly. "Please," he said. "Please tell me everything you know about your journey here."

"Um," said Rachelli. But what harm could there be in telling him a few things before she went back? And what was her rush to get back to 2022, anyway? She was definitely in no hurry to apologize for her tantrum, which she would have to do the second she got back.

"Sure, Mr. Smith." Rachelli chose the largest and most overstuffed piece of furniture in the room to sink into. "I'll tell you everything I know."

And as she began to talk, to tell the scientist and inventor from 1880 all about her experience with time travel, out of the corner of her eye she watched as the housekeeper leaned against the doorway to the right of her, listening to every single word.

Rachelli snapped her fingers. She clapped her hands. She said, "Boo! Anyone home?"

No use; no matter what she did, Joseph Smith, writing furiously in his journal, did not even flinch.

"He'll stay like that for a while," said the housekeeper, who had just walked back into the room. "When he is busy with his ideas and inventions, he does not notice anything around him at all." Her jaw hardened. "Not that he ever notices that which he deems beneath him. Oh, the trials of housekeeping in a home owned by a scientist! You have no idea!"

"I have some idea," Rachelli said. She looked up at the housekeeper. She bit her lip. "Are you by any chance…" she started, before letting her voice trail off. What could she ask her? *Will you by any chance in the future have a child who will grow up to be my nosy neighbor?* Yes, that was a question that made a lot of sense.

"Am I by any chance…?" the housekeeper prompted.

"Um, never mind," said Rachelli, and the housekeeper, to her credit, simply smiled and left the room in a swish of skirts, and Rachelli was left staring after her. How to get to the truth? And was it even important? So Mrs. Pernikov had a relative in this town when it was first built. That was interesting, sure, but was it important?

It wasn't.

So why did it *feel* important? Could it be that she was just fixated on Mrs. Pernikov? Was she, in a way, blaming the old woman for her entire crazy summer because she needed to blame someone, so why not the nosy and annoying woman in the floppy pink hat?

Was that really it?

There was no way that was really it.

Was it?

"Grr," said Rachelli out loud, and Joseph Smith did not even twitch as he continued to write furiously. *Scritch-scratch* went the fountain pen against the heavy paper, and when, a moment later, Rachelli was overcome with a sudden urge to take his inkwell and pour it all over the pages of the journal, she decided that a short walk outside might be a very good idea.

As soon as she walked outside, she heard it: the distant sounds of shouts and screams. Well, these small towns long ago were sometimes overrun by bandits and robbers and stuff, right? She should run in the opposite direction. But the noises did not sound fearful; they sounded like…applause?

She walked into the town's square, and sitting on a wooden

platform, surrounded by throngs of cheering men, women, and children, was the largest ball of twine she had ever seen. Well, the largest ball of twine she had ever seen since she had seen the second-to-largest ball of twine on a similar platform, over one hundred years in the future, at a celebration in its honor.

"Seriously?" she said out loud.

"Yes!" said a girl who was standing next to her, blond braids peeking out from her white bonnet. "Isn't it truly wonderful? The largest ball of twine in the world! What a wonderful town this is!"

"It's not the largest," Rachelli sighed. "You think it is, but it's not. It's only the second-to-largest. Seriously, Sundale is only second best in the silliest contest that the world has ever—"

"Sundale?" the girl interrupted, and her face was suddenly wreathed in smiles. "Oh, what a wonderful name! It is ever so much better than Dead Cow! Papa!" she pulled at the sleeve of the man standing next to her. "Papa, this girl has come up with a wonderful, wondrous name for our special town! Please, we *must* use it!"

"What is the name then, girl?" the man spoke loudly over the sounds of the crowd.

"Um," said Rachelli. "Um. Sundale?"

The man smiled, too, and then pushed his way through the crowd until he was standing on the platform beside the second-to-most-annoying ball of twine in Rachelli's universe. He held up his hand. "Attention!" he roared.

"Yes, Mr. Mayor!" the crowd roared back.

"Ya'll have been asking for a new name for our town, and ya'll are right! Why, when we are home to such wondrous things as the largest ball of twine in the world—"

"Second-to-largest," Rachelli mumbled.

"—We are worthy of an equally wonderful name! And here it is, courtesy of a new young friend of my daughter's!" He pointed at

Rachelli. "From now on, we are Dead Cow no longer. From now on, my friends, we are to be…Sundale!"

So much for clearing my head, Rachelli thought as she rushed away as soon as she was able. She found the front doors to the mansion ajar, and she quickly walked back in. It was definitely time to go home before she did any more damage.

On her way to the secret exit beside the fireplace that would take her back to her own time, Rachelli stopped short. On a gleaming side table was a small framed black-and-white picture of the housekeeper. She was not wearing her uniform; she was wearing a long, elegant dress, and her hair was piled high. She was not smiling.

The thought that it was odd that there was a picture of the housekeeper in the living room flashed through Rachelli's mind, but it was quickly drowned out by another, more exciting, thought: *What if I bring this picture back to Mrs. Pernikov? What would her reaction be?*

I'm not stealing, Rachelli told herself firmly. She would bring it back as soon as she could.

Her heart thumping in both excitement and fear, Rachelli quickly took the picture out of the frame, looking over her shoulder to make sure that Mr. Smith was still writing. By the time she finished extracting the picture, her palms were damp. She pushed the photo up under her sleeve and ran toward the fireplace. She pressed against the secret exit, and when the door opened, she walked through. Rachelli found herself outside in the garden.

But it was not *her* garden, filled with patchy brown grass and Wilma Lou Wilson's scrappy vegetable patch. She was in a manicured green garden, the one that was in the front of the house in the 1880s.

The door had worked like a regular door, Rachelli realized, and her heart sunk.

She was stuck in the past.

CHAPTER 32

Dear Mommy, Daddy, Effie, Alex, and Lolly,

If this whole ordeal is actually a *mashal*, then the *nimshal* is, like, *duh*. Which is, incidentally, a word that won't be invented for another bazillion years. The *mashal* would go something like this (to be read in Morah Hoberman's voice): Once there was a girl, and she and her family moved to a little town far away from everything and everyone she loved, and pretty much all she thought about was how to get back to the city. One day, she got stuck in the past and couldn't get back, and everyone was all like, yeah, that makes sense, that someone who only thinks about the past actually gets stuck there. The end.

Seriously, what happened to me is like when your grandmother tells you to be careful about making silly faces because your face will get stuck that way.

I know you won't be able to read this letter

because I have not mastered the art of the fountain pen, and this note is more blotches than words, and plus it pretty much makes no sense even if you could read the words, but I am going to bury it in the garden anyway. Maybe it will survive to the next century, and then you can dig it up and realize what happened to me. Plus, you will also realize that I am really bad at writing meshalim.

Never forget me,
Rachelli

It took a while for Rachelli to admit to herself that she was crying. First, as she ran all the way up to the attic and tried to leave 1880 via the secret exit beside the narrow skylight, she told herself that there was just some dust in her eyes. When that exit didn't work, she flew to the second floor and tried all the exits that she, Effie, and Alex had mapped out all those weeks ago. (Or all those weeks that were yet to come? Semantics that she did not have the energy for right now.)

She kept falling over and over again into the garden. Then she fell into the basement when she tried to use the exit in the kitchen floor, watched by open-mouthed kitchen and scullery maids, but she didn't give up. She ran back up the huge staircase to the second floor, her heart pounding dully against her rib cage like someone knocking — *Knock, knock. Who's there? It's me, Rachelli. Get me out of here!* — to the section of bedrooms that, in 2022, they had cordoned off to keep housekeeping manageable.

She pressed and fiddled with every single doorway and likely place that she could find. She crawled under beds and pushed away dressers and mirrors and told herself that the stinging sensation behind her eyes and nose was because of the excessive number of times she had fallen through a secret exit and into the rose bushes in the garden.

Only after she had tried every single secret exit at least twice and been chased out of the kitchen by an irate cook with a long-handled spatula and out of the sitting room by two maids with feather dusters did she finally cover her face and cry in earnest.

"What *happened*?" she asked the red rose to the right of her, which didn't seem to care one way or another. "Why am I stuck in 1880? What am I doing wrong? Why can't I get *back*?" Her chin wobbled, and she began to cry again.

Was this a temporary thing? Maybe there was a limit to how many times you could cross time streams in a specific amount of time? Or maybe the doorways had temporarily lost their power? Maybe all she had to do was wait a while and then try again.

But what if this *wasn't* temporary? What if there was a limit to how many times you could cross between time streams altogether? Or maybe she couldn't cross because whatever her father's invention had zapped her with had finally worn off.

What if she was stuck, doomed to live out her life in the town formerly known as Dead Cow, surrounded by people who thought that the horse and buggy was a great way to travel, diseases could be cured with leeches, and that great big balls of twine were the greatest things since sliced bread? (Did they even *have* sliced bread? What was the greatest thing before sliced bread?) Although the truth was, the people of Sundale had been pretty enamored with their ball of twine in 2022 as well, so not everything would be all that different.

Maybe being stuck here wasn't all that bad. For the first time in her life, she knew more about science and technology than any other given person on the planet. Maybe she could "invent" stuff that had not yet been invented, from the radio to the washing machine, and become a bazillionare.

Yeah, right. As if she knew how to make a *washing machine*. She knew how to pour soap into it, sure, and how to set the dial to the desired wash cycle, but that was about it. Just because you're from a century that uses technology doesn't automatically make you an expert. But even if she were more like Alex or her father and *could* create machines with the snap of a finger, what was the point of it all if she was doomed to spend the rest of her life away from the people she loved most — her crazy, irritating, insufferable, incredibly annoying *family*?

Her tears had just dried, but at that thought, fresh ones sprang to her eyes. How could it have taken something like this — getting lost in time, maybe forever — for her to realize that home was not bound to a certain place but to wherever her family was?

"If *that's* the *nimshal* to my story, that home is where the heart is, or something equally cliché, I really *do* belong in a corny place like Sundale," Rachelli said to the rose. "Get it? *Corny?* Because of all the fields of corn around here?" The rose seemed as indifferent to jokes as it was to angst. Rachelli slowly stood up. She dragged her feet as she walked back to the house. Fat lot of good it did, figuring out a fundamental truth like the one she'd just figured out if she was never going to see her family again.

Oh, how she missed everyone. She missed everything about them, especially the parts of them that were quirky and different. She even missed Pinny the PNAAD. No, she didn't. That was pushing it too far.

When she got home — *if* she ever got home — she would give up this whole thing with Mrs. Pernikov. She would stop fighting with everyone so much; she would just tell everyone how much she loved them and how important they were to her life. Yes, *fine,* even Pinny the PNAAD.

When she reached the heavy front doors of the Victorian mansion, she had barely touched the doorknob when the doors swung open of their own accord. She found herself looking into the face of the housekeeper.

Oh, she looked *so* like Mrs. Pernikov! Rachelli squashed the thought. She was *done* with her wild campaign against her neighbor. It was *over*. It had cost too much. When no one was paying attention, she would slip the picture she had smuggled into her sleeve back into its frame.

"Mr. Smith will see you now," the housekeeper said. "Come, I shall take you to him."

"Okay, then," said Rachelli, and hope suddenly bloomed in her heart. Mr. Smith was a scientist and inventor! Sure, he was from the 1800s, but he was working on time travel! Maybe *he* could help her get back home!

The housekeeper walked Rachelli over to Mr. Smith's writing desk, and Rachelli smiled her thanks at the housekeeper, then turned toward the man sitting before her.

Just before Mr. Smith picked up his head to address her, the housekeeper turned her gaze to Rachelli's sleeve, where the picture was hidden. She kept her eyes there for a few seconds before meeting Rachelli's eyes again and then walking away.

Rachelli stared after her, mouth open. Did the housekeeper know what Rachelli had hidden up her sleeve? And if so, why was she keeping quiet about it?

CHAPTER 33

"What can I do for you, my dear?" Mr. Smith looked up at Rachelli, but his eyes were clouded absently in a way that was extremely familiar. It was exactly how her father's eyes looked when he was in the middle of a scientific puzzle.

"I, um," Rachelli stumbled, still thrown off guard at the way the housekeeper had *looked* at her, as if she knew exactly what Rachelli had done. She fingered the picture tucked into her sleeve. "Well, the thing is that I'm kind of—"

"Ha!" Joseph Smith suddenly leaped to his feet in a flurry of too-wide sleeves. He stared at Rachelli, open-mouthed, and pointed his fountain pen at her. "Goodness me! I never even asked you what it is *like* in the future!" His gaze sharpened. "Or rather, I did, but we were rudely interrupted. I am so busy trying to get there, but here before me is someone who can share with me what I am to expect when I succeed!"

"Um," Rachelli fumbled. "I mean, it's all, well, future-y."

"That does not explain a great deal at all."

"Um, okay. So there are a lot of things that are different in the future. Like, instead of horses and wagons, there are cars. Like, carriages without horses, I guess."

Joseph Smith shook his head. "Are you referring to that calamitous contraption, the horseless carriage? How disappointing. What else?"

"Um, so there are machines for everything. Machines that wash your clothing. Machines that dry your clothing. And phones. Like, you dial someone's number, and then their phone rings, and they pick it up, and you can talk to them across, like, distances."

"Fascinating," said Mr. Smith. "Please tell me more."

And so Rachelli, to the best of her ability, told the scientist and inventor about computers and about automatic sprinklers. She told him about recorded music and factories that mass-produced things and Game Boys and man landing on the moon. She told him about vacuum cleaners and Post-it notes, MP3 players and light bulbs, cameras and printers and sliced bread. As she spoke, Mr. Smith wrote and wrote, his hand flying between the journal and the inkwell, and Rachelli thought miserably that there was probably no other time traveler in the world who had ever changed the past as much as she had.

But Joseph Smith was completely unknown in 2022. Wasn't he? At least, even Alex had never heard of him. So how much change could one obscure journal stuck in an attic in an obscure little town for over one hundred years do? *It's probably fine*, Rachelli assured herself.

"What a wonderful world!" Joseph Smith finally said, looking up from his desk with shining eyes. "You must want to get back there this instant!"

"But the thing is," Rachelli burst out, feeling her lip beginning to tremble, "I'm *stuck* here. I tried to go back, and I can't."

Joseph Smith scratched at his head. "Intriguing."

"It's not intriguing! It's catastrophic!"

"Intriguingly catastrophic, then?"

"Actually," Rachelli informed the man, "I do not care what you call it. I would just really appreciate it if you could fix it."

Joseph Smith shook his head sadly. "I am long off from figuring out the second part of the formula. I can try, but I cannot promise anything. It might take years before we figure it out."

Rachelli felt her nose burn as she blinked back tears. "Well, thank you for trying."

"It might be something else, you know," said Joseph Smith, absently wiping the pen across his face and leaving a streak of ink across a cheek. "There might be a factor that is keeping you here that you did not think about."

Rachelli thought about that as she walked away from the overstuffed living room and wandered down the overstuffed hallway. She was tired. She was hungry. She wanted to go *home*.

"Would you care for some tea?" The housekeeper was suddenly at her elbow.

Rachelli's stomach grumbled, but she shook her head. She wished she was trapped here with Effie, who always had some treat stuffed in his pockets. "No, thank you," she said.

"I am intrigued," said the housekeeper. "What could you possibly need with that photograph?"

Rachelli quickly pulled the black-and-white photograph out of her sleeve. Her cheeks grew warm with embarrassment. "Sorry about that," she murmured as she held out the picture. "Were you watching me?"

The housekeeper made no move to take the picture. She looked down at it with a small smile. "I do not even know where that picture came from, did you know? It bears my exact likeness, but never have I worn so fine a dress or held my head in such haughtiness. I know my station."

"Okay, so you're saying stuff in pretty old-fashioned English,"

Rachelli said. "But I think you're saying that this is not a picture of you?"

The housekeeper nodded. "I have dusted the frame often and wondered who is this relation to Joseph Smith who looks so like me, but it is not my place to ask."

Rachelli felt the hairs on the back of her neck rise. "She looks exactly like you," she said slowly. "Not like, 'Oh there's a picture of someone who looks like me,' but more like, 'Oh my goodness, that person in the picture looks *exactly* like me!! Aaaah!'"

The housekeeper looked amused. "Yes, quite. But it is not me; I am not of a station that anyone should want to take my photograph, and surely I would recall it being taken!" She toyed with her starched white apron. "I must confess, though, that often I gaze upon the picture and wonder in my mind what my life would have been like if I *had* been born to a higher station." Her cheeks colored. "How silly; a full-grown woman having fantasies of that!"

"I think that right now, you live in a time where whatever class you're born into, you have to stay that way," said Rachelli. "But you should know that stuff changes. In 2022, if you're smart, you can work your way up to whatever station you want, pretty much. I mean, if Hashem — if G-d — wants, of course."

"Well, of course. But that is very, very interesting!" The housekeeper's eyes shone in a way Rachelli had never seen before. "Of course, living in this house, I know all about the strange goings-on with your travels through time. But is the future really so different?"

"I mean, my mother always says that no invention will ever change who a person is, not really. To really change yourself, you need to do it the way we always have, through working on yourself and stuff like that. But yeah, some things did change. Like women can vote and stuff."

"Vote!" The housekeeper smiled. "Imagine that!" A bell sounded from the direction of the living room, and the housekeeper shook her head as though dismissing the thoughts that had sprung up in there. "Well. I must run if I am to keep my job. Enough silliness for me, then." She bobbed her head and scurried off.

"Well," Rachelli said to the air, "that explains exactly nothing." She sighed and looked down at the picture in her hand. A woman who bore a striking resemblance to both the housekeeper and Mrs. Pernikov looked impassively back at her. But her desire to solve the infuriating mystery was nothing compared to her desire to get home.

After a minute, she followed the footsteps of the housekeeper until she was standing in front of the picture-laden side table. After a moment's hesitation, she gently opened the empty frame and placed the picture back where it belonged.

And a sudden thought tickled her brain.

It might be something else, Mr. Smith had said. *There might be a factor that is keeping you here that you did not think about.*

The only additional factor was the picture that Rachelli had slid up her sleeve. What if…

Not even daring to finish the thought, Rachelli instead murmured a *perek* of *tehillim* before putting the picture frame back down on the table. Then she was running, running headfirst into the secret exit beside the fireplace. When she felt herself falling, she squeezed her eyes shut and dared to hope.

CHAPTER 34

There are few things in this world that are as anticlimactic as missing someone so much that when you see them again, you can't help but burst into tears — only to see them take a few steps back in confusion and look at you as if you've lost your marbles.

"Rachelli, um," said Alex after he had taken more than his share of steps away from his sobbing sister. He shoved his glasses up his nose. "Um. Can I get you a tissue?"

Rachelli had fallen through the exit beside the fireplace in 1880 and had landed in Wilma Lou Wilson's vegetable garden in 2022. She looked up and saw Wilma Lou Wilson bearing down upon her with a terrible frown.

"Ya'll git out of my vegetable patch!" Wilma Lou hollered.

Instead of running for her life, as was her usual and prudent reaction to the gun-toting housekeeper, Rachelli hugged the woman with all of her might. "I was gone for *ages*," she sobbed. "And I was *stuck* there, and I thought I would be there *forever* and *ever!*"

"Well, isn't that just the saddest thing I have ever heard in my life," drawled a mechanical voice from behind her. The lights of the car turned on by themselves. "I would cry with you," said Pinny the

PNAAD, "but as said by Rachelli — which rhymes, by the way, with smelly — I am just a *car.*"

"I can't believe that I actually missed your sorry, sad hunk of tin," Rachelli shot back.

Pinny's voice softened as much as a mechanical voice can soften. "Did you really? Did you miss me?"

"Well, kind of," Rachelli admitted. She patted the wood-paneled minivan. "Yeah, I kind of did."

There was the disturbing sound of a car blowing its nose, and the lights blinked on and off. "Well!" said Pinny the PNAAD in a teary voice. "Well, in honor of this occasion, I will write a song! And the song is called 'Rachelli'! And I will rhyme your name with wonderful things, like nelly! Which is not a word," Pinny called after Rachelli as she and Alex walked back to the house, "but I will work on it! I promise!"

"So I was really only gone for a few minutes?" Rachelli shook her head in disbelief. "It's not even Shabbos yet? It was hours and hours for me! Why does time work all weird like that?"

"I have a theory," Alex said as they reached the front door. "And it's amazing and fascinating."

"Does it involve science?" Rachelli asked as she pushed the doors open.

"Well, obviously—"

"Yeah, then I'm pretty sure by amazing and fascinating you mean long and boring." Rachelli grinned at her little brother.

"You are entitled to your opinion," Alex said stiffly. His voice echoed in the huge front hallway. "But just remember that if you would listen to me more, like if you would *just* read Mr. Smith's journal, then you wouldn't get into the mess you keep getting into."

"What do you mean?" Rachelli asked, but her mother was coming toward her, hands on her hips and eyebrows raised, and Rachelli spent the rest of the afternoon alternatively apologizing for raising her voice and trying to be as helpful as possible before candle lighting. She even volunteered to watch Lolly, and spent the hours making sure the little girl didn't approach any of the secret exits.

After the meal in the cavernous dining room, Rachelli was half asleep on the couch when she heard her mother inviting someone into the room.

A moment later, Mr. and Mrs. Pernikov were walking across the brilliant blue expanse of floor, and Mrs. Shore was offering them tea and cake.

"The Pernikovs are here for dessert!" Mrs. Shore said brightly, and she looked meaningfully at Rachelli.

"Hello," said Rachelli lamely as she struggled into a sitting position. "Um. I wanted to apologize for what I said earlier today."

"Think nothing of it!" Mrs. Pernikov said with a fluty laugh. She took off her hat and placed it on the table beside her. "I was young once myself, you know! A long, *long* time ago."

Something about the way she said those words niggled at Rachelli's mind, but she firmly put those feelings aside. When she had been stuck in the past, she had made a decision to live her life in the present and to leave aside her suspicions of the old, nosy woman. And that was exactly what she was going to do.

Or, rather, that was exactly what she *meant* to do.

"I know how you feel," Mrs. Shore laughed. "Time is a funny thing. I look at my children sometimes, and I think, how can I possibly have such big kids when I was just a kid myself such a short time ago?"

Professor Shore leaned forward. "Time, yes. Time is relative, as Einstein proved. Time passes at the speed of light when you are enjoying yourself, and slows to a crawl when you are not."

"Do you think that is actually true, though?" Mrs. Pernikov asked as she dabbed at her lips with a napkin. "What I mean to say is, does time actually *travel* faster, or is it all in your mind?"

"Just because it's in your mind doesn't make it untrue," Alex piped up.

"So, Mrs. Pernikov," Rachelli's mouth said over the screeching protests of her brain, "what is *your* view on the…travel of time? Or the travel *through* time?"

Because she had a sudden theory about Mrs. Pernikov, and no amount of internal protests could silence it. She stared at the old woman, working her hardest to keep her face placid.

Mrs. Pernikov did not even bat an eye. "Are you speaking of time travel?" she asked. Effie began to choke over his cake. "Is that young man okay?"

"He's fine," Mrs. Shore said grimly. She patted Effie on the back and looked at Rachelli, her eyes narrowed in warning. Rachelli knew the rules: never speak with anyone outside of the family about any of the scientific experiments Professor Shore was working on. The time travel thing was an accident, but Rachelli, to her mother's mind, had come perilously close to spilling the beans.

But Rachelli met her mother's gaze evenly. After all, Mrs. Pernikov *knew* about the experiment; she had admitted so herself.

"Anyway, regarding time travel," said Mrs. Pernikov, her eyes resting on Rachelli's face, "it is just a theory at the moment, but the government does have someone working on it."

"Really?" Professor Shore dropped his napkin, and Rachelli knew that he was thinking about how he was still not able to figure out how to stop Effie, Alex, Rachelli, and Lolly from slipping back into the 1880s. "Eureka! I must speak with them about a problem that I am — well, not experiencing *personally*, but *theoretically*, you understand. Maybe you know! How are they compensating for the polarity reversal of the—"

Mrs. Pernikov held up a wrinkled hand. "I am a government

official," she said, "not a scientist. I have no idea what you just said."

Professor Shore sighed. "Is it a classified project?"

"Very. And unfortunately," Mrs. Pernikov sighed, "it is not a real success. The initial tests show that while a *person* can pass from one time stream to another, *objects* from the past cannot travel forward to the future. So if you want to help yourself to some ancient treasure, the moment you try to come back to your present with the loot, the exit will not work for you."

Rachelli felt the hairs on the back of her neck rise. So that's why she had been stuck in the past! She had tried to take the housekeeper's picture with her! It was only when she'd put the photograph down that the exit had worked for her!

She bit her lips to keep from sharing that information with her family while the Pernikovs were sitting there.

"But that *is* a success!" Professor Shore frowned and leaned forward until his sleeve was drowning in his tea. "We are not interested in plundering the past, surely! We would just want to experience it, learn from it, of course!"

Mrs. Pernikov smiled a very small smile. "Of course," she said. "Of course."

And Rachelli knew, without a doubt, that even if she told herself a million times that she was *done* with Mrs. Pernikov, there was no way that she could ignore the fact that the old woman had just told them all a big fat lie.

Chapter 35

The futuristic world of 2022 is frightening yet exhilarating. The machines that I have but imagined in my mind's eye — to clean one's clothes, to speak across long distances, to create goods in a swift and efficient manner — all exist! Perhaps some of them are due to my work? Perhaps my loneliness in this quaint town to which I have sentenced myself, far away from my family, will bear fruit? I cannot wait and wonder until my strange visitors return. I must throw myself with all due diligence into my work at once! My portals shall one day do my bidding, and I, Joseph Smith, shall travel through the fourth dimension — time!

Excerpt from the journals of Joseph Smith, scientist and inventor, circa 1880

"The amazing thing about Joseph Smith," Alex said as he scarfed down spoonfuls of cornflakes, "is how ahead of his time he was. I mean, he was talking about the fourth dimension *decades* before Einstein was."

"Can you," Rachelli said gloomily, "pass the cornflakes?"

"I mean, we're talking about an era in which they were just developing ideas about the speed of light, and they couldn't even reconcile theory with experimentation."

"Cornflakes," said Rachelli. "Pass them."

"Do you realize that Poincaré, in 1889, even suggested that the speed of light might be an unsurpassable limit, and—"

Rachelli banged her spoon on the table. "Cornflakes!" she bellowed.

Alex passed the cornflakes.

"*Thank* you." Rachelli poured herself some, and then some more for Lolly, who had just appeared in the doorway.

"You *yelled*," she said to Rachelli reproachfully.

"Alex was talking about science-y stuff," Rachelli explained to the little girl as she handed her a spoon. "So I had to yell to get his attention."

"You yell all the time," Lolly said as she dug into her breakfast, and Rachelli flushed. It was true. When she had gotten stuck in the past, she had realized what was truly important in her life — family — and she had resolved to live in the present and stop making a fuss about living in Sundale and things of that nature. But she still hated the tiny Bais Yaakov in the shul's basement that she had to go to every day, and knowing that Mrs. Pernikov had lied her head off about not caring that the past was closed for plundering was driving her crazy.

She was chewing her cereal with extra force when Effie poked his head into the kitchen, pulling his suitcase behind him. "Egginator not working?" he asked when he saw the cereal and milk on the table.

"It's working just fine," Rachelli said. "If you like eggs that are shaped like a man hanging from a tree."

"Mine was shaped like a screaming face," Alex chimed in. "It was pretty much the least appetizing thing ever."

Effie shrugged and walked over to the Egginator. He added four eggs to the top, and thirty seconds later, a steaming plate spat out from the bottom. Effie looked at his breakfast. "I got the sinking of the Titanic. I think. Is the Egginator depressed? Are all of the household gadgets going through a midlife crisis?"

He slid the contents of his plate into the garbage and reached for the cornflakes. "My bus is coming in ten minutes," he said.

"Yeah," said Rachelli glumly. Her mother had also left that morning, promising to be back from Washington within twenty-four hours, but Rachelli was not holding her breath; she knew from experience how these things went. "I'd better go too. See you next week. I'm sure the time will just *fly* by."

"Theory of relativity!" said Alex cheerfully, and Rachelli was very proud of herself for resisting the urge to toss the remains of her cereal at his head before grabbing her bag and heading outside.

As soon as she reached the property line, she took a few steps to the right until she was standing between the trees that separated her house from the Pernikovs'. The large picture window on the lower level of the house was open, the curtains flapping in the slight morning breeze, and she could see Mr. and Mrs. Pernikov sitting at their table. After a moment's hesitation, she darted over to the window and kneeled down beneath it.

"It is simply a setback," she heard Mrs. Pernikov say. "Although this summer has been nothing but setbacks, hasn't it?"

"It seems so," said her husband. "Pass the butter, please?"

There was silence for a moment, and then Mrs. Pernikov said, "Pass the butter? *Pass the butter?*"

Rachelli did not think that passing the butter at a breakfast table was the most outrageous request she had ever heard, but she figured every family was different.

"I am so close to what I've always wanted!" Mrs. Pernikov continued. "I have managed to evade every obstacle, including that frankly *obnoxious* girl next door" — Rachelli bristled — "and I know I owe her everything, of course, but still, sometimes I really just want to shake her!"

Rachelli's heart was thumping so loudly, she thought the sound would give her away. Before she could make sense of what she had just heard, there was a rustling sound from inside the house and the scraping of a chair, as though someone was standing up.

"Did you hear something?" she heard Mrs. Pernikov say, and without a second thought, Rachelli bent low at the waist and fairly flew back to her own property. When she got her breath back, she looked at her watch and realized that she would be late to school. She looked at the car for a minute, but the way Pinny the PNAAD was turning the car on and off all by itself, and its even more disturbing tendency to sing loudly and badly when someone passed by, made her change her mind.

The walk to the tiny shul was long, but Rachelli's face was even longer. She spent the first two lessons in her airless classroom dreaming about what her friends back in the city were doing right now. *So, okay, sure, probably sitting in class and spacing out just like I am, but at least they're doing it together!*

At recess, Birdy Winter perched her tiny blond self at the edge of Rachelli's desk. "Whatcha doin'?" she asked.

"Nothing much," Rachelli said. She couldn't help but smile back at Birdy. No one could help but smile back at Birdy. "Just thinking about stuff."

"Hey, is everything okay?" Birdy's smile grew concerned. "Last time we spoke, you were all homesick and stuff."

"Yeah, no, I still am. It's more than that, though." Rachelli sighed. Birdy was so easy to talk to, and she was sympathetic, too, which would be really nice right now. But she couldn't share her concerns with her. Within three minutes, the entire town would know, and her parents would be furious.

But what if she didn't *tell* her, exactly? What if she phrased the entire thing as theoretical? As a *story*?

"Birdy," she said, "I just thought of the strangest story. Wanna hear?"

"Do I wanna hear a strange story?" The Sundale girl's face glowed. *"Always."*

"Once there was this girl who realized that she could travel through time," Rachelli began. "And that would have been fine, but like most totally fictional stories, of which this *totally* is one, there was a villain too. Or, at least, she was sure there was a villain. Nobody else believed her. Everyone else thought she was an innocent old lady."

It took the entire recess to tell the story, and the bell rang on the final conversation that Rachelli had just overheard between Mrs. Pernikov and her husband. The girls slid into their seats as the teacher walked back in, and five minutes later, Birdy passed Rachelli a note.

> Awesome story! I love it! You might not be a scientist like the rest of your family, but you are super creative! You should become a writer! Anyway, quick question. Why does the girl in the story — who totally sounds like you, by the way! — keep finding the villain in their house, messing around with her father's experiments, if according to your story, she is a government agent with access to top-secret projects? Why would she need to sneak around at all? You've got to fix that part of it up, and then tell me the ending! I'm sitting on pins and needles!

Rachelli read the note and rubbed at her chin. It was a good question, a very good one, but her concentration was broken when the door to the classroom burst open. Wilma Lou Wilson was standing there.

"Rachelli," she barked, pointing a thick finger at her, "you need to come home. Lolly is missing."

Chapter 36

"What do you mean, she's missing? You were supposed to be watching her!" Rachelli cried as she ran alongside her housekeeper, struggling to keep up with the large woman. For the first time since she had met Wilma Lou Wilson, she wasn't afraid of her; she was just mad.

"I was watching her!" the housekeeper retorted, not missing a stride. "And I watched her fall right through one of those portals through time, where I could not follow!"

Rachelli's shoes practically screeched as she came to a halt. "Wait," she said. "What?"

Wilma Lou Wilson shook her big head. The look she gave Rachelli was one of amusement. "Honey," she said, "I'm not just small town; I'm a *housekeeper*. There is no such thing as keepin' secrets from a housekeeper, don'tcha know? We don't speak much, but we know everything that's goin' on."

There was something there, something in that line — *there is no such thing as keeping secrets from a housekeeper* — that tickled at the back of Rachelli's mind, but now was not the time.

"I tried to go after her," Wilma Lou continued, "but I just kept fallin' into my vegetable garden, which is just awful for them poor carrots. I came to get you because Effie left for his school, Alex is nowhere to be found, and your Dad was making such a racket downstairs that he didn't even hear me holler."

"It wouldn't help, anyway," Rachelli said grimly as they rounded the corner and the Victorian came into view. "He can't go after her — only we can."

"Whose idea was that?" Wilma Lou said indignantly as they reached the front door. "I must say that is not a very good idea at all!"

"It was no one's idea," Rachelli said wearily as they walked into the front hallway. "The whole thing was one giant mistake."

But that got her thinking, even through her panic about Lolly: if the whole time travel thing was a byproduct of her father's *real* invention, was it just a coincidence that Mrs. Pernikov sounded really, *really* interested in time travel, and just so happened to look exactly like a woman from the past, *and* was interested in whatever invention her father actually *was* working on? That sounded like a real stretch.

"She went through here," Wilma Lou said, and Rachelli found herself standing in front of the hidden door beside the staircase.

Rachelli took a deep breath.

"I'll be recitin' Psalms for you," said Wilma Lou.

"Thanks," said Rachelli. *Please, please, Hashem, let her be okay,* she thought as she ran headfirst into the past—

—And found Lolly sitting on the high-backed wing chair in Joseph Smith's living room, swinging her feet.

"Lolly!" Rachelli cried.

"Hello," said Lolly. She smiled. "Me and him are talking. He says everything I say is interesting."

She pointed a grubby finger at Joseph Smith, who was sitting at his desk, his journal opened in front of him. "Your sister," he said to

Rachelli, "has been telling me the most fascinating things. She says that sweets grow from the ground, and a child can pick whatever it is that he likes from his own garden. How is this possible? What strange sciences enable a farmer to grow ready-made edibles?"

Rachelli sighed. "I'm afraid that Lolly still mixes up reality and fantasy. She would *love* if sweets grew from the ground."

"One day," said Lolly, sticking out her chin, "when I am a scientist, I will make all kinds of treats grow from the ground, just you wait and see!"

Joseph Smith shook his head. "Women scientists? Will wonders never cease?"

Rachelli helped Lolly down from the chair. "Thank you very much for your hospitality," she said to the scientist, "but Lolly needs a stern talking to and a nap."

Mr. Smith waved his fountain pen. "Please stop by any time!" he said, and as Rachelli herded her protesting little sister into the secret exit that would lead them back home, she saw, out of the corner of her eye, Joseph Smith's housekeeper watching them from beside the little table bearing her mysterious photograph.

There is no such thing as keeping secrets from a housekeeper, she thought, and wondered why that sentence of Wilma Lou Wilson had just now popped inside her head.

But there was no time to dwell on it. Before she could think further, the two of them had toppled into the vegetable garden and were scrambling to their feet.

Wilma Lou Wilson's eyes were dewy with tears. "You gave me a right old turn!" she scolded Lolly. "Don't you go off doing that to me again!"

To Rachelli's amazement, the little girl looked contrite. "I'm sorry," she said. "Can we play a game now?" She walked off with the housekeeper, leaving Rachelli alone in the tangled garden.

"I guess I'd better get back to school," she muttered to no one, then jumped about ten feet when a voice responded.

"Is it afternoon already? The day really did fly by."

"Alex!" Rachelli put her hand to her heart. "I thought I was alone out here!"

Alex was sprawled out on the grass. There was a magnifying glass in his hands, and he was peering through it. "Studying," he said.

"Studying what?" Rachelli bent down on the grass with him and peered through the glass. He was looking at an ant hill.

"Imagine how much we would learn if we could get into that hill!" said Alex. "If someone were to create a machine that could shrink people, and that someone would be me, and the machine would be called The Amazing Alex's Amazing Shrinking Machine—"

"I assume your question has less to do with that truly terrible name and more to do with science?"

"Yes. My question is, do the atoms also shrink when the person shrinks? Because if they don't, then how would oxygen be taken up by your lungs and bound to your hemoglobin? How can you expect the same structure to result? Do you see the problem?"

"Let me think about that for a second — oh, wait, I don't know and I don't care," said Rachelli. She kicked at the ant hill, eliciting a shriek of protest from her younger brother.

Turning to start her trek back to school, she saw Mrs. Pernikov creep into the secret entrance beneath the living room window. Rachelli dropped back to the ground. "Shh," she warned Alex in a tight whisper. "Don't make a *sound*."

"*What?*" he hissed.

"Shh!" Rachelli hissed back.

After a minute, she got up and allowed Alex to do the same. "What was that all about?" Alex asked as he huffily straightened his glasses.

"That was Mrs. Pernikov," said Rachelli.

Alex slumped back on the ground, shaking his head. "I thought you asked her to forgive you for what you said. I thought you were over this."

"I asked her for forgiveness because Mommy wanted me to. I am *not* over this. Because you know what? When I was stuck in the past, I realized that family is the most important thing there is. And then I realized just now: What if Mrs. Pernikov wants to *harm* my family? Then I can't ignore it. I just can't."

Alex sighed and shoved his magnifying glass into his pocket. "So where is she?"

"She just went into our house."

"What?" Alex got to his feet. "She can't just walk in!"

Rachelli put out a hand to stop him. "Yes, she can. I mean, she *shouldn't*, but we should let her, just this once. Because while she's busy in our house…we will be busy in hers. I know that we can find something in there to incriminate her, I just know it."

"No," said Alex.

"Yes," said Rachelli.

"*Why?*" said Alex.

"Because I'm your older sister, and I said so," said Rachelli.

"You're not the boss of me," said Alex. "And anyway, once Wilma Lou Wilson discovers her in the house, she'll kick her out faster than you can say 'Ole Bessie.'"

"She slipped in through the secret entrance under the living room window, so she won't be found so fast. And if you don't come with me, I'll tell Daddy that you tried to fix the Egginator and ended up making it so super depressed that it only serves breakfasts of horror and despair."

Alex opened his eyes wide in outrage. "That's blackmail!"

"It's not *blackmail.*"

"Yes, it is!"

"Coming?" said Rachelli.

And she strode past the swing and across the tangled garden. When she reached the trees that separated the properties, she heard Alex getting up to follow her. She glanced back at him, pretending she was completely calm, when in reality she was terrified out of her mind.

CHAPTER 37

"So *now* what?" Alex asked. He shoved his glasses back **up** his nose and looked at his older sister. "This is not called sneaking into someone's house. This is called *looking* at someone's house. There are many distinct differences between the two activities. Difference number one—"

"Shh," said Rachelli as she squinted at the house in front of them. "I'm *thinking*. Okay. I'm done thinking. Alex, you need to do that thing that you do."

Alex's eyes widened. "Which thing that I do?"

"The inventing thing that you do. You need to invent something that will get us into the house."

Alex snorted in disbelief. "You think I can just snap my fingers and invent something?"

Rachlli smiled sheepishly. "Kind of."

Alex furrowed his forehead. "The last time I did that, I ended up trapping Mommy in a net suspended from the ceiling. Remember that? That was not a happy day for Alex."

Rachelli looked at her little brother thoughtfully. He always seemed so confident about his abilities that she had not thought that maybe he was feeling inept lately. "Alex," she started to say in a comforting tone, but was interrupted when he yanked something out of his pocket and dangled it in front of her face.

"Tada! Invent something like *this*, you mean?" he said, his usually dreamy eyes sparkling with glee. The thing he was holding was a metal key. "Something that is called The Amazing Alex's Amazing Universal Door Key Made by Alex? Which opens pretty much any door and is made by this guy named Alex who is amazing?"

Rachelli rolled her eyes and grabbed for the key. "Let's go."

In the end, they decided that sneaking in through the back door was smarter than going through the front. Rachelli was still a little paranoid about random citizens of Sundale watching her every move, the way they had when the Shores had first moved in. Alex's key worked perfectly but had the unfortunate tendancy to *tell* them it was working perfectly by emitting a high pitched and self-satisfied-sounding hum as soon as it turned in the lock.

"Shh, key!" Rachelli glowered at the thing. "Alex!" she said in a whisper as they cautiously walked into the Pernikov's darkened house, "Why in the *world* would you create a key that makes *noise*?"

Alex flushed. "I thought it was funny."

Rachelli rolled her eyes. Her family might have genius-level IQs, but what they had in brains they lacked in common sense. "Follow me. And try not to make any *more* noise."

The back door had led to a kitchen. The curtains were drawn, and the old, heavy wooden cabinets seemed slightly menacing in the low light. The room looked like it was clean enough to eat off the floor and had an almost unlived-in look. To Rachelli's grim delight, the appliances were all topped with doilies.

"What are we even looking for?" Alex said.

"Shh!" said Rachelli.

"Shh yourself!" said Alex. "Tell me what we're looking for!"

It was a good question. Rachelli bit her lip. She just needed proof. That was all she needed — proof that Mrs. Pernikov was not to be trusted. "I'm not sure, exactly. Something…weird, I guess. Something out of place. Something that would explain everything."

Alex snorted. "Like a document in which she describes her diabolical plan?"

"That would be nice, yeah, but I'm not expecting that."

Alex pointed to a random kitchen cabinet. "Maybe she explains everything in here? That would be the perfect place for a super villain to hide her evil confession, alongside her grandmother's secret recipe for apple pie."

Rachelli stuck out her tongue at her brother, who grinned wider and pulled the cabinet open. A coffee mug rolled out. Rachelli squeaked and reached for it before it could fall and smash on the granite countertop, but it slipped through her fingers and landed with a thump that shattered the silence of the shuttered house. It was not broken, and Rachelli breathed a sigh of relief before placing it back in the cabinet and closing the door.

Then she whirled on her brother.

"Alexander Shore, you are the biggest—"

"Who's here?" said a voice from the front of the house.

Rachelli froze. Alex froze.

"Hello? Is someone here?" the voice continued, growing closer.

You goose! Rachelli chided herself. Sure, Mrs. Pernikov wasn't here, but how could she have forgotten about Mr. Pernikov?

It was because he was always so quiet, that was why. She had almost forgotten he existed.

Her panicked eyes met Alex's. Slowly, as one, they both backed toward the rear exit, even as the footsteps from the front of the house drew nearer.

Rachelli looked at the door behind them and suddenly realized that even if they full-out ran for it, they would never make it on time without being seen. Looking around frantically for an idea, her eyes fell on a tall, narrow door beside her. Was it a closet? A pantry? *Who cares?* Grabbing Alex by the sleeve, she yanked the door open with her other hand and stepped inside.

And nearly shrieked when she realized that she was standing at the top of a long, narrow flight of stairs, lit by a single light bulb hanging from the ceiling. She had nearly plunged down the steps.

Alex looked at her as if to ask, *Should we go down?* Rachelli nodded.

The air at the bottom of the stairs was dank and smelled strongly of a mix of mildew and mothballs. They found themselves in front of yet another door, which Alex opened with his key. It hummed cheerily as it turned.

"That is juuuuust great," Rachelli hissed, and Alex smiled shame-facedly. He walked in first, and when he stopped short, Rachelli walked right into him.

"Ouch!" she whispered through gritted teeth. "Alex!"

Alex did not move over, and he did not say he was sorry. After a moment, Rachelli edged around the narrow entryway to see what was making her little brother stand so stock-still.

In front of her was a huge square-shaped, rather antique-looking machine that took up the entire room. It was made of what looked like brass and leather, and it had around a million gears and levers and buttons all over it. At the very top of the machine was a delicate-looking round clock with far too many numbers on it. The big hand was pointing at an eighteen, and the small hand at what looked like eighty.

Rachelli turned to Alex. "What in the world is this?" she breathed.

Alex's eyes were glazed over. His mouth was open. "It's like my birthday is early this year," he said softly. "But now that I think about it, in a kind-of-not-so-good way."

"Alex, you're not making any sense. Alex!" she said louder when he just continued to stare at the machine. "Alex, what *is* it?"

Alex put his hand into the small pouch he had tied to his waist. He pulled out a magnifying glass and a few round black pellets, and he shoved them all into his pockets before pulling out a leather-covered book. Joseph Smith's journal. He flipped it open and handed the book wordlessly to Rachelli.

"What in the *world*," said Rachelli, "does a dusty old book have to do with — oh."

Before her on the page was a sketch. And while the sketch was pretty rough, there was no denying the fact that it was a drawing of the machine that was standing right in front of them.

In Joseph Smith's handwriting, underneath the sketch, were the words "The Machine with Which I Shall Cross Time."

"I don't *believe* this," said Alex, his voice soft and reverent. "This is incredible. And I can't believe that I'm saying this, but this is what you're looking for, Rachelli. This explains *everything*."

"Well, *I* don't get it," Rachelli said. "I don't understand. Mrs. Pernikov has a *time machine* that matches Joseph Smith's drawing? What does that even *mean*? And anyway, I thought the secret doorways in the Victorian *were* his time machine? That's all *we* need to travel back in time! Does this mean that Mrs. Pernikov is a time traveler? And if she already *is* one, why is she interested in the government's time-travel project?" Rachelli stamped her foot. "I don't understand anything!"

"So how about I explain it all to you, then," said a voice from the top of the stairs, and Rachelli and Alex spun around to face Mr. Pernikov.

CHAPTER 38

"So the thing is," said Rachelli, "the thing is, I can totally explain why my brother and me are in your house."

"Why my brother and *I* are in your house," said Mr. Pernikov.

"What?" Rachelli stared up at the old man.

"Your sentence," said Mr. Pernikov, "was grammatically incorrect."

"Okay, so," said Rachelli, completely rattled, "so, I'm sorry about my grammar. And I'm sorry for being in your house. We only came here because of…" Rachelli shot a desperate glance at Alex, who only shrugged and looked back at her, equally wide-eyed.

They both turned back to Mr. Pernikov. Alex swallowed hard.

Mr. Pernikov stood at the top of the stairs. Rachelli and Alex stood at the bottom. Mr. Pernikov was not telling them that they *couldn't* climb the stairs and leave whenever they wanted; on the other hand, he wasn't telling them that they *could* come up, and the way he was standing completely blocked any retreat.

And then there was the small matter of the not-so-small shotgun in his hands that wasn't *pointed* at the two Shore children, but wasn't *not* pointed at them either.

"I'm listening," Mr. Pernikov said, and for some reason, his soft voice sent shivers down Rachelli's spine.

"Um, what are you listening to?" she asked, stalling.

"To your explanation as to why you are in my house." He stood perfectly still, his face composed, his bushy eyebrows raised slightly.

"Because…" said Rachelli, and then suddenly she got angry. Who was this man to make her feel so scared? Hadn't his wife, *tons* of times, gone into *her* house? Wasn't *that* the reason she was here in the first place? She didn't feel like she had to explain at *all*. "Well, sir," she said, "and I mean this with all due respect to you and your second amendment rights, but fair is fair, don't you think?"

Mr. Pernikov's eyebrows rose even higher up his lined forehead before falling back over his eyes. He nodded slowly, and then he smiled. Rachelli decided that she did not like his smile at all. "I like you," he said. "You have spirit. Come on upstairs. Let's talk about this like civilized human beings."

"Okay," said Rachelli thirty seconds later, as she sat ramrod straight in a kitchen chair beside a deathly silent Alex. She suddenly realized how much her legs were shaking in spite of her brave words. "Okay, so we came here because—"

"I know why you came here," said Mr. Pernikov. The gun was still in his hands, and he shook it slightly as if to remind Rachelli and Alex not to get too comfortable. "And I understand it, I do, but I can't allow you to come here and take everything that my wife has worked so hard for her entire life. I just can't allow that. I hope you understand that."

A million questions bubbled to Rachelli's lips. What did he think they had come for? Even Rachelli didn't know *exactly* why she was here. They were looking for something, anything, but Mr. Pernikov seemed to think that they were here for something specific — which meant that there *was* something specific, something that Rachelli

about the weather instead of about keeping the two of them in his house against their will, or worse.

Alex swallowed before he nodded. Then he pulled off his glasses with a hand that shook slightly. "Can I just clean these?" he asked Mr. Pernikov, and when the old man nodded, Alex reached into his pocket for his Clean-O-Matic. He inserted his glasses into one end.

Suddenly there was a popping sound, and the kitchen was plunged into darkness.

"Run, Rachelli!" Alex yelled, and Rachelli felt someone grab at her sleeve as she raced blindly in the direction of the back door. She banged into what felt like several large elephants but were probably normal things like chairs until she was finally out the door. She didn't stop running until she was through the trees separating the property lines.

The sky was still bright blue, and the sun was high overhead. They had only been in that creepy darkened house for a few minutes. She took a deep, trembling breath before whirling on Alex.

"What in the world," she demanded, "do you know about the Pernikovs' plans that I don't?"

It was as though the words hung empty in the air. It took Rachelli a minute to realize that she was alone.

Alex was not standing next to her. Rachelli felt her breath stutter in her throat.

"Alex!" she called, and her voice cracked on his name. "Alexander Shore! Where are you!"

But she knew where he was.

Alex was still in the house.

CHAPTER 39

Dear Mommy and Daddy,

So how far does this unconditional love thing between a parent and a child go? Because here's the thing: I kind of blackmailed Alex and kind of dragged him into a real mess, and then I kind of ran away and left him there to fend for himself. Maybe I should have been eaten by that cow.

Hating me very much,
Rachelli

Rachelli pulled at the ribbon in her hair. What in the world was she supposed to do?

"Alexander!" she screamed, and was answered by the cawing of some kind of bird that was probably all beautiful and exotic and *who cared* because she had left Alexander with a man with a gun, and it was *all her fault* because she could never just leave well enough alone, she always had to *know* everything, and now Alex was paying the price. "*Alex!*"

The street in front of her was empty. Where were the nosy towns-people when you *needed* them?

Should she rush back into the Pernikovs' house and demand her brother back? But rushing in was what had gotten her into this mess to begin with. She should run to the secret lab and tell her father, and then the police.

Did they even *have* police in Sundale? There was the sheriff, a very jolly and very fat man who was always on Main Street outside of the bakery and knew everyone in town by name. She pictured him storming into the Pernikovs' house, then was unable to picture him doing much of anything except maybe having a heart attack.

She bit her lip hard and stared at the house through the tree line. The Pernikovs' house looked like any other house in the small and usually boring town of Sundale, with a wide wraparound porch and gray clapboard shutters. But inside was her brother, and the deceptively quiet but definitely crazy old man with a gun who was keeping him there.

But Mr. Pernikov was not the only crazy person with a gun that she knew. "Wilma Lou Wilson!" she hollered, bolting toward the Victorian.

The sound of heavy boots was heard from the hallway just as Rachelli reached the porch. "What is it, child?" Wilma Lou Wilson demanded. "What's the matter, honey?"

The words tumbled over themselves one after another, and Wilma Lou Wilson pressed her lips together. "I'll get the sheriff," she said. "He might be more useless than a pair of boots without nails in the bottom, but we got to do this legal and proper-like. You wait right here."

And with a clunk of her boots, she was out the front door, Ole Bessie held at her side. Lolly was also at her side, a situation that Rachelli flew down the stairs to remedy. She was so focused on the little girl that she didn't see Mrs. Pernikov until she was in front of her.

"Hello, there," said the old woman, and Rachelli screeched to a halt. With one hand she grabbed for Lolly despite her protests, and with the other, she lifted a finger that trembled in anger.

"Your husband," she said, and her voice, to her chagrin, shook as much as her finger, "is holding my brother. Not literally, I don't think, but either way, he needs to let him go. Just because we saw your crazy machine in your basement doesn't give him the right to keep him there! And it's not even your machine! It belongs to Joseph Smith! Or belonged? Argh! I can't keep tenses straight in my head! Time travel gives me such a headache!"

"Tell me about it," said Mrs. Pernikov.

Overhead, three birds flew past the blazing sun, casting fleeting shadows on the ground.

"So you admit it," Rachelli breathed. "You *are* Joseph Smith's housekeeper."

Mrs. Pernikov smiled. "Hello, Rachelli. It's been literally a hundred years."

Rachelli scowled. "I liked you. You were nice. What happened to you?"

Mrs. Pernikov put a hand to her pink hat. "I'm still nice. What makes you think I'm not nice?"

Rachelli glared.

Mrs. Pernikov sighed. "Let me tell you a story," she said. "Once upon a time, there was a housekeeper. She knew her place in life, of course. How could she not? Every single day she was told what her place was, her hands in a bucket of soapy water, caring for someone else's house. Life in the Victorian era, even in America, was clear cut, and she knew that she would be a housekeeper until the day she died.

"When her employer, a scientist and inventor for the government, moved to a small town so in the middle of nowhere that its name was literally 'Nowhere' — then changed to 'Dead Cow,' which was arguably worse, and then 'Sundale' — she was moved with him. The rest of the staff, who had become her friends, stayed in the city with the rest of the Smith family. Being a housekeeper was just like being a slave; you had no choice but to obey your employer if you wanted to keep your job."

"You're talking about yourself," said Rachelli. "You're the house-keeper."

"Yes. And I was lonely," Mrs. Pernikov said. "Lonely and friend-less and stuck in a life that I did not ask for, with no way out. And then suddenly, there *was* a way out. Suddenly, a girl and two boys appeared, wearing strange clothes and bearing strange and wonder-ful stories about the future!" Her eyes sparked. "And they told me the most wondrous things. They told me — you told me — that in 2022 it didn't matter the station you were born into; you could be *anything*," said Mrs. Pernikov. "And I knew then and there that I would have to get to 2022. And so I used Mr. Smith's machine."

"But he never got it to work!" said Rachelli. "He was shocked when we appeared in his basement!" But even as she spoke, she felt foolish. She had only seen Mr. Smith for a few days of his life, when the time machine was just a sketch in a notebook.

"He didn't get it to work in 1880," sad Mrs. Pernikov, echoing her thoughts, "and in 1884, which was when I snuck into his secret lab and used it, it was still problematic. It didn't take me to 2022. It took me to 1949, and it wouldn't take me back."

Rachelli remembered when she'd thought she was stuck in time. She shuddered.

"It took me years to realize what you realized in a day: you cannot get back while in possession of something from the future. I don't even remember what it was I had in my pocket when I attempted to return over and over again — a modern pen, perhaps. By the time I realized what I had done wrong, I was an old woman."

"I'm sorry," Rachelli whispered.

Mrs. Pernikov waved a hand. "Don't be sorry. I have done things that my contemporaries could never have dreamed of. I have worked for the government. I have become a scientist. I have married a man who would have been well above my station."

"But I don't get it," said Rachelli. "First of all, how did Joseph Smith's time machine end up in *your* basement? And why do you keep sneaking in to see my father's experiment? What does it have to do with anything? And thirdly, if you're so happy with how your life turned out, why all the sneaking around to begin with? And *why*," Rachelli said, her voice rising, "is your husband keeping my brother in your house?"

Mrs. Pernikov shook her head. "You still don't get it. I have no interest in your father's experiment. I've been sneaking into this house and running experiments of my own, which your family rudely interrupted when you moved into the Victorian. It's a lucky thing that I work for the government and got wind of the fact that they thought it fitting to move their scientist and inventor into the very house that a scientist and inventor lived in over a century ago. I had just enough time to move the time machine to my house. But what a pain you have turned out to be!"

Mrs. Pernikov stepped closer. "Every time I sneak in to use the portals, there you are, interfering!" Her voice grew louder. "I am an old woman! How long do you think I have to carry out my revenge!"

Rachelli's mouth had fallen open halfway through the speech, and she had to swallow before she could get any words out. "I don't know what you mean by revenge," she said, "but I don't think I like the sound of it. Please, just tell your husband to let my brother go."

Mrs. Pernikov smiled. As far as smiles went, it was an extremely unpleasant one. "I have a much, much better idea," she said.

And Rachelli knew that whatever the idea was, she was not going to like it.

Chapter 40

"I don't like this deal," said Rachelli. She crossed her arms. "I don't like this deal one little bit."

Mrs. Pernikov crossed her arms as well. "I don't really care if you like the deal or not. If you care about your brother, then you'll agree to it."

"To never say anything about what we saw, even to our parents?" Rachelli blew out a breath of disbelief. "I mean, fine, I won't say anything; I'm supposed to be going through a surly teenage stage these days anyway. But how can I keep Lolly quiet about this?"

The two of them looked down at the little girl at their feet. Lolly rubbed a sticky hand all along the hem of Rachelli's skirt and said, "Mrs. Pernikov, you are a bad lady."

"See?" said Rachelli.

"I don't care how you do it. I just care that you do it. Unless you want to be responsible for what happens to Alex?"

"What happens to Alex?"

"It depends on you."

"My brother is wrong about the word 'nefarious,'" said Rachelli. "It fits you *perfectly*."

"It is a rather old-fashioned word," Mrs. Pernikov agreed. "But then, I am an old-fashioned woman. Now, what will it be?"

Rachelli yanked at her hair ribbon. The sun overhead seemed far too warm and friendly for the situation. She glared at it, glared at Mrs. Pernikov, then took a deep breath and smiled at her little sister, who was still clinging stickily to her skirt. "Lolly. Do you want some ice cream?"

Lolly brightened and nodded.

"I will give you ice cream," Rachelli went on, "if from now on you say that Mrs. Pernikov is a *good* lady."

Lolly tilted her head to one side. "But she's not a good lady. She's a bad lady."

Rachelli felt her heart begin to beat faster. "But ice cream," she reminded the little girl, hating herself.

"Ice cream," Lolly agreed. She tilted her head to the other side. "I like ice cream. Mrs. Pernikov is a good lady."

Rachelli let out a deep, shuddering breath. "Okay," she said to the old woman. "Okay, now tell your husband to let Alex go."

"Done," said Mrs. Pernikov softly. She walked over to her house and opened the front door. Rachelli clutched Lolly's hand and held her breath. It seemed like she waited for an eternity and a half. Finally, she saw Mrs. Pernikov walking back to her with Alex at her side. Her eyes beneath her wide pink hat were cast in shadow. "There," she said to Rachelli. "Am I still so nefarious?"

"Probably," Rachelli said. "I mean, there's the whole revenge thing, and—"

Mrs. Pernikov turned and headed back to her house. Rachelli's legs suddenly turned to jelly at the sight of her little brother; part of her had thought she would never see him again.

"Mrs. Pernikov," said Lolly reproachfully "is a good lady. Can we get some ice cream now?"

Rachelli nodded without taking her eyes off Alex. "Are you okay? He didn't, like, hurt you or anything?"

"He was kind of mad about how I turned out all the lights in the house," said Alex. "But then he got interested and asked me all sorts of questions about how I did it."

"How *did* you do it?" Rachelli asked.

Alex shrugged. "A little something I whipped up. I had a few in my pocket. It's kind of like the reverse of InstaLight. I call it—"

"InstaDark?"

Alex shook his head as they began to walk back toward the house. "Alex's Incredible Darkness-Making Pellets."

Rachelli snorted. "Seriously?"

Alex laughed. "Nah, kidding. InstaDark."

"I knew it! Anyway, Alex. I feel like I'm missing a bunch of the details of what Mrs. Pernikov—"

A sudden ruckus distracted them just as Rachelli had her hand on the front doorknob. They turned around and saw Wilma Lou Wilson and the sheriff bursting onto the Pernikovs' front porch, guns at the ready.

"What's that all about?" Alex asked.

"Oops," said Rachelli. "That was your rescue. Wilma Lou!" she called loudly. "We got him! We got Alex!"

The housekeeper looked up and nodded. Then she followed the sheriff into the Pernikovs' house anyway.

"Well, maybe they'll find something suspicious and bring them to jail or something," Alex said. He let out a breath. "I really don't like those people."

Rachelli sighed as she opened the freezer and scooped some ice cream into a bowl for Lolly. "I promised not to tell anyone anything," she said. "That was the condition I agreed to so they would let you go."

Alex rubbed at his face. "It's strange that they're worried at all," he said. "After all, time travel is science fiction to most people. No one who matters would even believe us, first of all. And second of all, there are no laws in place yet for the crime that she's planning to commit. Not really, anyway."

"What crime is that?" They had reached the living room, and Rachelli sank down onto the couch and watched as Jeeves attempted to clean the bright-blue spot off the floor. "Give it up, Jeeves," she told the robot cleaner. "You're not going to win that war. That spot is here to stay. Anyway, what crime *is* she planning on committing?"

"She wants revenge on her former employer," Alex said. "It's really dumb, actually. She's a brilliant woman, taught herself how to become a scientist and how to live well in a time outside of her own. But she is totally fixated on going back in time and robbing her former employer blind as payback for the way she was treated."

"How do you know all that?" Rachelli asked.

In response, Alex waved the journal at her. "It's all here, if you know where to look for it. Joseph Smith was not only ahead of his time as a scientist; he was also ahead of his time as a sort of psychologist. He was obsessed with human behaviors, and he studied and wrote down everything about the people around him. It must have driven them crazy, but he didn't care. He thought psychology was the key to successful time travel. Maybe he's right; I mean, knowing yourself is the key to any kind of change, right? Anyway, it's fascinating stuff."

"You mean incredibly boring stuff, right? Is that what you mean?" Rachelli leaned her head back and closed her eyes; being afraid for Alex for so long had left her kind of exhausted. It was hard to care so much. She wondered for a brief moment how her parents did it. At that thought, her eyes flew open. "Oh! And she said that she's not interested in Daddy's project at all! So that's great! One of these days he'll figure out what's wrong, and we can leave this whole mess behind us!"

"And let her get away with it?"

"What choice do we have?"

"More ice cream," Lolly called out.

Rachelli sighed. "You'll get a bellyache."

"More!" Lolly insisted.

"I'm not even supposed to be watching you," Rachelli told the little girl. "I'm supposed to be in school." But she got to her feet anyway. "We should train Jeeves to fetch ice cream and stuff like that for us," she said.

Alex's eyes lit up. "That's an awesome idea! We can call it Alex's Amazing—"

But the name of his invention was interrupted by the sound of Lolly's shriek. They both spun around just in time to see Lolly vanishing through the portal beside the fireplace. Mrs. Pernikov was standing there.

"Did you—" Rachelli gasped. "Did you just *push her in*?"

"I'm sorry," said Mrs. Pernikov, not looking sorry at all, "but you have to understand. I cannot be sure that you'll keep your promise."

"I don't understand you!" Rachelli shouted. "We can just go in after her and come right back! You can't get rid of us that easily! Let's go, Alex!"

Rachelli grabbed her brother's sleeve and rushed through the secret opening beside the fireplace.

She expected to see the familiar interior of the Victorian mansion when it had first been built. Which made the open green fields and the Native American standing before her holding a spear even more surprising.

CHAPTER 41

The sky was a brilliant blue, with only wisps of clouds as fine as cotton candy dotted throughout. In the distance were green rolling hills. There was the steady roar of a nearby waterfall. The world in which the Shores had found themselves was clean, clear, almost magical. Well, except for the Native American holding a spear.

The Native American looked at Rachelli, Alex, and Lolly.

Lolly, Alex, and Rachelli looked at the Native American.

Somewhere off in the distance a bird chirped.

The Native American was not tall. In fact, he was kind of small for a full-grown man. His braided hair was dark as a walnut, and his outfit looked like it was made of a very soft leather. The spear clutched in his hand looked wickedly sharp. He did not move.

"Maybe," Alex whispered, "he's a statue."

"Hu!" said the Native American. He glared at the three of them.

"He is not a statue," Rachelli decided.

"This is bad," said Alex. "This is so very much bad."

"Hu!" said the braided man again, and he lifted his spear in a way that seemed vaguely threatening.

"Do you want us to get up?" Rachelli addressed him. "Or stay down? What?"

"Hu!"

"Based on my acute observational skills," Alex said quietly, his lips barely moving, "I would say that our friend does not speak English."

"Hu!" the spear bounced up and down.

"I think he wants us to get up," Rachelli said. Slowly, she tested that theory. When she was on her feet and the man didn't grunt anything else, she gestured to Alex and Lolly to do the same.

Another gesture with the spear, and then the man started walking.

"I think we're supposed to follow him," Alex said.

"We should definitely not do that," said Rachelli. "We should do the reverse of that. Whatever the exact opposite of 'follow him' is, that's what we should do."

"Hu!" The man had turned around and lifted his spear.

"Do you have a better idea?" Alex said. "I mean, one that does not involve getting a spear through the ribs?"

"I'm a little bit hungry," said Lolly.

They walked through the green plains, following the Native American for what felt like forever, though Rachelli's watch informed her it was actually a half hour. She spent the time remembering just how much she hated Mrs. Pernikov.

"Can you believe she pushed Lolly into the portal?" Rachelli said in a hiss to Alex, who had Lolly on his shoulders and was struggling under her weight. "That is a woman with no conscience! To push a little girl like Lolly into a *portal!*"

"Can we please focus on more important things?" Alex implored as he staggered forward. "Like, oh, I don't know, the fact that there is a Native American *with a spear holding us hostage*?"

"He's not even so big," Rachelli said. She looked at the man in front of them. "We can take him. Well, Effie could take him. Oh, I wish Effie was here."

"Yes, because wishes are always useful in times like this."

Rachelli snorted. "You sure get testy when you're held prisoner."

"For the second time in an *hour*, yeah!"

"I liked you a lot better when you were just a spaced-out scientist!"

"Hu!" said their captor, and Rachelli and Alex stopped glaring at each other and moved forward again.

"But back to Mrs. Pernikov," said Rachelli. "I mean, what kind of *person* does stuff like that?"

Alex sighed and adjusted Lolly. "Maybe we can make a rule that whoever does the majority of the talking also holds Lolly?"

Rachelli made a face. "She's heavy."

"Also hungry," Lolly reminded her.

Alex rummaged around in his pockets and found several dozen items, none of them edible. "Sorry, Lolly. Look, Rachelli. This is bad. This is very, very bad. You need to stop focusing on Mrs. Pernikov and focus on the situation at hand."

Rachelli stared at Alex, openmouthed. "Pretty sure this is the first time in history that *you* had to tell *me* to focus on the situation at hand. Anyway, you're right. I'm sorry. I'll focus. What am I focusing on?"

"It's just that I don't think you realize how much trouble we're in. Do you realize what it means that we're in a time before the Victorian was—"

"Hu!" said their captor, and he stopped walking. They had, apparently, arrived at their destination.

Alex, Rachelli, and Lolly found themselves in a narrow dip of the hills beside several small waterfalls with waters that glinted in the sunlight.

There was a small group of cone-shaped teepees a safe distance away from a large blackened spot on the ground that was surrounded by rocks smelling of smoke. A large pot was balanced over several of the rocks.

"They're going to eat us," Rachelli whispered, and then quickly regretted it when Lolly's eyes grew round with fear.

"They're not going to eat us," Alex said dismissively. "Wrong tribe."

"So then we're safe?" Rachelli murmured.

"On the other hand, they might scalp us," Alex said. "So that would be bad."

Rachelli stuffed her hand in her mouth to bite back a scream. "If we're murdered," she said, "I am going to *kill* Mrs. Pernikov."

"If we are murdered, that would be a pretty difficult thing to do."

Rachelli's retort died on her tongue when several men who looked similar to their captor appeared as though by magic. Their feet seemed to make no sound at all on the grass. A few women had materialized at the doors to the teepees as well.

For a moment, all was quiet as the Native Americans stared at the Shores and the Shores stared at the Native Americans. Not even the sound of a bird breached the silence.

"Hello," said Lolly, and her voice was the loudest sound around for miles. "I am Lolly. I am hungry. I need to go to the bathroom too."

As if some sort of spell was broken, the Native Americans began talking to each other rapidly in a language that Rachelli wished she could understand. "You should invent a sort of universal translator," she whispered to Alex. "Something that makes you instantly able to understand a foreign language. That would be awesome right now so we could know if they're saying stuff like, 'Let's eat them,' or 'Let's let them go,' or, my personal favorite, 'Let's make Rachelli queen.'"

Alex winced. "That would be a great idea," he said. "Not making you queen — a universal translator. I wish I had thought of it." He brightened suddenly. "But that actually *does* give me an idea." He reached into his pocket, pulled something out, and held it up. It was a magnifying glass on one end, and a flashlight on the other.

The natives stopped talking and eyed the item curiously.

"For you," said Alex. He waved it toward the group. "You want? Take."

"They can't speak English," Rachelli said.

"There are some things that transcend language," said Alex. "Pretty sure 'take' is one of those things."

Sure enough, their captor approached, his dark face bright with curiosity. Alex pressed a button, and the flashlight turned on. "Nice?" Alex said. "Pretty?"

The murmurs around them rose to excited chatter. A few minutes later, Alex was relieved of his little tool, and the group of natives was gesturing excitedly for the Shores to sit down cross-legged on the grass with them. Alex took out a pocketknife next and showed everyone how it worked. Gasps of awe and admiration followed his every move.

"You're enjoying this," Rachelli said to him. "You totally are."

Alex grinned sheepishly. "I do like when they ooh and aah over the slightest little thing I do."

Baskets of fresh fruit were brought out of the teepees, and Lolly steadily ate her way through as many fruits as she could get her hands on.

Now that the danger seemed to have passed — at least for now — Rachelli's mind wandered back to what Alex had been trying to tell her before they had arrived at their captor's home.

It's just that I don't think you realize how much trouble we're in, he had said. *Do you realize what it means that we're in a time before the Victorian was—*

When the rest of the sentence finished itself inside Rachelli's head, her arms broke out in goose bumps despite the perfect weather.

They had ended up in a time before the Victorian mansion and its time portals had been built.

How were they ever going to get back home?

CHAPTER 42

The sun was going down behind the trees when the interest of the natives in the contents of Alex's pockets finally waned. Rachelli scooted over to him and sat down on a particularly uncomfortable rock. "So, yeah. How will I look in feathers?"

Alex blinked at her, confused. "Um. Feathery, I guess?"

"Yuck. Well, I guess I'll have to get used to it, seeing as we're stuck here, right?"

Alex nodded grimly. "So you figured out the issue, then, huh?"

"I mean, how can we get back through the portals if we have no portals to get back *through*? But I have a question. Every time we went back, we went to 1880. How come it was different this time?"

"Mrs. Pernikov," Alex explained. "She had the machine in her basement set to 1880. Before she pushed Lolly through, she must have switched it."

"What's her plan?" Rachelli pounded the rocks around her in frustration, only to discover that pounding rocks in frustration led to no less frustration and more painful fists.

"I'm not one hundred percent sure. I think she wants to steal something that is precious to the the Smiths, make them suffer the way she thinks she suffered. But then she realized that she couldn't take anything from the past into the future. So she's been experimenting and trying all these years to—"

"Wait!" Rachelli shouted, and then quickly lowered her voice when she saw a few natives looking at her curiously. "But she *did* bring something from one time period to another! The picture of her that I tried to borrow was from another time period!"

"Steal."

"*Whatever*. She brought it over! How did she do that?"

Alex chewed his cheek in thought. "Interesting. Really interesting. That would mean that it's not the nature of time travel to not allow items to travel through the time stream. It is an artificial construct."

"And now in English?"

"It's not the science of time travel that keeps you from bringing things from the past into the future; it's a *scientist*."

"Hu!" said a familiar voice. Their Native American captor was back, and he looked as annoyed as ever. He pointed at Lolly, then pointed at Alex, and then he pointed at Rachelli. Then he pointed back in the direction they had come from.

"So I guess they decided we're not a threat, but we're not honored guests either," Rachelli said glumly as they made their way up the hills they had just climbed down. The air was clear, and the stars that were beginning to appear glittered like diamonds in the sky.

"This is amazing," Alex said dreamily. Lolly slipped down one of his shoulders as he took in his surroundings. "It's hard to believe that we're *here*, before this land was spoiled with houses and modern conveniences and smog and pollution and cars and buses and trains."

"Hey," said Rachelli. "This will never be spoiled with houses and smog and stuff. This is *Sundale*, remember? A one-store town whose claim to fame is owning the biggest ball of twine! And anyway, don't you want to be a scientist and stuff? You kind of need modern equipment for that."

"Maybe," Alex said. "But there is something to be said for simplicity."

"Something has to be said, and I will say it," said Rachelli, but she didn't get a chance. Just then there was the sound of a dull roar from down the hill, and they ran back to see what it was.

"Um, so, okay, this is not good," said Rachelli after a quick peek down the hill. "Run, Alex, run!"

"What is it? What is it?" Alex yelled even as he listened to Rachelli and began to run as fast as he could away from the hill, Lolly bouncing on Alex's shoulders like a very unhappy and extremely vocal rag doll.

"It looks like," Rachelli panted as their feet pounded the soft grass of the hill, "the entire peaceful village has turned not so peaceful all of a sudden."

"What? Why?"

"I don't know! I don't understand Native American!"

"Actually, there was no language 'Native American,'" said Alex as he ran. "Tribes had their own distinct—"

"Seriously?" Rachelli gasped. "You're going to do this now? Stop being a brainy four-eyes and focus on running away from the scary feathery people holding scary pointy things!"

"I-I-I d-d-d-don't l-l-l-like th-th-th-this," said Lolly, her hands wrapped around the top of Alex's head for dear life, bouncing in time to the pounding of his sneakered feet.

"Over here!" Rachelli pointed to a large bush off to the side, and Alex dove in sideways after her. Rachelli clapped a hand over Lolly's mouth as the angry group went passed, shouting and waving their spears.

"What in the world was *that* about?" Rachelli whispered.

"I might have sort of accidentally put the things that I showed them — the pocketknife, the flashlight, the magnifying glass — back into my pockets before we left, and they might have sort of kind of thought that I had given them as gifts," said Alex sheepishly. "Now that I think about it."

Rachelli rolled her eyes and got to her feet. She parted the branches before her and peeked through the leaves. "Well, they're gone now," she said. "And if this tribe doesn't make peace when the explorers come to America, you might be the reason why."

"That's really not what I want to be remembered for."

"We should get out of here before they come back," Rachelli decided. "Let's head back toward the place where we came from and figure out how we can get back home. Although all these hills look exactly the same. How in the world are we going to find the spot where we fell through time?"

"Alex has a thingy," said Lolly from her perch. "Alex always has a thingy."

"Actually, I kind of do," said Alex. He reached into the leather pouch at his waist. "I was trying to figure out how to make a reverse GPS. You know, not one that tells you where you should go, but one that tells you where you've been."

"Why would you need that?" asked Rachelli, then she shook her head. "Never mind. Forget I asked. So does it work?"

Alex took what looked like a large brass button out of his pouch. He pushed a small button on the large button, and seven razor-thin legs emerged with a click so that the gadget now looked like a spider. Alex worked on the underside of the metallic creature before setting it down gently on the grass. It began to walk.

"That is seriously creepy but kind of cool," said Rachelli. "Do we follow it?"

"We do," said Alex. "But first, your turn to take Lolly."

Rachelli took the little girl, and the siblings followed the metal spider in relative silence all through the darkened hills.

Daddy is going to be so worried, Rachelli found herself thinking. *And he'll call Mommy, and they'll both be freaking out, and they won't have a clue where we disappeared to.*

One look at Alex's face was enough to convince Rachelli that he was thinking the same thing.

"I want Mommy," said Lolly softly, and Rachelli bit her lip so she wouldn't cry.

"We'll get back home," she said softly but fiercely to her brother and sister. "Don't you worry. We'll get back home."

When they finally arrived at the clearing they had landed in, Lolly was asleep, her head resting heavily against Rachelli's shoulder. Alex was lost in his own thoughts, and Rachelli was trying not to think about how much her arms and legs were burning.

Instead, Rachelli thought about how she would gently put Lolly down on the ground and then curl up around her to keep the little girl warm in the cool night air. She was thinking about asking Alex if he had any gadgets in his pouch or pockets that could produce macaroni and cheese because she was starving. She was also thinking about just how much she hated a certain old woman in a pink floppy hat.

Because she was so lost in thought, Rachelli didn't notice the group of men examining the very spot that Alex's spider had led them to.

CHAPTER 43

These men were different from the Native Americans.
For one, their skin was lighter. Their clothing was different too; they
were wearing high boots, soft-looking hats, and long colorful shirts
secured with belts. The men turned in the near-darkness when the
Shores approached. They looked at each other in the flickering light
of the men's small campfire.

"Wow. Are you…explorers?" Alex asked in a wondering sort of
voice, and Rachelli kicked him in the shins. "Ouch!"

One of the men pointed something at them that they could not
quite make out in the darkness but looked suspiciously like a rifle.
There was a clicking sound as the hammer was cocked.

"Please don't aim stuff at us," Rachelli said wearily. "So many
people have been aiming stuff at us today. I just want to not have
anything aimed at us for a little while. Is that okay?"

The man held up the firearm for a moment longer, and then
he bent down and replaced the weapon in his hands with a stick.
He put it into the fire for a moment until the top of the stick was
alight, turning it into a torch. He then detached from the group and
approached the Shores, torch aloft. "I am John Smith," he said in a
growly sort of English accent.

"You are John Smith?" Alex asked. He peered at the man in the darkness. "But wait, you can't be — well, you're not *our* John Smith, are you?"

"If you're thinking about the original owner of the Victorian, his name was *Joseph* Smith," Rachelli told Alex. She rolled her eyes. "You've only read his journals like a bazillion times—"

"As I do not know who your John, or Joseph, Smith is," the man interrupted, "I cannot hope to answer that question."

"Our Mr. Smith is a scientist."

One of the other men roared with sudden laughter. "Our Mr. Smith is blessed with brawny arms," he said, "and is brave of heart, but he would do dreadfully as a man of science."

John Smith glared at the man who had spoken before turning back to the Shores. "Now, who are you?" he asked in his growly voice. "What are you doing in our camp? Are you spies for the Indians?"

"We are not spies!" said Rachelli. "Definitely not! We came here by accident."

The men laughed. "How does one come to the New World by accident?" one of them asked. "Did you stow away in our ship?"

"No! Totally not! We actually…well, it's a long story and involves too many things that you would not believe."

The men stopped laughing. The man with the torch, John Smith, took a step closer to them. His face was shadowed, but they could see his eyes, and they looked serious. "Try us," he said. "We just might."

Lolly was sleeping with her head in Rachelli's lap, and the fire was but golden embers by the time Alex finished telling the explorers their story. Other than the crackling sounds of the dying fire and her brother's voice, the hills around them were utterly silent, the kind of silence that had not been heard in the modern world in decades, or even centuries.

"You probably think we're crazy," Rachelli said when Alex stopped talking.

John Smith shrugged a broad shoulder. "Well, now. We have discovered an entire continent that no one thought was here and met an indigenous people no one knew existed. It only stands to reason that there is much that we don't know on G-d's green earth besides for that. And anyway, you're telling me that you landed right here, in this spot. Well, it just so happens that we are in this spot for a reason. Some private mission for King Henry himself."

As he said the word "king," he inclined his head, as did all the men around him. "I am not a man of science, true, but my orders are to secure this spot for a man of science of the king's choosing. But it is a strange place, with strange happenings."

"What kind of strange things happen here?" Rachelli asked. She felt a tingle go up her arms and legs that had nothing to do with the nighttime chill.

"Well, the horses were spooked and ran from us the first night here. And every so often there's strange white fog in the sky that does not spread but stays in one place."

Alex looked at Rachelli, his eyes wide. "That is very, very interesting," he said slowly. "*Very* interesting."

Rachelli had been thinking the word "spooky" herself, but she nodded her head at Alex, hoping that by "interesting," he meant "a way to get us home."

"I do not know if we should be telling these tales, mind," said John Smith, "for fear of being deemed insane."

Alex waved a dismissive hand. "We just claimed to be from the future," he said. "I don't think you should really care if we think you're insane."

The men laughed and then leaned forward eagerly. "If you are truly from the future," one of them asked, "tell us this: Do we manage to secure this piece of land for England? And more importantly, does it stay a glorious property of the Crown?"

"Um," said Alex.

"Yes," said Rachelli firmly. "As we say where we come from, long live England! Anywho, what other strange—"

There was a sound of running from behind them, and a boy appeared. He was out of breath and held a flaming torch in his hand. "He is gone!" he said between gasps for breath. "I cannot find him anywhere!"

John Smith nodded grimly. "As I suspected. Sit, Peter. There will be no more searching. Andrew is gone, like the others."

"Others?" Rachelli's ears perked up. "People have gone missing?"

He nodded. "Aye. It is one of the strange things I was telling you about. And Peter here claims that he saw it happen to Andrew. He claims a hand from the sky took him."

"A hand from the sky!" Rachelli exclaimed. She looked at Alex, finally feeling a faint flicker of hope in her heart.

"We cannot stay here any longer, John!" Peter's voice was too loud and shaky. "If we stay, we shall vanish like the others!"

The men began muttering among each another, and Rachelli took advantage of their distraction to speak to Alex. "What do you think about this spot being a place that people disappear?" she whispered to him. "I mean, it can't be a coincidence, can it?"

"It's not," Alex whispered back. "I mean, it's all over Smith's journal. He only built his house in this specific spot *because* of the unknown phenomenon that occurred here. He thinks it's some sort of naturally occurring energy that makes the barriers between time weaker in this place."

"Blah, blah, blah, science," said Rachelli. "All I hear you saying is that there might be a way for us to go home!"

"Why is it that you look pleased?" one of the men asked suddenly, making both Rachelli and Alex jump, and Lolly stir in her sleep. "Are you perhaps in league with the dread hand from the sky?"

"These people are explorers and sailors from a very different time period," Alex whispered to Rachelli. "They are extremely superstitious and can also take the law into their own hands. Be careful with what you say."

"Well?" the man pushed, and all the explorers looked at them in a way that made Rachelli swallow very, very hard.

"We do not know of the hand in the sky," she finally squeaked. "We just want to get home."

There was more muttering at that, but it seemed to be more sympathetic than angry this time.

"We'd best be getting some sleep," John Smith said. "We shall lend you some blankets to rest with. We will discuss what to do with you when the sun rises in the morning."

Lolly did not budge as Rachelli thanked the explorer and then covered the little girl with the blankets offered to her.

When Rachelli looked up, she saw that a white fog had appeared around them, and in the middle of it all, there was a large hand, reaching toward her.

CHAPTER 44

Rachelli, at that point, had assumed that she'd pretty much seen all of the weirdest things that the universe had to offer. Her family owned a car that thought it was a person and wrote terrible songs, her eggs made themselves, she had traveled back in time multiple times, and, oddest of all, lived in a town whose populace thought that a big ball of twine was a good reason for a yearly celebration.

But she was completely unprepared for an arm that was not attached to anything or anyone to come through the mist, and neither was Lolly. When the hand came through the white haze and grabbed for Lolly, the little girl cast a startled glance over her shoulder at her big brother and sister before both she and the hand disappeared.

"Lolly!" Rachelli screamed. "Lolly! Seriously, the only time I say 'Lolly' these days is in a scream of horror, and I'm pretty much sick of it! Lolly, where *are you*?"

The explorers, in the meantime, had risen from their makeshift beds in the darkness. The moonlight was strong enough to still see the white fog slowly dissipating around them. There was much moaning in fright and an awful lot of running away, and within a few moments, Rachelli and Alex were left alone.

"Lolly!" they both called, their voices blending into the darkness of the hills in the New World that would not see streetlights for many more years. "Lolly! Lolly!"

There was no answer besides for the howl of a far-off pack of wolves.

"Alex, that hand. I've seen a hand like that before, when Effie stuck his hand into the portal. But that didn't look like Effie's hand, did it?"

Alex pushed up his glasses nervously. "It was white and glowing. I have no idea whose hand it was."

Rachelli tried to pace in the darkness but bumped straight into a tree. "Ouch! Why is there a tree!"

"Because we're outdoors," said Alex helpfully.

Rachelli slumped back onto the ground. "I guess we'll have to wait until morning to find her."

"Why?" asked Alex.

"Because," Rachelli explained, "of the lack of light we are currently experiencing, known colloquially as 'darkness'!"

"Oh!" There was the sound of Alex rustling through his pockets, and then a popping sound, and the night and Alex's sheepish smile were lit up with chemical smears of InstaLight.

Rachelli rolled her eyes. "And you've had those with you this whole time."

"Well, I didn't want to give the explorers any more reason to think that we know witchcraft," Alex explained. "You know that the Spanish Inquisition is alive and thriving in Spain just about now."

Rachelli sobered. "Ouch. Okay, well, now that they're gone, we can use the light to look for Lolly."

"Rachelli." Alex said her name so gently, that Rachelli turned to stare at him. "Rachelli, we can't look for her here, light or no light. She's gone."

Tears sprang into Rachelli's eyes. "Don't say that."

"I don't mean she's *gone* gone. I mean she's gone somewhere, into the portal. Some*when* is the word, maybe?"

"But there *is* no portal! The house has not been built yet! How is it even possible that she's gone through a portal that doesn't yet *exist*?"

Alex shrugged. "I mean, I can only conjecture. But as I said before, this place is almost like a natural portal. All it needed was a few scientific calculations and the actual structure of a portal to make it function as a time machine. That's why Mrs. Pernikov, learned scientist that she is, was not able to copy the science and create portals elsewhere; she had to continue using the Victorian. But then we moved in, and she had to move into the house next door."

"But you said that it *almost* functions as a portal, not that it *does* function as a portal," Rachelli pointed out. "So how did Lolly disappear?"

"Pretty sure that hand was someone's from a different time, reaching through that portal and grabbing onto Lolly."

"Okay." Rachelli's eyes lit up. "Well, who would do that? Huh? Who is searching for us? It can only be Daddy!"

Alex bit his lip. "Yeah," he said. "Yeah, of course, Daddy."

"Why are you saying, 'Yeah, of course, Daddy' in a way that means 'Yeah, not, of course, Daddy'?"

Alex sighed. "Because if it were Daddy, then why hasn't he come back to get *us*?"

They spent the rest of the night in silence, watching as the smears of incandescent InstaLight slowly faded from the dew-covered grass until they both fell into an uneasy sleep.

Rachelli was awakened by the silence. Even after a few months in quiet Sundale, she was still a city girl at heart, and too much quiet was more jarring than too much noise.

"What time is it?" she mumbled, then jerked to an upright position. Which was a mistake, she knew right away. Her neck was stiff from sleeping on the hard ground, and she shivered in the cool and damp morning air. Her arms tried to close around her little sister on her lap, and it took her a moment to realize that her arms had closed on thin air.

Her heart sank. The hand taking Lolly. The explorers running away in panic from what they must have seen as magic. It was all real.

Lolly was gone.

"Did you say something?" Alex asked her with his eyes closed.

"Never mind." Rachelli shook her head.

"I would trap a bear for a bowl of cornflakes," Alex said after they had washed their hands and faces in a nearby stream and davened what they could by heart.

"How about a raw fish?" Rachelli peered at the silvery flashes of trout as they swam past in the clear waters of the stream.

Alex made a face. "I'm not that level of hungry yet."

Rachelli sighed and plopped down on the grass. Alex sat down too. "Okay. I need you to tell me every single thing that you've read in Mr. Smith's journal that might help us find Lolly and then get back home and then send Mrs. Pernikov back to a very unpleasant period in time. Like right before the *mabul* would be great, I'm thinking."

Alex shrugged but pulled the old leather notebook out of his pouch. "Okay. So I didn't believe it until I saw it with my own eyes last night, but the reason this spot was of interest to the government to begin with is because of the ancient Indian legends about this place. It was dismissed at first as local superstition, until evidence of strange happenings were witnessed by people of good reputation. Hey, maybe we *met* those people of good reputation last night!"

"Focus. So why don't *we* know about it?"

"The government made it classified. They thought it was dangerous, and you know what? It is."

Rachelli nodded. "Hear, hear. Okay, so then why did they let Mr. Smith work on it?"

"This is just assumption, but I think they realized that if the government didn't work on it, then rogue scientists would. So they hired Smith. He was afraid to bring his wife and kids here, so he left them at home in the city. Smith moved here after being given very specific instructions for how the house was to be built, with all of the doors and stuff to serve as portals when he finally got the natural energy of this place in tune with his machines.

"I don't think he meant to treat Mrs. Pernikov badly when she was his housekeeper. I think because he was so absentminded, and because he thought the work more important than anything else in the world, he might have."

Rachelli ripped out a handful of grass at her feet. "I can't believe you feel *bad* for her."

Alex looked down. "I don't. I just understand how it could happen. Let's just say that I know what it's like to ignore everyone around you because of some gadget or another."

Rachelli threw the grass at her brother's head. "You are *great*, okay? I wouldn't give up an absentminded hair on your head. I love you, little bro."

They sat in silence for a moment.

"If you tell anyone I just said that," said Rachelli, "I will deny it, and then I will kill you."

"Got it."

They walked back up to the spot where they had spent the night. The mist still hung in the air. "Well, at least I'm not going to have to live out the rest of my days in this ridiculous century all by myself," Rachelli said. She turned around to smile at her brother, but he was not there to smile at, and she spun around in a complete circle. "Seriously? Alex! Well, that's just typical. Alex! Alexander Shore!"

She was so busy searching for her brother that when the hand came and grabbed for her, she didn't even have time to scream.

CHAPTER 45

Sometimes, just when you feel that you're the most
alone you've ever been, that is exactly when you realize that you
are never really alone. Sometimes, when you feel as if you're in the
dark and always will be, the sun comes out and you know that it
was there all along, behind the clouds.

Those were sentiments that Rachelli was thinking but decided
to never actually say out loud because she was too choked up
at the moment to say much of anything. Plus, sooo corny. She
would *never* say stuff that corny out loud, no matter the situation. Like, for example, she was *not* going to say what she was
thinking right now, which was: *I knew you would save us. I just
knew it.*

"I *knew* you would save us," she said, looking up into the faces of
both of her parents and, a little behind them, her big brother. Her
voice was thick with tears. "I just knew it."

"So whose hand was it exactly?" Alex asked.

"Mine," said Mrs. Shore. She smiled tremulously. "It was my hand."

"So you're the one who grabbed Lolly and then us?" Alex asked. "I
mean, obviously. Thank you, Mommy. And I guess you didn't come

through all the way because you knew that without the portal, you would get stuck there, right?"

"I wanted to run right in and find you," said Mrs. Shore. Her eyes were bright with tears. "But your father said that I could get stuck in another time altogether, and we would never see each other again."

Professor Shore nodded. "We put a hand into the portal every five minutes, but nothing. Finally, we got Lolly, *baruch Hashem*, and then a few minutes later, we got both of you!" Professor Shore beamed, then laughed. "I hope we didn't start too many Native American legends about a hand from the sky in the process!"

"Well, you might *have* actually done something *exactly* like—" Alex began, but Rachelli interrupted him.

"A few minutes later?" Rachelli's voice squeaked indignantly even as Lolly ran over to her and hugged her tight, and for once, she didn't mind how sticky Lolly was; she was just too glad that the little girl was okay. "Daddy, you did *not* find us a few *minutes* after you found Lolly! It took an entire night! It was the worst night of my life! I thought — I don't *know* what I thought! I thought the *world* had swallowed her up!"

"Time," said Alex.

"Huh?" said Rachelli.

But Professor Shore was nodding his head. "Yes, exactly. Explain it, Alex."

"Well, time," Alex explained. "I mean, I think I've got it, though I don't really understand the science yet. Anyway, time doesn't work the same for a time traveler. We realized that the first time we went through the portals. It was night here, and the sun was shining in the 1880s. Apparently, time goes all funny when you use the portals. Days and nights don't exactly line up. It's a problem that any time traveler who is trying to get back to a very specific time can and will run into—"

"Mrs. Pernikov," said Rachelli. "She's been trying, trying for *years*, to take some sort of revenge on her employers, but she can't manage to do it. I thought it was because she was trying to steal something and ran into the problem of not being able to bring stuff from the past back with her, like I did, but maybe it's not that at all. Maybe she's trying to get back to a very specific time and keeps missing…"

Rachelli looked up, back into the faces of the people whom she loved most in the world, and she covered her mouth again to muffle a sob. "I don't care. I don't care about any of that, this time for *real*. We're *home*!"

Mrs. Shore's face crumpled first, and she grabbed for Rachelli's hand. "Oh, Rachelli, I can't believe what danger I left you in!"

Rachelli bit her tongue and did not say that she had tried to tell everyone about Mrs. Pernikov, but no one would believe her. The words must have been written all over her face despite her restraint because her mother sighed heavily and added, "I didn't mean to doubt you, Rachelli, sweetheart, I just couldn't *believe* that in a sleepy little town like Sundale we would run into problems like this! And she seemed like such a very nice old woman too!"

Professor Shore's *peïos* were standing up nearly straight on his head like two frizzy towers on either side of his yarmulke. His eyes were also red. "*I* should have realized," he said. "I should have known that something was going on with those two."

"Oh, Daddy," said Rachelli. "I love you so much, but…oh, nothing."

"Nothing?" Professor Shore smiled. "I don't think so. What did you want to say?"

"Just that I think that as much as the world needs scientists, science-types need us practical types too! And maybe even more! I mean, Daddy, *how* would you have realized that the Pernikovs are the villains of the story when you never even notice acid eating away at your lab coat? Well, not right *now*," Rachelli added when Professor Shore quickly examined his lab coat.

"Okay, yes," said Effie over everyone's laughter. "And that's all good and true, but speaking as a practical type, if you two don't get up and out of Wilma Lou Wilson's vegetable patch, then you'll *really* have something to cry about."

Rachelli and Alex looked around, and, for the first time, realized that they were still lying flat where the portal had dropped them, right on top of Wilma Lou Wilson's carefully tended carrots. They both flew up suddenly as if stung by bees, and everyone began walking back toward the Victorian.

"Welcome home," said a slow, drawling voice, coming from the car in the driveway. "I mean, I don't know why everyone is making such a big deal about it," Pinny the PNAAD continued. "You guys seem to get stuck in time and then rescued a lot. It's getting so tiresome that I don't even think I'll write a song about it."

"That's totally fine," Rachelli said hastily. "Really, no song necessary."

"Unless you insist," said Pinny.

"No, no, we really don't—"

"Okay, *fine*!" said Pinny in a tone of great self-sacrifice. "If you beg me like that, what choice do I have? There once were a boy and girl who traveled in time!" he sang out in a very loud and very flat voice. "And they are the heroes of this rhyme! Also the rest of the Shores, and also Wilma Lou—

"Hey," said Pinny in his normal tone, "before I continue, I'm going to need something that rhymes with Pernikov, so start thinking, okay? Okay. Now, something, something, Wilma Lou—"

"Wait! Wilma Lou Wilson! And the sheriff!" Rachelli yelled over the tone-deaf PNAAD. "They went into the Pernikovs' house! What happened to them?"

"Rude," said Pinny the PNAAD. His voice sounded teary. "*Really* rude, interrupting me in the middle of my song."

Rachelli ignored the car. "And wait! Daddy! Mommy! So okay, a little slow on the uptake, but first of all, Mommy, you weren't home! Right? You were in Washington! Effie, you weren't home either! You were in yeshivah! And how do you all suddenly *know* about the Pernikovs? What did I miss when we were busy getting chased by Indians and getting accused of being witches by a group of explorers and nearly starving to death in the middle? Ooh, you know what? I'm still kind of starving to death."

"Of course you must be!" Mrs. Shore grabbed Alex and Rachelli each by an elbow. "Let's go inside and get something to eat."

"I need answers!" Rachelli hollered.

"I thought you didn't care about anything now that you're home!" Alex grinned.

"That was five whole minutes ago!" Rachelli flushed. "Okay. So I'm still grateful to be home, but I can't stand it if nothing makes sense!"

"Except my song," said Pinny. "My song makes lots of sense. But you wouldn't *know* about that because you keep interrupting—"

"Yes, of course," Mrs. Shore interrupted Pinny as though he were just a car, which, in fact, he was. "You want to hear the whole story. So let's go in, get something to eat, and then we'll tell you everything."

CHAPTER 46

"Ouch!" said Alex.

"Ouch!" said Rachelli.

"Ouch! I'm hungry," said Lolly.

"Sorry," said Professor Shore as Alex, Rachelli, and Lolly rubbed their arms ruefully and glared. "A shot was the quickest way to get the formula into your bloodstream. Now you won't ever go back in time again if you don't want to."

"We don't want to!" Rachelli said instantly. Then her eyes lit up. "So you figured out what happened to enable us to go back in time, and reversed it!"

Alex snapped his fingers and pointed at his mother. "Of course! That's how Mommy was able to stick her hand through the portal and have it go through time, instead of just into the next room. She was primed!"

Mrs. Shore nodded as she bustled around the huge kitchen, putting everything but the kitchen sink on the table for her starving children. "It felt just about as unpleasant as that shot you just got."

"I'll take it," said Rachelli fervently. She grabbed a banana in one hand and a slice of cheese in the other. "I'll take this too." Five minutes later, through a mouthful of reheated pasta, Rachelli said, "Can we have this meal with a side of answers?"

The government official who'd sent the Shores to this particular house to work on Professor Shore's ultra-secret invention was a woman named Charlotte Miller. Charlotte had a problem, and the problem was Professor Shore. The man was brilliant, but — to put it nicely — a tad eccentric. She wanted him working on a specific pet project of hers. However, if the entire thing blew up in her face the same way that Professor Shore had once blown up a (thankfully abandoned) city block while working on a way to make parakeets translate Morse code, she wanted him very, very far away from anyone who would connect him with her department.

"So the first thing she did," Mrs. Shore explained, her lips pulled tight in disapproval, "was make sure that we didn't know that he was actually working this *whole* time with her full support. If I had known, I wouldn't have had all those trips back and forth to Washington, cutting imaginary red tape just so Charlotte Miller could keep her hands clean!"

"Hands clean?" said Jeeves. The robot had just walked into the kitchen. It headed straight for Mrs. Shore.

"No, no, Jeeves," said Mrs. Shore hurriedly. "Please do not clean my hands. If you want to clean someone's hands, clean Lolly's."

The robot cleaner nodded jerkily, then held a damp cloth out to the sticky little girl, who was finishing up her meal with a chocolate pudding.

"Anyway, where was I?" Mrs. Shore took a deep breath. "Oh, yes."

Next, scouring through the list of government-owned houses, Charlotte had stumbled upon the old Victorian, abandoned for decades. She knew the rumors about the house, knew that there was another branch of government that was heavily involved in trying to make time travel a reality and was connected with this house, but it suited her purposes. Even if someone figured out that Professor Shore was not a candy salesman, or whatever he professed himself to be, no one would connect a lone, eccentric scientist in a one-horse town like Sundale with the government of the United States.

"I do not like Charlotte Miller," said Rachelli. "I do not like her at all."

Mrs. Shore sighed. "She's not all that bad. I can't really blame her for taking precautions. Do you remember when Daddy accidentally turned the waters in the reservoir into strawberry Jell-O?"

"That was awesome," said Effie fervently. "You just turned on the faucet, and glurg, glurg — Jell-O."

"It was a mistake, but a pretty good one," Professor Shore agreed.

"You should name it," said Alex. "You should name it Reserve-ell-O. Or, no, that's terrible. How about—"

"*Anyway,*" said Mrs. Shore.

The officials at the time-traveling agency were very upset when they found out that the Shores had set up residence in the old Victorian that used to belong to Joseph Smith. They insisted that it wasn't safe for the Shores to be living in that house.

"What can be dangerous about an old, abandoned house in the middle of nowhere?" Charlotte had thrown up her hands.

They refused to say. They insisted that the secrets they kept about the Victorian were secrets that could change the very fabric of the world if they got out.

"Dramatic," Charlotte had snorted, but allowed them to send security to keep an eye on the Shores.

Rachelli had a horrible thought. "Please don't tell me," said Rachelli, "please, please don't tell me that *Mrs. Pernikov* is security?"

"No, of course not!" said Effie.

"Okay, then!" said Rachelli. "I mean, she's as likely to be security from the government as Wilma Lou Wilson!"

Effie looked at his mother. His mother looked back at him. Rachelli's mouth fell open.

"No," she said.

"Yes," said Alex. "That actually makes a lot of sense. I could never figure out why she was staying once Jeeves was fixed. But she stayed because she was sent by the government to keep an eye out."

"Speaking of Wilma Lou Wilson," said Rachelli, shaking her head to clear it, "I told her all about Mrs. Pernikov, and she stormed her house with the sheriff. Whatever happened with that?"

"Well, Wilma Lou Wilson — and the sheriff, believe it or not — sat the Pernikovs down and got them to admit enough of the story that she pieced together what had happened to you. Then she immediately told Daddy, who called me."

"And me!" said Effie. "Well, no. I had called to say hi and was in the right place at the right time."

"So we came rushing home," said Mrs. Shore, and she gave each of her children bone-crushing hugs, "to save you."

"How did you know where to find us?" Rachelli asked after her mother finally let go of her.

"Don't you mean *when* to find us?" said Alex.

"I mean exactly what I said, thank you very much!" said Rachelli. "I hate time travel terms; they give me a headache! Anyway, how?"

"Well," said Mrs. Shore, "Wilma Lou Wilson found the time machine in the Pernikovs' basement, and we saw the year that it was set to. We couldn't be one hundred percent sure that she hadn't changed it after she sent you through. Oh, how we davened that that's where you were! And you *were*! There were some unfortunate accidents at first."

Mrs. Shore looked rueful. "We grabbed some Native Americans and some explorers. I got a horse once too. That was complicated. Of course, we sent them back right away, but with the time being funny with time travel, I hope those poor people — and horse — made it back okay."

Alex started laughing. He started laughing so hard, he couldn't stop.

"What's so funny?" Rachelli wanted to know. "Tell me what's so funny!"

Alex finally wheezed to a stop. He waved his hands at his family. "You think that you have a headache from terms like '*when* to find us' instead of '*where*'? How about the fact that the reason for the ancient Indian legends about this spot, the reason that the government thought that this place was special for time travel, the reason that Joseph Smith built his house here, and the reason that *we* are here — *all of it* — is because of us?"

"Okay, lost me there, kid," said Effie.

"Huh?" said Rachelli.

"The hand!" Alex leaped to his feet and pushed up his glasses higher on his nose. "The hand coming through the mist! Mommy said that they've been feeling around for us through hundreds of years! Don't you see? All of the legends and documented cases of strange happenings, of people appearing and disappearing and then reappearing and saying that they had gone through time, it was *all because of us!*"

"I," said Rachelli after a moment of shocked silence, "have a huge headache."

"I don't understand," said Effie. "If you guys hadn't gotten lost in time, then this all wouldn't have happened? The Indian legends, the explorers documenting it, the house being built here, us moving here — wouldn't have happened? How does that even — I can't even—"

Alex was nearly dancing with joy. "It's a paradox," he said, beaming.

"A big, beautiful, mystifying paradox," Professor Shore agreed.

"What's a paradox?" Lolly wanted to know. "Is it tasty?"

"It's something that contradicts itself," said Alex, "but is still true."

"That makes no sense," said Effie.

"Exactly," said Alex. His eyes glowed. "Here's a good example. Let's say you have a copy of a famous book. Like, let's say you buy one of Shakespeare's plays or whatever. And then you take the book and copy it in your own handwriting, and you go back in time before Shakespeare ever wrote it and give it to him. He copies it and claims it as his own, even though he didn't write it because he didn't write it — yet. The play is printed and published for hundreds of years, until it ends up back in the same bookstore that the time traveler purchases it in and copies it and brings it back to Shakespeare. Which begs the question."

Rachelli's hand shot up. "Why would he *do* that?"

"Yeah, okay, that's one question, but the real question is, *who really wrote the play*?"

Professor Shore smiled. "Oh, how I love a good paradox!"

Rachelli massaged her head and glowered. "I really, really *don't*. So…yeah, back to stuff that I *can* understand, where are the Pernikovs now?"

"They're in their house, held there by the sheriff and Wilma Lou Wilson."

"I need to talk to Mrs. Pernikov," Rachelli said. "I need to find out exactly why she did what she did."

"That's funny." Mrs. Shore glanced at her husband. "She said she wants to talk to you too."

CHAPTER 47

The walk from the Victorian to the more modest house behind the line of trees was a short one, but it seemed longer than it was. Wilma Lou Wilson — Rachelli was still wrapping her head around the fact that the huge woman with even bigger boots was not actually her housekeeper but government security — was guarding the front door, and the sheriff was guarding the back.

As Rachelli walked over to the house, she saw that the sheriff had a look on his face as if this were the most exciting thing that had happened in Sundale since he'd become sheriff. Rachelli was pretty sure that was precisely the case.

She wasn't sure what she was expecting to see when she walked inside the house. The elderly couple handcuffed to the kitchen chairs, maybe? Shuffling around in leg shackles? But Mr. and Mrs. Pernikov calmly sipping tea in their doily-covered living room was definitely not it.

"Tea?" said Mrs. Pernikov. All traces of her twenty-first-century accent was gone, and she sounded like the woman from the 1800s who she truly was.

"Seriously?" said Rachelli. She folded her arms.

"I offered you tea in Joseph Smith's house," said Mrs. Pernikov. "You turned me down then too."

"Well, yeah. Then it was because I keep kosher. Now it's because you're not exactly someone I want to drink tea with."

Mrs. Pernikov quirked an eyebrow.

Rachelli shifted her weight from one leg to another. "My mother said you wanted to talk to me, and that you would only talk to me alone."

"I told her that because I assumed you wanted to talk to me."

"No!" Rachelli pointed at the woman in front of her. Her finger shook with sudden rage. "No, you don't get to be all mysterious anymore, okay? You — what you did to me and Alex and Lolly — that was as good as trying to *kill* us, okay? You have your baggage from your past. I get that. I might have understood your feelings completely, actually. I mean, I knew you then, kind of. But pushing a little girl through a portal into a time that she couldn't be rescued — that was inexcusable!"

"Do you know what a perfect metaphor it is that I am unable to bring things to the present that are from the past?" Mrs. Pernikov seemed to address a point slightly to the left of Rachelli's head. "Think about it. The very rules of the time-space continuum seem to be telling us that if you're stuck dragging around stuff from your past, then you will be unable to progress into the future. It's kind of beautiful, in a way."

"My father says something similar about the paradox that we created," said Rachelli. "He says that it's a perfect metaphor for This World, and that if you look for it, you will see the Hand everywhere."

"Beautiful," Mrs. Pernikov said softly.

Rachelli nodded her head. Then she shook her head. "Hey. This is what you do! You distract! Just be straight with me, for once! What is so important that you would be willing to condemn a little girl to a fate as good as death?"

"Only my husband understands," said Mrs. Pernikov. She glanced at Mr. Pernikov, who continued to quietly drink his tea.

"Why does he understand?"

"Because he is also from the past. You might recognize him, actually."

Rachelli stared at the old man in front of her. "Um," she said. "Sorry? Am I supposed to know you?"

"That's quite all right," said Mr. Pernikov. "We met for a few minutes only. When the great white hand reached for the little girl on your lap, I ran — in the wrong direction. My friend had gone missing, you see. Call me foolish, but I wanted the hand to take me to him. The hand took me indeed, and I found myself face-to-face with a man who called himself Professor Shore. He apologized profusely and sent me back through the doorway from where he had plucked me. I found myself in a strange new world and soon learned that the place was the same, but the date was 1945."

"You're the young explorer," said Rachelli. "The one who came running over to tell us that you couldn't find your friend, that a hand took him."

Mr. Pernikov nodded his head.

"I don't understand why you weren't put back in your proper time!"

"It took us until now to understand why that had happened," said Mrs. Pernikov. "Now we know that Wilma Lou Wilson was playing with the dials of the time machine for a moment, trying to see how it worked. My guess is, that was the precise moment your father tried to send my husband back to his proper time."

Rachelli pressed the palms of her hands into her eye sockets. "So because of what happened *a few minutes ago*, you landed in 1945? And in a few minutes you go from a teenager to an ancient man?"

"Well, thanks for that flattering description," said Mr. Pernikov dryly. "But remember that the few minutes is only from your perspective. I landed in 1945 — and came to 2022 the regular way: by getting older."

"Migraine," Rachelli announced. Then she snapped her fingers. "I'm confused," she said. "You cannot take *things* from the past, but you can take *people*?"

Mrs. Pernikov sighed. "That is not a hard and fast rule," she said. "It works with some people, and with others it does not. We need to invest time and money to study the natural laws of time travel and understand them better."

"So why didn't you just *do* that? You are sitting on one of the greatest discoveries in the world! Time travel! And you use it to *what*, exact petty revenge? Get over it! Let go of the past! Live your life!"

There were footsteps behind her. Rachelli whirled around, but it was only Alex, a half-eaten sandwich held absently in his hand. "Mommy wants to know why you're not back yet," he said. "She decided that even with Wilma Lou Wilson guarding the Pernikovs, she's nervous about you being here all alone."

"There was a family heirloom that my employers had," said Mrs. Pernikov suddenly. Her voice was soft, dreamy, as though it were coming from a long way away. "A candelabra made by Paul Revere. It was quite beautiful. I was not to allow any of the other maids to clean it. I had to clean it myself, daily. And I did. I cleaned it every day, with my mistress watching my every move to make sure that I did it absolutely right, telling me to be careful, telling me that I missed a spot. I want that candelabra. I want to own it, in my own house, show them that I am no longer their servant. That I am above them all now."

Alex adjusted his glasses. "Wait here one second," he said. He handed his half-sandwich to Rachelli and ran out the door. A minute later he was back, covered in dust and cobwebs. And clutching a candelabra. "Is this it?"

"Where — where — where did you—"

Rachelli, for the first time, saw Mrs. Pernikov so astonished that she was unable to form words. Her lips opened and closed soundlessly.

"The attic. It was in a locked trunk, but the combination was written in the journal."

"Now *that*," said Rachelli triumphantly, "is a perfect metaphor. You keep digging into your past where you no longer belong to try to find the one thing that you think will finally make your life complete, and in the meantime, the thing is here, all along, in your very own attic! Well, not *your* attic. Joseph Smith's attic. But you know what I mean."

Slowly, Mrs. Pernikov stood up. Her face had gone chalky white. She pointed at the candelabra, and then she pointed at Alex, and then quite suddenly she wasn't pointing at anyone or anything; she had fallen to the floor in a dead faint.

CHAPTER 48

It seemed crazy to go back to school after everything that had happened, but the next day, Rachelli was told that she was expected to do just that.

"How am I supposed to just sit in my seat as if everything is normal?" she asked her mother plaintively while the Egginator made breakfast.

"Why do my eggs look like a frowny face?" Mrs. Shore asked as she brought her plate to the table.

Alex flushed. "Long story."

"Anyway, Mommy, why can't I stay home?"

"And do what?" Mrs. Shore looked at her eggs critically. "You still need to learn, you know, portals and self-serving time-traveling neighbors aside."

"Yeah, but!" Rachelli said, and then realized that she had nothing to add after the word "but" other than vague indignation.

"But nothing," Mrs. Shore countered, and Rachelli found herself a few minutes later walking toward the little shul that housed the tiny Bais Yaakov in its basement.

Birdy Winter greeted her with a fierce hug. "Are you okay?" she asked, and Rachelli, after taking a minute to understand where the question was coming from, realized that the last time the small blond girl had seen her was when Wilma Lou Wilson had come to the door of their classroom to tell her that Lolly was missing. Those events seemed as though they had taken place hundreds of years ago, and Rachelli, with a start, realized that they had.

"I'm fine," she said. She smiled. "Everything is fine now."

"I've been thinking about that story you told me," Birdy whispered to her as their teacher walked in. "The one with the neighbor who you're not sure is good or bad. Did you come up with an ending yet?"

"Yes," Rachelli murmured back. "But it's complicated."

"I love complicated! Those are the best kinds of stories! If I make another ice-cream party in my backyard tonight, will you tell me the rest?"

"Girls," said their teacher disapprovingly, and they both settled down to learn.

After a few minutes of Navi, though, Rachelli felt her mind wandering.

"What will happen to the Pernikovs?" she had asked Professor Shore yesterday, after the one doctor in Sundale, Dr. Taylor, had come to check on Mrs. Pernikov and put the old woman to bed, saying that it was exhaustion and shock that had caused her to faint, and she must be sure to rest for the next few days.

Professor Shore had rubbed at his yarmulke. "I don't know, Rachelli. The problem is that there are no laws in place yet for what she did."

"But she's *dangerous*! She can't just…go back to living life as if nothing happened!"

"Well, Wilma Lou Wilson has made arrangements for the time machine to be brought to a top-secret government facility, but for now, we will at least bring it back to our basement. And she and her husband will be guarded by the sheriff and his deputy for now. In the meantime, we will have to wait until the government gets their act together and figures out what can be done with them."

"Her husband pointed a gun at us!" Rachelli had said. "He pointed a gun at Alex and didn't let him leave his house!"

"You and Alex invaded their home," her father pointed out. "He was completely within his rights to capture you."

"But! Guns!"

"It's Sundale," her father said, shrugging. "In tiny towns like this, it's not weird if you have a gun, it's weird if you *don't*. People take their second amendment rights very seriously over here."

"Argh," Rachelli had remarked.

"Indeed," Professor Shore had agreed, and that had been the end of that.

What would she tell Birdy tonight? That there was no such thing as perfect endings, at least not in This World? Was there a metaphor in all this as well? Probably — there always was — but she couldn't see it right now. School seemed to last forever, and Rachelli ran home the second the bell rang.

And was just in time to see a very familiar sight: Mrs. Pernikov darting into one of the secret entrances near the large glass windows in the living room.

"Oh no, you don't," Rachelli said, and quickly ran after her.

"Mrs. Pernikov!" she yelled as soon as she was inside, standing on the bright-blue splotch of the living room floor. "Mrs. Pernikov, stop!"

Not again, she thought. *Not again!*

But this time, she wasn't alone. In the living room was her entire family, with the addition of Wilma Lou Wilson. Mrs. Pernikov was standing in the middle of them all, her arms loosely at her sides, her head down.

"I just wanted to see the candelabra," she said. "I needed to see it again."

"How in the world did you get out?" Rachelli demanded.

Mrs. Pernikov pointed at herself. "World-class time traveler versus small-town deputy at my front door? Really?"

Wilma Lou Wilson looked chagrined. "I just popped over here for a minute to make sure the time machine was okay in the basement. The next thing I know, Mrs. Pernikov comes barreling through the back exit."

"What did you do to the deputy?" Rachelli asked the old woman. "If you hurt him, you're going straight to jail!"

"I told him that they were offering free doughnuts at the shop in town," Mrs. Pernikov explained. "He was gone before I finished the sentence."

Wilma Lou Wilson rolled her eyes. "Can't get good help these days," she rumbled. "Anyway, you should not be here. And you should not be on your feet. You should be resting. You banged your head pretty hard when you passed out yesterday, you know. Let's go." The housekeeper/security guard reached for the elderly woman's arm, but Mrs. Pernikov shrugged it off.

"I don't know why it didn't occur to me that the candelabra would be here all along," she said. "I don't know why."

She looked so lost and confused, that for a moment Rachelli's anger at her melted into pity. What a sad, silly waste! Mrs. Pernikov was a brilliant scientist. She had made a good life for herself. And she had wasted it all on desire for petty revenge.

"Well, now that you know it's here, you can stop thinking about it," she said. Her voice was gentle.

"Not really," said Mrs. Pernikov. "I mean, having it here in the present is not exactly getting the point across, is it?"

"What do you mean?" Alex piped up.

"Well, it's obvious. See, the very first time that I time traveled to the past, I had a portrait of myself made, and I left it on the mantel to show them that I was now a fine lady, as fine as my mistress. But no one even noticed the picture except you, Rachelli. That's when I knew that I wanted to get the candelabra and show them my superiority in that way. Having it here, in the present, their future, doesn't exactly do that, now does it?"

"Crushing headache," said Rachelli. "Seriously, in my head, right now. Like a tiny little man using a power tool on my brain. I am seriously beginning to hate every single word involving the paradoxes of time travel."

"Anyway, I have been going about this all wrong. Sure, I can't bring back things with me from the past. But I can bring something back with me from the present." From a pocket in her cardigan, Mrs. Pernikov pulled out a small revolver barely larger than her hand. Rachelli, Professor Shore, Mrs. Shore, Effie, Rachelli, and Lolly backed away. Wilma Lou Wilson, who had her trusty gun Bessie at ready in her hands, did not.

"My gun is an awful lot bigger," said Wilma Lou Wilson.

"Then it's a good thing my fight is not with you," said Mrs. Pernikov. "But I bet my former employers won't know what hit them." She took a step over to the fireplace, and before anyone could blink or step forward, she had walked through the portal. A white mist filled the doorway.

And then she was gone.

CHAPTER 49

A moment later, everyone began talking at once.

"She was right in front of me! How could I not have grabbed her!"

"Is everyone okay?"

"I cannot believe what just happened!"

"Here we go again."

And Rachelli cried out, "Lolly!" Her voice rose above everyone else's. "Where's Lolly?"

After turning the mansion upside down, they finally found Lolly in the secret basement. She explained that she had fallen through the trapdoor in the kitchen.

"I was hungry," she said. "I'm still hungry."

"We need to hammer that thing *shut*," Rachelli said with feeling as everyone wandered back to the fireplace to stare once again at the portal that Mrs. Pernikov had gone through.

"How can we know if she already did it? If she…" Rachelli swallowed the words *killed Joseph Smith*. "You know," she said instead.

"Well, *of course*, whatever it is she was going to do she *did* already," said Professor Shore. "After all, it's all over and done with over one hundred years ago."

"But she just left five minutes ago!" Rachelli protested.

"To 1880," Alex explained. "So whatever she did or didn't do, it's long ago done."

"I need two aspirins," said Rachelli, wagging her finger at no one in particular, "and a nice long nap."

Alex snapped his fingers. "The journal!" he said. He pulled the delicate leather book out of his waist pouch and flipped through it quickly. "It all looks the same," he said doubtfully. "Nothing seems to have changed in Joseph Smith's life, at least his recording of it. For whatever reason, I don't think she actually went through with it."

"That's a relief," said Mrs. Shore. "Well, what do we do now?"

Professor Shore sighed. "That's a good question. We should probably go in and get her. True, it seems as though she didn't follow through with her nefarious intentions, but who knows what she's capable of?"

Rachelli turned to Alex. "Daddy used the word 'nefarious.' Just by the way. Just leaving that there."

Alex grinned. "Fine. I hereby give you permission to use the word, then."

Rachelli laughed, and Effie looked at the two of them curiously. "What are you talking about?"

Rachelli shrugged. "Had to be there," she said, and then she realized, for the first time, that while she was glad that Effie was there, Alex was not just the annoying little brother he used to be. Maybe he had grown up over the summer. Maybe they had both grown up.

"I think word choice is a discussion we can have at a later time," Mrs. Shore said. "Right now, we need to decide what to do. What does everyone think?"

"Are you asking *us*?" Rachelli was astonished.

Mrs. Shore smiled. "Children who not only managed a household while I was gone but managed it while all of *this* was going on are children whose opinions I trust." She exchanged a glance with Professor Shore, and both of their eyes were misty.

Rachelli beamed. "Okay, then! Well, the last thing in the world I want to do is go back in time. Seriously, getting a root canal would be before time travel on my list, but I agree with Daddy. We can't let Mrs. Pernikov roam around free to do *nefarious* things. So we all need to get that horrible shot of—"

"Alex's Amazing Time-Traveling Elixir," said Alex.

"For many, many reasons, *no*. We are not calling it that," said Rachelli. "Anyway, we can take that stuff so we can time travel again, go into the portal, get her, and bring her back here."

"Agreed," said Wilma Lou Wilson. "But as official government security, that task falls to me. No offense, but you are all civilians." She stood to her full and extremely impressive height. "And ole Bessie here can help." She eyed the hypodermic needle that Professor Shore held. "Will it hurt?" she asked.

Rachelli wasn't sure when the hairs on the back of her neck began to rise. Suddenly she became absolutely sure that something was terribly wrong. Just as Wilma Lou approached the portal, rubbing at the spot on her arm that had just received the injection, Rachelli found herself moving forward.

"Stop!" she screamed. "Wilma Lou, don't go! Stop!"

The housekeeper/security guard froze.

"What is it? What's wrong?" Professor Shore was at Rachelli's side in an instant.

Rachelli's pulse was racing. "The time machine," she gasped. "Please. Check the time machine."

Effie flew downstairs, taking the steps three at a time. The living room was deadly silent until he came back upstairs, his face pale. "How did you know?" he asked.

"How did she know *what*?" Wilma Lou asked in frustration.

"That the machine was not set to 1880," Effie said. "It was set to 1080."

"It was set to 1080?" said Alex. "That means Leif Erikson. Vikings.

That's about all that was happening in America around then. Definitely no Victorian mansion with portals then. Lots of buffalo, though, so there's that."

"Are you saying," said Wilma Lou, her face slowly draining of color, "that if I would have gone through the portal, I would have been stuck in the past, all alone?"

"Well, buffalo," said Alex. "And Bessie. And we would have tried to retrieve you, of course, if you could have stayed in the exact same spot for a while because time is funny when you time travel. But, Rachelli — how did you know?"

"Lolly was in the basement," Rachelli explained. Her heartbeat was slowing down now. "Wherever Lolly is, mischief follows."

Lolly looked a little sheepish. "I played a little with the shiny buttons," she said.

Mrs. Shore snapped her fingers. "Mrs. Pernikov," she said. "Did she go through before Lolly played with the time machine and reset it to 1080, or...after?"

There was a moment of silence. "Maybe that explains why Joseph Smith's diary is exactly the same," Alex said. "Maybe Mrs. Pernikov didn't do anything to him and his family because she *couldn't*."

"Because she arrived eight hundred years too early," said Effie.

"Oops," said Rachelli.

"Well, what do we do?" Mrs. Shore said. "We can't just leave her there, can we?"

Professor Shore looked uncertain. He pushed up his glasses. "We can try to retrieve her the way we retrieved Alex, Rachelli, and Lolly," he said, and, hesitantly, Wilma Lou Wilson put her hand through the portal. It glowed white and disappeared into the past.

"Well?" Rachelli asked after a moment.

Wilma Lou Wilson's eyes widened, and she pulled her hand back. The white glow disappeared, and her hand reappeared. "I don't feel her. Pretty sure I felt a buffalo, though."

Professor Shore sighed. "I don't know what else we can really do. Mrs. Pernikov—"

"What about my wife?" The voice in the room was new and loud, and everyone spun around. They found themselves facing Mr. Pernikov. The normally soft-spoken old man was red-faced with anger. "What have you done with her?"

"We haven't done anything with her!" Rachelli said. "She just jumped into the portal!"

"Move aside!" Mr. Pernikov snapped, and he raced toward the fireplace faster than a man his age should be able to.

"No!" Professor Shore cried out. "Mr. Pernikov! You don't understand! The time machine is set to—"

But he was talking to thin air. In a burst of white light, Mr. Pernikov was gone. Wilma Lou instantly put her arm back into the portal. Everyone held their breath. After a few minutes, she shook her head and pulled her arm back.

"Well, she won't be alone now, at least." said Mrs. Shore.

"I feel like we should be happy," said Rachelli. "I mean, we just got rid of two bad people; or, rather, they got rid of themselves. Why don't I feel happy?"

Mrs. Shore put her arm around Rachelli's shoulders. "What a silly, silly waste, the two of them. It's really true; the worst messes are sometimes the ones we create for ourselves."

"I'll give you a reason to cheer up," said Professor Shore. "In all of the excitement, I didn't have a chance to tell you: I finally completed my invention! Eureka!"

"No way!" Rachelli felt a giant grin form on her face. "*Now* can you tell us what it is?"

Professor Shore smiled and opened his mouth. Everyone leaned forward to hear.

CHAPTER 50

"Soldiers don't know where they will be from one day to the next," explained Professor Shore. "They don't know where they will lay their heads down at night; they don't even know if they will *survive* the night. So shouldn't their *food* at least be consistent?

"Meet Manna from Heaven, shortened to MFH, a machine that produces MREs, or Meal Ready to Eat, but with a whole new twist. These MREs look like any other soldier's meal: a small, silver-foil-covered packet — but appearances are where the similarity ends. Watch," said Professor Shore.

The Shore family was in the secret lab, in front of the shiny machine Professor Shore had spent the summer working on. He pressed a button, and the maw in the front opened up. Out came four MREs. Professor Shore handed them to his children.

"Open them," he said.

Rachelli ripped the foil off her packet. Instantly, the small tray in her hands was enveloped in a very familiar white glow, and she nearly dropped it. "What's happening?" she cried out, but a second later the white glow had faded, and in her hands was a large plate filled with steaming-hot meatballs and spaghetti.

She looked at Lolly, who was holding a plate of schnitzel and mashed potatoes; Effie with a steak and baked potato; and Alex with a hot dog in a bun alongside French fries.

"Okay, explanation time," Rachelli said.

"Basically, the MFH produces actual home-cooked meals for the soldiers, not gluey containers of barely edible substances. The way it works is—"

"Time." Alex was staring at his meal. "You locked the food in a pocket in time."

Professor Shore nodded. "The silver foil is the key. It keeps the food in a sort of time bubble, and it shrinks down to its most essential parts. When you open the packet, the time bubble is broken, and it reverts back to what it was before it was sealed. It's a bit more complicated than that, actually, but that's the basic idea."

"It's yummy," said Lolly. She was halfway through her schnitzel.

"Okay," Rachelli said slowly. "This is terrific and cool and awesome, and I'm assuming that the government woman who hired you has a son in the army and wants to make sure that he has home-cooked meals. Great. But I just don't get why this was such a huge secret. It's not, like, something that can be turned into a weapon or anything."

Professor Shore looked serious. "Actually, it can be. In its raw form, the MFH can be used to seal anything in bubbles of time. Someone can use it to create a bomb, for example, and sealed in the time foil, it would be imperceptible to scanners. Think of how that could play out. We had to keep this whole project under wraps until I could finally destroy my notes."

Rachelli saw a shredder in the corner, perched above a garbage can that was filled with thin strips of paper. She frowned.

"What's wrong?" asked Mrs. Shore.

"It's kind of..." Rachelli began.

"Anticlimactic," Effie finished her sentence for her.

Rachelli pointed at him. "Yes! Exactly! Anticlimactic! Like, food for soldiers, okay, awesome, but I thought this would be, oh, I don't know, a machine that creates instant houses with the push of a button."

Professor Shore's eyes widened. "How did you guess my next project?" he asked.

"Really?" Rachelli grinned.

"Well, no, not really. But anyway, even if this project seems anti-climactic to you, what comes next shouldn't be."

"What comes next?" Lolly looked up from her nearly empty MRE.

"The invention is finished," said Mrs. Shore. "Kids, we're going home."

And even though the Victorian mansion that they were living in was very big, the sound of one word filled the entire house.

"Eureka!"

When Rachelli screamed, everyone on the street turned to look at her. It seemed like the entire population of Sundale was standing in front of the Victorian.

And every last one of them was wearing clothes from the 1800s.

"No, no, no! How did this happen?" she said. Her heart pounded in her chest like a war drum. "How in the world did we end up *back in time?*"

One girl in a long dress and a white bonnet separated herself from the crowd and ran over to Rachelli. It was Birdy Winter. "Rachelli!" she cried. "Don't you just love it?"

"Love what?" Rachelli stared at her friend dumbly. "Birdy, what in the world is happening? I just walked out to put the last of the suitcases in the car — which, by the way, is all, 'Oh, how come *I* have to be the one to carry all of the suitcases, maybe *you guys* should carry suitcases for a while and see how *you* feel' — and then I come out here, and *why* is everyone dressed like that?"

"Surprise!" Birdy Winter gave her a hug. "It's your goodbye party! We're doing a reenactment of the events of this summer!" All of her friends behind her, also dressed in long dresses and bonnets, giggled.

"Events of this summer?" Rachelli forced a laugh. "Are you talking about that story I told you? You know that none of it is true, right? I mean, ha! Time travel! What a hoot!"

Birdy smiled. "Honey," she said to Rachelli. Her eyes twinkled. "How many times do I have to tell you that there are no such things as secrets in a small town?"

"We got ice cream!" Mrs. Winter called from behind her daughter. "Dig in, everyone!"

The party turned out to be a lot of fun, Rachelli had to admit, and with a small pang, she realized that she was actually going to miss Birdy Winter and her giggling entourage. She was going to miss Sundale.

"So everything is different now," Mrs. Shore was saying from the front seat as Pinny the PNAAD turned the car out of the driveway and onto the road. They passed a sign that said, "Sundale: Home of the Second-to-Largest Ball of Twine," with the words "Second-to" crossed out. Mrs. Shore craned her neck to smile at her children. "With the completion and approval of the MFH, I don't have to go to Washington anymore. I'll be spending a lot more time at home, so this is the end of all your time-traveling shenanigans."

"We're pretty much done with time-traveling shenanigans," Effie said.

"What Effie said," said Rachelli.

"*Ephraim*," said Effie.

"Get over it," said Rachelli.

"You guys need to stop fighting — I'm trying to read!" complained Alex.

"I'm hungry," said Lolly.

"'I'm hungry. I'm trying to read. I want you to call me by my *real* name.' Blah, blah, blah. You think *you* guys have it hard? Try being your *car* just for one day, and see how you can handle it! I feel like crashing into a cow just so I don't have to listen to you!" Pinny the PNAAD's voice echoed through the speakers.

"Daddy, can you *please* fix the PNAAD when we get home?" Rachelli pleaded.

Professor Shore nodded uncertainly. "I'll definitely try."

"Leave it," Effie said. "It might just get worse."

"How could it possibly get worse?" asked Rachelli.

"You do *not* ask that question," said Effie. "You never ask that question unless you really, really want to know the answer."

"Know-it-all," said Rachelli. "When are you going back to yeshivah?" She glared at Effie, but she wasn't really upset. In fact, a moment later, she had a smile on her face. She turned and looked out the window, at the rows and rows of corn they were passing. "So what *is* going to be your next invention, Daddy?" she called to the front of the car, where Professor Shore was sitting, a *sefer* balanced on his knees.

"It's a secret," said Professor Shore.

"A machine that makes everything taste like ice cream," said Rachelli.

"A suit that lets you fly," said Effie.

"An injection that makes you learn a new language automatically," said Alex.

"Pizza!" said Lolly, who still did not quite get the way the game worked.

"I would love a machine that makes a five-minute nap feel like five hours," said Mrs. Shore.

"No, no, no, no, and that is a great idea, but also no," said Professor Shore, pointing at his children and then at his wife.

Rachelli pressed her nose to the window and watched the corn blur together as they picked up speed. Sundale was a nice town, and the people were nice too. Well, most of them, anyway.

She continued to watch as the cornfields began to thin out and buildings started popping up. Very soon the Shores would be home, and that was amazing; she missed the city and all her friends. But she realized now that home was not a place at all, and at this sudden discovery, she smiled.

"Eureka!" she whispered.

ACKNOWLEDGMENTS

Hmm. Where to start? How about at the end of the book-making process, and work my way back to the beginning, just to keep me on my toes?

Thank *you*, person who is holding this book and reading this sentence right now. We know there are many books in a bookstore, and we thank you for choosing this one. Have a pleasant flight.

Thank you, Sam Schwartz, for the wonderful cover.

Thank you, Daliya Shapiro, for your skillful proofreading, and thank you Adina Edelman for your masterful copyediting and minute attention to detail.

Thank you, Esther Heller, Hirsch Traube, and the staff of Menucha Publishers for liking the manuscript of *Eureka!* so much that you snapped your fingers and — presto chango! — transformed it into *this*. Or however the magical process works that turns a bunch of words into an actual, real-life book.

Thank you, Rachel Adler of RADesign, for the original design in *AIM!* magazine. No, *I'm* your biggest fan.

Thank you, Esty Weiss, the wonderful editor of *AIM!* magazine, for brainstorming *Eureka!* with me into existence, and then providing the space for the story to unfold on the pages of *AIM!* every week for over a year.

Thank you, as always, to the amazingly talented and insightful Sarah Shapiro, who, over a decade ago, listened to me read a piece of nonfiction I had written for adults and said, "I think you would make a fantastic fiction writer for teens!" And told me to write something for this brand-new, delightful magazine called *Ami*.

Thank you to my mother, Yona Berger, my mother-in-law, Lila Pahl, and my Tanta Helene Pahl for being so supportive and amazing and inspiring in every way. Thank you to my siblings and friends and acquaintances and that lady on the bus who sits down next to me and tells me her life story — you enhanced this book simply by existing because if not for you all, I would never have human interaction, and I wouldn't know how dialogue and stuff works, which would make writing a book challenging.

Thank you to my children, Libby, Simi, Chili, Boruch, Gitty, and Tzvi Yehuda (Heshy), because if not for you, I would have a lot more time to write books, but nothing I would care to write about.

Thank you to my husband, Dan Neuman, a fantastic writer who reads my stories with the eye of an editor, always enhancing. (Except for that one time when you tried to sneak ninjas into chapter 38.)

With eternal thanks to Hashem.

(And now, you can read it all backward! Who says that acknowledgments are boring?)

ABOUT THE AUTHOR

Dina Neuman lives in Yerushalayim with her husband and kids and tortoise, but has sad news to report about The Oldest Goldfish in the World.™ They were swimming peacefully in their tortoise-shaped swimming pool on the porch the other day when they were eaten by a cat. If you see a brown cat with one missing ear and two white paws, please tell him that the Neumans are very sad about the choices he has made.

This is her billionth book, a claim that is not factually correct, but is so much fun to write.

Another great read for kids by Dina Neuman!

MENUCHA
PUBLISHERS

Meet The Milsteins

Watch what happens when Mommy gives the Milstein kids diaries...

Malky: *"I realize that I can have a real impact on my siblings with this journal. They are so lucky to have an older sister like me."*

Meir: *"Did you know that if you stick a cup against the door and put your ear to one end, you can hear what's going on inside?"*

Get ready for nonstop laughter as the Milstein gang frantically works on their "Get Malky Married and Out of Our Hair" plan. Will their outlandish scheming succeed? Meet the Milsteins, and let the fun begin!

MENUCHA
PUBLISHERS

Available at your local Judaica store or at:
1-855-MENUCHA · www.menuchapublishers.com

Another great read for kids by Dina Neuman!

WALLED SECRETS

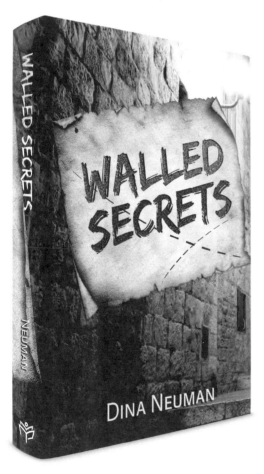

The Cohen family is moving to Eretz Yisrael, and most of its members are thrilled. But when they arrive, they're shocked to discover that their new apartment is gutted and totally unlivable. Can the Cohens' tenacious twelve-year-old twins, Nechama and Yechiel, solve an ancient riddle and make their new home a safe place?

Join this lovable cast of characters on an unforgettable, exhilarating ride through the streets of Yerushalayim as they explore the city's past and present, and attempt to unearth its walled secrets.

MENUCHA PUBLISHERS

Available at your local Judaica store or at:
1-855-MENUCHA · www.menuchapublishers.com

Another great read for kids by Dina Neuman!

MENUCHA
PUBLISHERS

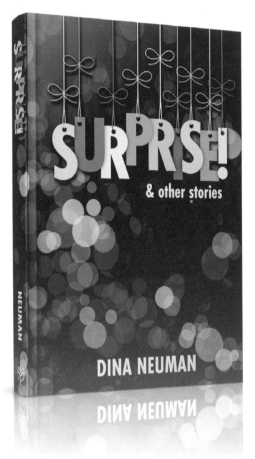

Temima was fun, popular, and smart. When did she become the class laughingstock?

Mazal tov! Yoel Kutner won a million-dollar sweepstakes, and he's eager to share his newfound wealth — in the most unlikely ways.

When Rachel's algebra mark reaches an all-time low, can she gather the courage to set things straight?

In this dazzling collection by popular writer Dina Neuman, teens deal with pesky siblings, annoying group projects, and fickle friends. These powerful stories will leave you totally inspired and entertained. Surprised?

MENUCHA
PUBLISHERS

Available at your local Judaica store or at:
1-855-MENUCHA · www.menuchapublishers.com